Going to the Dogs

Other books by Dan Kavanagh

Duffy
Fiddle City

Going to the Dogs

Dan Kavanagh

PERENNIAL LIBRARY

Harper & Row, Publishers, New York
Cambridge, Philadelphia, San Francisco
London, Mexico City, São Paulo, Singapore, Sydney

Library of Congress Cataloging-in-Publication Data

Kavanagh, Dan, 1946–
  Going to the dogs.

  "Perennial Library."
  I. Title.
PR6061.A898G6   1989   823'.914   88–45605
ISBN 0-06-080953-1

89 90 91 92 93 OPM 10 9 8 7 6 5 4 3 2 1

to Ruth and Don

I am grateful to Mickey 'the Grass' Sissons for slipping me the words of 'The Dogs'.   D. K.

BUCKINGHAMSHIRE/BEDFORD-SHIRE BORDERS. Classic rural neighbourhood with easy access M1. Outstanding detached period residence standing in 40 acres of its own land. Substantially modified in mid-1960s but many original features remain. Three reception rooms, 8 bedrooms (2 with en suite bathrooms), study, family room, kitchen/dining-room, billiard room. Gardens comprise own wood and lake. Outbuildings include stable block and former squash court (currently recording studio for well-known pop star who must sell) with opportunities for reconversion.

**Freehold. Sole Joint Agents:
· Madley and Burton Wood.
Viewing and offers by arrangement.**

1 ● LIBRARY

There was a body in the video library. It was hard to miss, as these things are, and Mrs Colin spotted it the moment she pushed open the panelled light-oak door on which someone had humorously painted a large pink *trompe-l'oeil* keyhole. Mrs Colin recognized Ricky at once, recognized equally that he was dead, and put her hand to her throat. Beneath the white poplin blouse she had ironed that morning at 6.30, she felt the bump of her crucifix. She always wore Our Saviour inside her clothes, next to the skin, and the few people who knew wondered if it was because she was ashamed of her religion. Mrs Colin was not ashamed of her religion, but she was often more than embarrassed by some of the things she found herself looking at in the course of her daily duties at Braunscombe Hall. If you had been born in Davao thirty-five years ago and were sending money home every month, you did not question the way people chose to behave on the Buckinghamshire/Bedfordshire borders. But this did not mean you should allow such behaviour to be inflicted upon Our Saviour, even upon an image of Our Saviour. There were times, as Mrs Colin set the breakfast tray down in certain bedrooms, when the gold figure at her throat seemed to burn in anger, and with the pressure of her hand she would try to reassure it that such things had nothing to do with her, and that she would in due course pray for the slumbering sinners. Part of the money she sent back to Davao always went to the Church of Our Lady of Penitence, where the holy sisters regularly chivvied the Lord about the moral safety of those in service overseas.

This time, however, as Mrs Colin gazed into Ricky's cold, dead eyes, the crucifix did not burn, and after the first shock she began to look calmly round the room. The several thousand videotapes – a collection of which Vic Crowther was exuberantly proud – lay undisturbed. They were enclosed in special boxes with tooled plastic spines, and had their titles printed in gold leaf. This made them look, Vic would explain, as if they were real books. Some of the tapes were pretty rare, and some of the fruitier items in Vic's collection masqueraded under such titles as *Chess for Beginners: The Middle Game*, or *Cooking with Spices, Part 2*. But whoever it was that had killed Ricky hadn't been interested in old films, or the middle game in chess, or cooking with spices, or even in what really lay behind such innocent titles.

The curtains over the french windows were drawn back, which was not unusual in Mrs Colin's experience: nobody in this household seemed to bother much about keeping out the dark, or the light, or the draughts. But the fact that the curtains were open meant that when the man, or men, had thrown Ricky's body through the window, it, or he, had travelled further into the room than if the curtains had been there to slow his, or its, progress. This elaborate thought took some pedantic time to travel through Mrs Colin's brain, and it was swiftly followed by the awareness that standing there trying to work things out was not at all her job. She shook her head at herself, released her grasp of Our Saviour, quietly closed the door of the video library and went in search of Mr Crowther.

Belinda Blessing was also Mrs Vic Crowther, but she preferred to keep her professional name. It always seemed a bit silly when some sly gawper still at work on his first moustache turned shyly to her in the pub and asked, 'Excuse me, you *are* Belinda Blessing?' for her to slap his face with a 'No, I'm Mrs Crowther.' Belinda stopped on her way to the video library and checked her side view in a long mirror. She'd always known she'd look good in riding clothes, but they also did something to her bum that she wasn't entirely happy with. Jolly girlfriends used to say that you couldn't have too much money or too much bum, but she wasn't sure, and stared quizzically into the mirror, shifting from one leg to the other, studying the effect on what Vic would jokingly refer to as her other pair. Belinda smiled, as if to camera, tapped her riding crop against her thigh (naughty, naughty), and walked quickly to the library, where she found those members of the household who believed in rising by 8.30 on a Sunday morning. She cast a quick look at the body, coughed sharply and observed, 'Looks like he was thrown through the window.' Then she turned away and went off to ride. A good gallop, with some of your long black hair escaping from underneath your hat and flowing out behind so that you might be recognized from a distance, made you forget all the nasty, sick things in life, she found.

Jimmy thought this was rather hard on Belinda's part, but then no one had ever compared Belinda to a duvet, except in respect of where she frequently used to find herself; at least in the old days. Now . . . well, Jimmy wondered a bit about all that, how Vic and Belinda were managing in the bedroom department after what was it, seven, eight years? Had there been a bit of extra-curricular activity? I mean, given their pasts, and given the fact that Vic's rev-counter probably didn't climb into the red zone all that often these days, what would you expect? It was a subject to which Jimmy occasionally turned his mind. He was not bright, Jimmy, and with a head that sloped away at top and bottom he didn't look bright either; but he was a tenacious thinker. For instance, he sometimes reflected on the fact that he came from a good family but seemed, as far as he could work out, not to have a bean to his name, whereas old Vic Crowther, his host, who was as common as muck (well, that was Jimmy's phrase – Vic would have preferred something like salt of the earth), had large amounts of the folding stuff which bought you a jolly good time. In short, he was stinking rich. Harry stinkers, in fact, as Jimmy would have put it. He dragged his brain back to the matter in hand, a process which made his right arm naturally extend and firmly enclose the shoulders of Angela. This was a harder business than it sounded, since Angela was crying a lot and shaking up and down. The grieving widow, thought Jimmy, and watched his arm being propelled up and down by Angela's back, as if he were operating a pump on the village green.

It was rather like that: Jimmy's arm pumping up and down, and water sluicing out of Angela's eyes. The bastards, the bastards. She'd loved Ricky. The tears were now interfering with her proper view of Ricky's body, but she didn't have to see him to feel the presence of those gentle eyes, that sweet expression, that lovely curly hair. The bloody bastards. She'd paid, and they hadn't ever mentioned Ricky, so why had they done it? The bloody bastards. What had Ricky ever done to anyone? Her sobs became fiercer, and Jimmy felt her pulling at his arm, as if she wanted to throw herself on the body. We can't have this, Jimmy thought, and held on more tightly, at the same time catching Mrs Colin's eye and making a drinking gesture with his free hand. Mrs Colin quietly disappeared.

Nikki, who was six, and who had been rather surprised when her mother had simply walked off, held her father's hand and wondered if Ricky was in Heaven. Mrs Colin had said she wasn't to go into the video library but everyone seemed a bit distracted so she had just slipped in and put her hand into her father's. What a mess the window was in, all broken like that. She wondered if this meant she wouldn't be able to come in and watch videos for a few days. She usually said she wanted to see *Bambi* or *Supergran* or *The Hundred and One Dalmatians*, but recently she'd found that if she climbed on a chair, some of the other films could be a lot more interesting. She didn't tell anyone about her discovery, though that Mrs Colin had caught her the other day and threatened to tell Mummy. Nikki had had to cry a lot and pretend a video had got in the wrong box by mistake. Nosey Mrs Colin. Actually, she thought she'd recognized Mummy in one of those films, but she didn't have the right colour hair, and Nikki couldn't be sure. She held her father's hand, looked at Ricky's stiffened limbs, and wondered if he was in Heaven.

Vic Crowther, a stocky man in his mid-fifties, had a ruddy complexion, chain-store clothes, and a cheerful expression which the coppers always used to take for cheeky. On this occasion he wasn't looking so cheerful. 'I'm going to have to bollock Duffy about this,' he said to Jimmy. 'Christ, try to give a mate a leg-up and look what happens.'

'Who's Duffy?'

'Fellow who put in the alarm system. This was his big break. Never exactly been the John Paul Getty of the security business. But there it was, nice job, big country house, don't count the pennies. Told him he'd be doing tripwires at Buckingham Palace next. And what happens? He screws up. Someone throws poor old Ricky through the french windows and the bell doesn't even go off. I'm going to give that Duffy a right bollocking.'

'Maybe it's out of guarantee.' Jimmy's suggestion was made in a worried voice.

'Guarantee? Guarantees are a guardsman's tit where I come

from.' Vic was sounding really angry. 'Guarantees are for stockbrokers and schoolmasters. I don't count the pennies and I don't keep files, but if someone does me a job of work, then someone does me a job of work.'

'Check,' said Jimmy.

Vic grunted. He didn't count the pennies, and he didn't keep files, and he did despise stockbrokers and schoolmasters – indeed, sometimes he'd have a chuckle about how he'd started lower than the lot of them yet ended up in the big house with a girl they'd give their right sperm-bank for. But he wasn't really thinking about this, and he wasn't even thinking about Duffy. What he mainly felt, as his daughter's hand squirmed like a mouse in his palm, was relief that no one had gone messing with the films in his video library. What if someone had come through that bloody great hole in the window and nicked his tape of *Naked as Nature Intended*? That was a real collector's item, that was. One of these days those old naturist movies were really going to come back into fashion.

Mrs Colin was not a drinker. She was a good Catholic who had come all the way from the Philippines to the Buckinghamshire/Bedfordshire borders and who regularly sent half her wages back to her mother, some of which was forwarded to the holy sisters at the Church of Our Lady of Penitence. You didn't come all this way to waste money on yourself, least of all by pouring it down your throat. Even after five years with the Crowthers, two in London before Miss Blessing retired and three in the country, she was still amazed at how much people drank in this cold, damp, grey-green land where the money was good. Perhaps they did so precisely because it was cold and damp and the leaves seemed to be falling off the trees all year round. In her country, among her people, they drank San Miguel beer, and that was enough. Here they drank everything, and more kinds of different everything than Mrs Colin had ever imagined. She stood behind the sitting-room bar – all deep-buttoned leather with brass accessories – and wondered what to get for Miss Angela. The array of bottles and tins and mixers and squirters, the prodders and crushers and pokers and pounders, plus the cheery colours of all the different drinks, made her feel like a pharmacist in a dispensary. Maybe that's why the English said things like, 'What's your medicine?' or, for a change, 'What's your poison?' Perhaps Miss Angela needed a little of each of her favourites. Mrs Colin poured an inch of crème de menthe into a large tumbler, added an inch of white wine, and topped it up with an inch of gin. She paused, thought of Miss Angela's tear-lined face, and added another inch of gin. She picked up one of Mr Crowther's novelty cocktail stirrers – a policeman's helmet at one end to hold it by, and a big pair of policeman's boots at the other with which to do the agitating – and mixed Miss Angela's medicine. Then she hurried back to the video library. Jimmy took the glass from her, raised an eyebrow at the colour, and wordlessly held it in front of the now quieter Angela, who drained half its contents without comment. It seemed to Mrs Colin that she had chosen wisely.

Almost in an undertone, but with a firmness of enunciation which made all those who heard it realize that it was an instruction, Vic Crowther said, 'I don't think we'll inform the gentlemen of the law just yet.' Then, one by one, those who had risen at Braunscombe Hall by 8.30 on a Sunday morning filed out of the video library with the cautious step of penitents leaving church. Mrs Colin closed the door and was alone with Ricky.

The fact of the matter was, Mrs Colin had always disliked him. He had frightened her. She hadn't ever told anyone, and it was probably more to do with something that happened once in a backstreet in Davao after dark than with Ricky himself; but there it was. Now, looking at him stretched out in death, she felt a little guilty about having disliked him. His eyes were empty of life, and his limbs were stiff, all four of them, and his tail would never wag again.

2. DRIVEWAY

It was 8.45 on a Sunday morning on the Buckinghamshire/ Bedfordshire borders when Mrs Colin from Davao slipped Ricky into a large blue plastic laundry-bag, stood for a minute or two pondering the etiquette of putting him in the freezer, decided against it, and went instead to the back cloakroom. Nobody much visited the back cloaks. The room contained a large number of wellington boots, none of which appeared to fit members of the household, a fairly new croquet set which Belinda had ordered and quickly become bored with, a wash-basin with a dripping tap, and a Victorian lavatory whose porcelain interior was decorated with a dark-blue flower pattern. A botanist, even an amateur one, would probably have been able to identify the flowers etched into the porcelain, but Mrs Colin had never tried: there were certain things, she thought, which ought to be decorated, and certain things which oughtn't to be, and lavatories fell into the second category. She had never heard of decorated lavatories in Davao. Ignoring the decadent bowl, Mrs Colin looked instead at the row of hat-pegs on the right of the cloakroom. On one of them hung a mud-splashed trench coat which some weekend guest had never bothered to claim. Occasionally, a shooting friend of Vic Crowther's would give him a brace of pheasant, and it was here – two pegs along from the discarded trench coat – that they always hung for a few days. Mrs Colin lifted the plastic laundry-bag and was about to slip its handle over the pheasant peg when she wondered if in some way this might be wrong; she hesitated, and chose the next peg along instead. Ricky's tail, or at least six inches of it, protruded from the bag. Mrs Colin tried pushing it down, but without any success.

Duffy's laundry-bag was made of bright yellow plastic, and at 8.45 on a Sunday morning he was carrying it down Goldsmith Avenue, Acton W3. A stray policeman on the lookout for murdered dogs would have found the contents of his bag innocuous. In legal terms, that is, though some of the contents were far from innocuous where the sense of smell was concerned; some of them might have constituted a minor health hazard; some of them – had the right public official been handy – might even have been taken away from Duffy and buried in a lime pit. Duffy was aware of this problem. It wasn't that he didn't change his clothes often enough; it was simply that he didn't get down to the launderette often enough. He carefully stacked his dirty clothes away in plastic bags at the bottom of his fitted cupboard; after a few weeks, when he thought the bags must be so familiar with one another that they might start breeding, he would empty their contents into his yellow laundry-bag and set off down Goldsmith Avenue.

Duffy quite liked this Sunday chore. Partly it was the release from guilt; partly it was the quiet of the streets. Saturday night had gone home. Saturday night was still snoring away in bed waiting for Sunday morning's hangover to come and wake it up. There was nobody about as Duffy turned in to the huddle of shops which contained the launderette. Light-heartedly he kicked at a few discarded styrofoam burger boxes. Some careful drunk had stacked up a pile of eight empty lager cans on the pavement outside the bookie's. Some less careful drunk had decided that the recessed entrance to the bookie's was well-suited for use as a urinal because, if it wasn't to be the bookie's it would have to be the next shop along anyway, and hadn't he lost a tenner on some three-legged nag here only last week? Duffy wrinkled his nose, aware that the reek from his laundry-bag came in a close second to the pong from the doorway, losing only by a short head.

Duffy consigned his clothes to the tender chomping of the wash, crossed the empty street and pushed open the door of Sam Widges. Sam was a middle-aged Chinese, who had always been called Sam and who had spent thirty years in the British catering business. After ten years in its lower echelons, he had acquired his own establishment, whereupon he changed his surname by deed poll to Widges. At the time Sam Widges had, not surprisingly, sold nothing but sandwiches. In the last ten years he had extended his cuisine, and was now proud of his skills with the microwave; but he remained stuck with the name.

'The usual, please, Sam.'

'Righty-ho-coming-up.'

The usual was a British breakfast cooked in the British way.

It had taken Sam some years to master – visits to rival eateries had even been necessary – but now he was able to handle the separate skills of undercooking the bacon while overcooking the egg, allowing the tomatoes to collapse while the sausages stayed *al dente*, and making sure that the baked beans, when they hit the plate in a sticky mass, retained the original shape of the serving spoon. As Duffy was a favoured customer – indeed, at that time of the morning he was the only customer – Sam threw in a slice of British fried bread: thick-cut, sopping in grease, not too crisp, not too brown.

'Delicious,' said Duffy, thinking a little about his pre-season training. Duffy played in goal for the Western Sunday Reliables and the first match was only five weeks away.

'Thank-you-coming-up.'

The fried bread slipped around the plate as he pursued it with his fork and left a broad snail-trail of grease. Duffy thought of young Karl French, lean as a whippet, who would be out pounding the road even now. Still, you didn't need so much speed to be a goalkeeper, Duffy consoled himself. You needed . . . solidity. He trapped the delinquent sausage against the curve of his plate; with a mixture of cunning and brutal strength he succeeded in piercing its skin.

On his way back up Goldsmith Avenue, with the yellow laundry-bag held rather more proudly beside him, Duffy pondered the eternal question posed to those who frequent launderettes: what happened to the other sock? You put twenty-four in, you got twenty-three back. You put thirty-six in, you got thirty-five back. You put two in, you got one back. At least the machines were fair: they stole equally from those rich in socks and those poor in socks. At first you merely assumed that you had left one stuck to the washer or the drier like a piece of chewing-gum, but this obviously wasn't what happened. However scrupulous you were – you counted them all out and you counted them all in – you always lost one sock. Perhaps there was a little trap-door at the back of each machine, which opened for just long enough to snaffle it. Perhaps this was the owner's way of increasing the profit-margin on these establishments. Duffy had long since given up trying to fight the extra tariff. Instead, he played along with it. He owned only two kinds of sock: the black cotton/nylon mix from Marks & Spencer, and the red cotton/nylon mix from Marks & Spencer. That way, if you lost one, you didn't worry too much, and when you lost another you were laughing.

'Telephone,' said Carol sleepily as he shut the door of the flat.

'Breakfast,' Duffy replied to the mound of curly black hair on the pillow. He got the yoghurt, the muesli and the skimmed milk out of the fridge, fetched the granary bread, the brown sugar and the honey from the cupboard. You needed your health and strength, that's what everyone said. The breakfast at Sam Widges' was for his strength; this one was for his health. Besides, you should always give yourself a reward for going to the launderette.

As water began to gurgle in the bathroom, Duffy switched on his answering-machine. The message was brief, and easily understood. 'Duffy, this is Vic Crowther. If I pay four figures for a fucking alarm system I expect it to work. Now get your fat bottom down here.'

Fat? What was Vic going on about? Vic Crowther hadn't seen his bottom for three years, so how could he tell? Duffy thought of himself as short, admittedly, but muscular; his face was broad, sure, but jowl-free. He examined his hands: square-ended, a little stubby, but no sign of podge. Nervously, he took an extra spoonful of yoghurt, as if that would help the problem. Well, at least it might help the anxiety about the problem, which was a beginning.

'I'm off to see Vic Crowther,' he said as Carol poured her second cup.

'So you're not taking me out to Sunday lunch?'

Duffy grunted. Of course he wasn't. When had he ever taken her out to Sunday lunch? How long had they been together, or half-together? Seven years, something like that? Ten years? Eighty-four years? He'd *never* taken her out to Sunday lunch. Why was she suddenly expecting it? He looked across at her; she was grinning.

'Well, at least you've got some clean shirts,' she said. 'Or is it black-tie country down there now? Iron your cummerbund, sir?'

'It's work,' said Duffy. 'The alarm's buggered.'

'Probably Vic trying to break into his own house for the insurance.'

'Now, now,' said Duffy, suddenly protective about his former client. 'Vic's never been sent down for anything.'

'Nor was Pontius Pilate,' said WPC Carol Lucas.

'Really? You know, I never knew that. How did you know that?'

'It's on the police computer, Duffy, what do you think? Pilate, P., age, very old, distinguishing features, Roman nose, suspected attempting to pervert the course of justice, manslaughter and going equipped for crucifixion.'

'No, how do you know that?'

'I don't know, Duffy. Telly, I expect. They said he killed himself in the end, but no one's ever proved it.'

'I don't see Vic taking a handful of pills.'

'Or falling on his sword.'

'I didn't know he had a sword.'

'Duffy.' Carol leaned across the table and rapped gently on the side of Duffy's head, 'Is there anyone in today?'

'Oh, I get it.' All that laundry had clearly taken it out of him.

'By the way, how's Miss Tits?'

Duffy wondered briefly if he ought to feel guilty. He didn't think he knew anyone who particularly answered to this description at the moment. 'Eh?'

'Little Miss Tits. Belinda Whatsit.'

'Ah. Blessing.'

'Blessing. What a terrible name. Belinda Blessing. You'd have to take your clothes off if you were called that, wouldn't you?'

'It's not her original name. She had it altered.'

'So that she could take her clothes off.'

'Suppose so.'

'I wonder what else she had altered at the same time.'

'*Carol.* What's got into you?' He looked across at her pretty, morning Irish face with its frame of dark curls.

'You?' She grinned again.

'Ca-*rol*.' He got up. 'There's stuff in the freezer. Pizzas. And some fish bits with a low-calorie sauce.'

'Terrific. Drive carefully. Kiss.'

Duffy would have driven carefully even without Carol's advice. For one thing, he wasn't crazy about the M1: biggest unofficial race-track in the country, if you asked him, full of mad lorries and flashing headlights; even your family saloons thought it the right place to have a crack at the world land-speed record. For another thing, he was driving his new Sherpa van, sitting high in the seat and worrying about getting sideswiped. It had been a relief to junk that rusting F-reg number and get something new. Well, 'new' in the sense of new to him, not absolutely new: he wasn't doing as well as that. So, if it hadn't been for the other traffic, he'd have enjoyed sitting up proud in his white Sherpa with DUFFY SECURITY painted on each side, heading up the middle lane at a steady fifty-five.

There'd been that good scam up the M1 not long ago. Duffy, as an ex-copper, didn't really approve of coppers being villains; but he couldn't find it in him to do anything but laugh at this one. Some petrol company, instead of giving away wine-glasses or little koala bears to hang in your rear window, had come up with a different scheme for attracting customers. Every month they circulated their garages with a list of car numberplates, fifty or so. If you owned a car whose plate number was on the list, you could win anything from a hundred quid to a thousand. Of course, you had to buy some petrol at the garage first; the cashier wouldn't let any old Tom, Dick or Jimmy Fiddler run his finger down the numbers.

The scheme certainly brought in the customers, but it also set a few philosophers thinking. In particular, a group of coppers based near the M1 who liked a little challenge. All done in plain clothes, of course, and mostly out of hours. Two of them would drive to a garage, buy some petrol, all above board, and ask for the list of numbers. They might not find their own, but would come away having memorized a couple of others. Of course, if they'd only bought a gallon or two of petrol, they soon might need another garage, and be forced to squint at the numbers again. The next day, back in uniform, they might find themselves – in the course of duty, what else? – obliged to check the odd numberplate with the police computer. Owner's name and address, please. And then, if it was in the area, they might drive over and ask the fellow if he knew how he could pick up a couple of hundred quid, quite legit, all for a short drive? Of course, there'd have to be a drink in it for them, let's go halves, shall we, after all without us you wouldn't be picking up a penny, would you? They didn't even need to say they were policemen.

Duffy supposed it was dishonest, but found it hard to get indignant. Who was losing? Not the petrol companies, who were risking that amount of money anyway. Not the motorist who couldn't be bothered to check the numbers every month and was now getting a bonus: half of something was always more than nothing. Nor were the boys in blue exactly losing. They were merely showing the spirit of commercial enterprise which was supposed to be the making of the nation. Who was losing, who was actually losing? That was what crime was – one person gaining wrongfully from another. Here there were only winners. Until the day it had all come out, and a few bottoms had been smacked. Then the petrol company closed down the scheme for a bit, and everyone went back to collecting wine-glasses and miniature toy koala bears instead, which was a lot less fun to Duffy's mind.

Cruising the middle lane at fifty-five, he turned his mind to Belinda Blessing and Vic Crowther. Little Miss Tits, Carol had called her. Duffy smiled. The Little applied only to the Miss, not to the Tits. Very much not to the Tits. Belinda Blessing had been one of the earliest Page Three girls un-leashed on the nation. At several million breakfast tables men would have a quick glance at the headlines, then turn the page to be coshed with delight and awe by Belinda's . . . by Belinda's . . . well, tits, you couldn't call them anything else: Tits, in fact, with a capital letter. There would be throat-clearing at a million breakfast tables across the country, and sometimes there would be crossing of legs. Belinda had done her morning's work again.

She had long black hair, a neighbourly face, eyes of an

indeterminate colour, which didn't matter as Page Three was in black-and-white, plus what the caption-writer ingeniously referred to on her first appearance in the paper as BELINDA'S BLESSINGS. Not surprisingly, the invented surname allowed the roster of caption-writers full scope to demonstrate their inventiveness. BELINDA COUNTS HER BLESSINGS, followed – just in case the reader didn't get it – by ONE! TWO! Then there was BLESS ME - IT'S BELINDA and a dozen others. Readers became fond of her and wrote in to complain if they hadn't seen her Tits for a month or so. Cynical detractors, loosened by a couple of jars, maintained that Belinda without her Blessings would be just an ordinary-looking girl. But that, her passionate defenders across the beer-mat replied, was exactly what was special about her. She looked really friendly, you know, sort of girl who might have poured that pint for you, who you might have grown up with, who you could show off to your mum without worrying – that sort of girl. Except, except that she had these . . . Blessings.

After six months or so of newspaper fame, Belinda's Tits sacked their agent. They acquired instead a career promoter and personal publicist, who was only one person and still took the same twenty per cent. But he got her a celebrity spot at the Motor Show (she wouldn't lounge about on any old car), he had her opening a few supermarkets, he stage-managed her front end for photographers outside night-clubs, he was thought to have been behind that incident when she threw champagne at a well-known actor who had tried to go snorkelling in her cleavage, and he got her on to a number of TV chat-shows. Here her effervescent homeliness and prepared jokes endeared her even to those who had expected to disapprove. She acquired a boyfriend, and soon after disacquired him. The boyfriend sold his memoirs the following month to a rival paper: 'Why did I buy an MG? Well, I thought I needed a topless car to go with my topless bird.' Readers of Belinda's paper were loyally shocked at this vile piece of opportunism and applauded her magnanimity in not immediately taking revenge by telling the world what a tiny cock the fellow had.

Belinda, flattered by crimpers and lensmen, enjoyed every minute of it. But she also remembered her mum and two sisters that she'd only just managed to move out of the council house, and she knew the time would come when fellers would no longer be quite so interested in seeing her without her bikini top. What would happen then? Would she be able to make the jump to being a proper celebrity? From somewhere inside her came a mutter of fear and doubt. She looked around the men she knew and saw only two kinds: the ones who were scared of her fame, and the ones who were turned on by it. The first type you had to lasso even if you only wanted to have tea with them; the second type were merely booking you for another notch on their bedstead.

And then she met Vic. Oh, of course people said the obvious things; that Belinda had lost her dad when she was a teenager and was still looking for a father figure; they said she broke up Vic's marriage; they said she deliberately got pregnant. But it wasn't really like that. She and Vic just got on from the start; he made her laugh – that's always important, isn't it? He wasn't scared of her because she was famous; he was a success in his own field, so he didn't feel threatened; and when she said to him, 'You know, Vic, sometimes I just want to throw it all up and live in the country and have a horse,' he didn't say, 'Silly cow,' but just nodded and patted what he called her other pair and answered, 'That'd be nice.'

Of course Vic's marriage had been on the rocks for years, and she didn't deliberately get pregnant: it was just one of those things that happen when people fall in love, wasn't it? It had given her publicist a bit of a headache, too, but what in other circles might easily have been HUSBAND ABANDONS WIFE FOR PREGNANT GIRLFRIEND was transformed into BELINDA'S LOVE-CHILD, and that made it all more acceptable. Of course, the modelling dropped off a bit, though there was a patch of leotard work, showing young mums-to-be how to keep fit; but Belinda's heart wasn't really in it, and as she grew fatter with little Nikki she sometimes looked forward with dismay to getting the weight off and seeing if they still wanted to look at her without her top now she was a mum. She carried on doggedly for a year or two after Nikki's birth, until one day, as she was uncapping the piña colada mix, she said, without really meaning it any more than usual,

'You know, Vic, sometimes I just want to throw it all up and live in the country and have a horse.' To which Vic gave a grin and said, 'Well, I have seen this little place, you know.'

Exit 13, that's the one, Duffy thought, and cautiously edged his white Sherpa van into the slow lane. He hadn't ever really gone for Belinda – not even when she'd come out at him from the newspaper like a police snatch-squad. And when he'd turned up to install the alarm system three years ago, she'd been a bit too Lady Muck about the place for his taste. I mean, Braunscombe Hall may not have been one of your top-drawer, ermine-and-pearls country houses, but it was still Braunscombe Hall. And Belinda Blessing and Vic Crowther were still very much Belinda Blessing and Vic Crowther, weren't they? You had to laugh really, and in his quiet way Vic did have a chuckle about it; but it seemed to Duffy from his first visit that Belinda Blessing had solemn ambitions to become Belinda Braunscombe, Dowager Lady Muck.

Vic wasn't likely to change. For as long as Duffy had known him (and that was going back a dozen years), Vic had been the same. He'd played at being over fifty – one who'd examined a lot of life and wasn't going to be impressed any more – when his birth certificate still insisted he was under forty. He coupled this with a cheery public manner of the kind that union negotiators affect when chummying up to the TV camera. Such stolid affability made those with ungenerous minds suspicious. Duffy had once tried to run Vic Crowther in, years ago. Vic, apparently uninsulted, had just laughed, then called in Laski & Lejeune, his favourite firm of bent solicitors, to explain how the watches in their client's warehouse may very well have been quite by coincidence a perfect match to the ones in Duffy's report, but they still weren't stolen, oh dear me no, fat chance.

This had been in the old days, when Duffy was a junior South London copper and Vic Crowther was . . . what, exactly? On his occasional appearances in the paper, he was always referred to as 'local businessman Vic Crowther'; but when asked to specify what sort of business he would give his candid smile and answer, 'Oh, a little bit of this and a little bit of that.' He'd started in the building trade, and switched to installing fitted kitchens when he spotted that construction work was nicer if someone else did the hard part for you first. Then he began to reckon that it was always nicer if someone else did the hard part for you first. Franchises, sub-leases – this seemed to be Vic's favourite area: get the other fellow to put up his life savings, take ten per cent and, if the operation folds, well mugs will be mugs, won't they? At one stage Vic had owned a string of launderettes: hey, thought Duffy, I bet it was Vic who dreamed up the idea of the washing-machine that nicks one of your socks every time. There had also been a couple of Crowther-operated funeral parlours; he'd had a bite of the local fast-food business; and stepped into video hire pretty early on. Quite how legit he was had often been a matter of debate among the local CID, but no firm conclusion had been reached except the obvious one: that if Vic Crowther was clean, then the Queen of England peed standing up. A few coppers had tried to pin things on him, and Vic had always been friendly, then a bit less friendly, then called Laski & Lejeune, who were downright off-putting. If Vic did walk both sides of the street, it was probable he'd be just as canny when being wicked. And no doubt the principle remained the same: franchises, sub-leases and, if the operation folds, well mugs will be mugs, but I was down at the Duke of Clarence at the time, Officer, as most of the Rotary Club will confirm.

Duffy stopped his van at the turn-off to Braunscombe Hall. Those entrance pillars are new, he thought. Two square red-brick jobs, each topped off by a flaking stone globe; the right-hand one had a stone animal, also flaking, clamped to its curving side. A weathered ferret, as far as Duffy could see. There was something odd about the mixture of bright, new brick and old, pitted stone. Duffy stared at the fat orbs until they brought back the days when he used to open his paper and get a double-barrelled blast of Belinda between the eyes. Hey, perhaps that was it. The family arms of Belinda Blessing and Vic Crowther. Two Tits Rampant with an old ferret crawling over them.

Duffy was still grinning at this as he stomped on the brake and scattered the gravel in front of Braunscombe Hall. Vic Crowther came out to greet him.

'Do you want me to go round the back, boss?' asked Duffy cheerfully.

'This isn't the bloody British Grand Prix,' said Vic. 'Look what you've done to my gravel. I'll have to get that raked.'

At this moment a small woman in glasses, who Duffy thought must be Japanese, came round the side of the house in a half-run. 'Mr Crowther,' she said as she got up to them, then stopped and assessed Duffy before continuing. 'Mr Crowther, sir. Someone just stole Ricky.'

3 • KITCHEN/DINING-ROOM

The eye-level cupboards in the kitchen were much posher than any Vic Crowther had ever fitted in the old days. They were made of polished German oak, and their price implied that the polishing had been done by little men in lederhosen rubbing their bottoms around on them for thirty days or so. Beneath the cupboards lay a smart bank of domestic machinery which might have been nicked from Mission Control at Houston. What could they all be for, wondered Duffy, whose own kitchen leaned towards the spartan. A plump middle-aged woman, evidently not from the East, whom Vic identified as Mrs Hardcastle, pirouetted from one machine to another, occasionally springing open some hatch and plucking from it another glistening pie, another bubbling quiche. With a kitchen like this, you could start a hotel.

'Planning a big family?' asked Duffy.

'There's only Nikki,' said Vic. He was a bit heavier and a bit ruddier than Duffy remembered; perhaps he was getting to like his booze. 'I think Nikki's the lot. I think any more might interfere with the riding.' He sighed, and looked as if he were going to say more, but the various permanent and temporary inhabitants of the house began drifting into the dining area. If the kitchen was Mission Control, the dining-room was tourist/rustic. There was a long refectory table, oak beams which Duffy reckoned must have been at least two years old, an open fireplace whose surroundings were emblazoned with horse brasses, a cast-iron chandelier which had either been converted to electricity or most likely had started off like that anyway, a set of wheelback chairs and a pair of petit-point footstools. In the corner stood an oak spinning-wheel, just in case Vic and Belinda wanted to start making their own clothes or something.

The ex-Page-Three girl shook Duffy's hand and gave him a distant, chatelaine's smile, as if completely puzzled why Vic had asked him to eat with them: surely he had a pickled onion and a slice of cheese wrapped up in a red spotted handkerchief which he could take out and eat on the back steps while the farm dogs chewed his boots? My my, thought Duffy, she has come up in the world; mind you, those jodhpurs didn't exactly do wonders for her bum.

'This is Duffy,' said Vic to those already seated round the table. 'Old mate. Come to fix the alarm system.' The five guests all seemed to be in their thirties, and you could be sure they hadn't yet in their lives touched kitchen installation or the franchising of launderettes. Duffy was presented to Angela, who seemed rather puffy about the eyes and whose red hair had a strange gild to it that might have come from a large bottle; Jimmy, balding and slightly short of chin, who stood up and shouted, 'How d'ye do, officer'; Damian, in a velvet suit, who didn't rise, but turned instead to the blonde Lucretia, who nodded briefly at this tradesman who'd come to share their lunch; plus Sally, a cascade of giggles and black curls, who said, 'Is that your van?' As Duffy was about to sit down, Nikki skipped in, came across to him and looked up at his face. 'Shall I do my dance for you?'

'Later, sweetheart,' said Vic quietly.

'But I want to do my dance. He hasn't seen my dance.'

'Lunch,' Belinda insisted. Nikki sat down grumpily, and when Mrs Colin tried to adjust the napkin round her neck, stabbed the Filipino woman in the arm with a fork. Mrs Colin didn't complain; nobody rebuked the girl, or seemed to notice. Duffy noticed.

'Where's Taff?' Vic asked. 'Where's Henry?'

'Taffy took a sandwich to the woods,' said Damian, as if it were the quaintest piece of behaviour he'd ever heard, 'where he is attempting to slaughter the local wildlife with the help of a carbine. Though why he doesn't simply pick up the poor little furry things and bite their heads off with his metal teeth, I'm sure I don't know.'

'And bloody Henry's bloody not here,' added Angela.

Every so often through lunch Duffy had to stop himself from nearly choking – a reaction which would not have been caused by Mrs Hardcastle's pies. Damian did most of the talking. He had long lashes and wavy brown hair, and the tip of his nose waggled very slightly from side to side as he spoke. His chubby face seemed to shine with the simple pleasure of being Damian. He held forth about topics and people unfamiliar to Duffy, occasionally breaking off to wave aloft an empty bottle of wine as if he were in a restaurant; whereupon

Mrs Hardcastle would come and replace it. Jimmy listened to him with his mouth hanging agape, and laughing just a little after the others. Vic didn't speak; Belinda spoke, but not to Duffy. Well, if they wanted him to play the tradesman, that was fine by him. Fix the alarm after lunch and join the mad-men back on the race-track. He wondered if Carol was having the pizza or the fish in low-calorie sauce for her lunch.

'Is that your van?' It was Sally, from across the table. She had lots of black curls down to her neck and large black eyes which didn't seem to be focusing exactly on Duffy. Maybe she needed glasses; or maybe it wasn't that at all. In either case, it was the second time she asked him that question.

'Mmm,' he replied.

'Duffy Security,' she continued, drawing out the syllables and giggling when she reached the end of the phrase. 'Are you secure? I like a man that's secure.' She giggled again. 'Are you secure?'

Duffy didn't know what to answer. What did she mean? Did he have any break-ins at his place? Did he have a mort-gage? Did he have a steady girlfriend? Cautiously, he answered, 'Sometimes.'

'I always assume,' said Damian in a voice that addressed the whole table while somehow ignoring Duffy, 'that policemen and all those people who deliver one's money to the bank in crash helmets, all that Wells Fargo crew, must have very peculiar sex lives. I mean, *truncheons* for a start.' Sally giggled. 'And *handcuffs*. What one could do with handcuffs . . . And those lovely big *dogs* . . .'

Angela, who had been silent for most of the meal, stood up suddenly and ran to the door. There was a silence.

'Berk,' said Lucretia.

'Oh, *whoopsie*,' said Damian. 'A bit tactless. But it just slipped out, as the actress said to the bishop. Oh God, I'll have to eat humble pie now. By the way, Mrs Hardcastle,' he raised his voice towards the kitchen area, 'the pies are magnificent.' Mrs Hardcastle smiled. 'My felicitations to the chefette.' She smiled once more; she looked quite fond of Damian.

'Have you got a dog?' It was Sally again.

'No.'

'I mean, for the business. You must have a dog for the business.'

'No.'

Sally took a while to assimilate this response. She was seen thinking it over carefully. 'I suppose the fact of the matter is that your dogs have been taken over by technology. Technological advances have eliminated . . .' She paused; these long words were taking it out of her. '. . . your use . . . for . . . the dog.'

'No, I just don't like dogs.'

Sally thought this the funniest thing she'd heard in ages; she yelped, she whinnied, she yodelled with laughter. 'He doesn't like dogs,' she repeated, and her eyes seemed to diverge even more from the parallel. Duffy squinted down the table. Lucretia was watching him impassively; she didn't blink when he caught her eye, merely continued to examine him. With her flowing blonde hair and firm, neatly cut features, she looked the sort of girl you only came across half-way through a fashion spread in one of the posh magazines. The models there had spent months being coached in the art of the frank, disdainful, fuck-you glance; this girl had it in real life. She looked way out of his league.

'Given that you don't like dogs . . .' It was Damian, addressing Duffy for the first time. '. . . then perhaps you're the fellow we're looking for. Can you explain your whereabouts on the night of . . .'

'Knock it off,' said Vic rather sharply. 'Ricky's gone. I mean, Ricky's body's gone. Mrs Colin put it in a laundry-bag and hung it in the back cloaks and someone nicked it.'

'Well, you do make a lot of meat pies around here,' said Damian brightly. 'Perhaps the moving finger of suspicion points at Mrs Hardcastle.' He pretended to examine a large home-made chicken-and-ham pie, then acted a bout of nausea.

'Leave it, Damian, old son,' said Vic. 'I suppose someone had better go and fetch Angela.'

Belinda went to look for her, and after a few minutes they returned together. There was trifle, plus fried-up Christmas pudding which must have been in the deep freeze for eight months or so. As coffee was being served, the door opened and a large, red-faced, square-headed man of about forty came in. He was wearing a bright hound's-tooth check suit, a mole-skin waistcoat of ancient cut, a check Viyella shirt and a red spotted bow-tie. He looked enthusiastically across the table at his fiancée.

'Henry darling, where have you been?' said Angela, with a sweetness Duffy hadn't thought anyone at the table capable of. 'I've been trying to get hold of you for hours.'

'Sorry, old girl,' Henry replied. 'You know how it is. Had to see a man about a dog.'

Angela screamed. The room fell silent. Henry shifted awk-wardly from one fat brown brogue to the other. 'What have I said?'

●

After lunch, Vic took Duffy along to the video library. A large sheet of brown paper had been taped over the hole in the french windows.

'That's where they threw Ricky through,' Vic explained.

'Cor.' In a curious, distant way, Duffy was rather impressed. Coppers, and ex-coppers, get so familiar with crime that any minor innovations are almost to be welcomed. Duffy had certainly never seen this before. 'Big dog, was he?'

'Mmm, well,' said Vic. He looked a bit vague and helpless. 'He was, sort of, you know, dog-sized.'

'Gotcha,' said Duffy. 'Was he any particular make?'

'They're not called makes, Duffy, they're called breeds. Even I know that. No, well I expect he was, he was just a sort of standard . . . dog. Curly hair, tail.'

'Four legs?' asked Duffy.

'Yeah. One of those ones with four legs. I can't say I'm a great student of dogs.' This was one of Vic's less necessary remarks.

'Was he dead when he came through the window?'

'Well, he was certainly dead by the time Mrs Colin found him.' He paused a moment. 'I suppose you don't get finger-prints on a dog?'

Duffy considered the question briefly. 'Not if it's disappeared.'

'Right.'

'So, when do the coppers arrive?'

'Coppers? I'm none too keen on coppers.'

'So I remember.' Duffy smiled. He wondered how much of a villain Vic had been in the old days, how much of a villain he still might be. Did the launderettes and the funeral parlours and the video-hire shops pay for a place as big as this? Or had there been the odd source of income on the side?

'And in any case, now that Ricky's disappeared, it'd just be a waste of their time coming, especially at the weekend. I thought, I just thought I'd . . .'

'. . . let sleeping dogs lie?'

'That sort of thing,' said Vic, and chuckled. 'You know, it's always nice to talk to someone who speaks the same language.'

'Not many of *them* were born in Catford,' said Duffy, nodding back in the direction of the dining-room.

'Yeah, well, they're mainly Belinda's friends. Anyway, you have a big house, you meet the other people from big houses. They're not as bad as you think,' said Vic. 'They're a bit loud sometimes, but they're young.'

'Well, I guess I just don't like posh people.'

'They're not all that posh.'

'They're all posher than me,' Duffy insisted rather grimly.

'That's usually a fair enough starting-point with everybody, I'd say.' It was Duffy's turn to chuckle. 'I mean, that Damian, for instance. He's just a vicar's son, clever boy, went to college somewhere, got in with a smarter crowd. *Damian*'s not a posh name.'

'It's posher than Vic.'

'Right, but that's your England nowadays, isn't it, Duffy? Your Vics can mix with your Damians, and your Damians can get to know your Hugos. All this class stuff, it's out the window now. It's what you are, not who you are. I mean, Belinda and me, look at us. When I grew up – you remember, no, you'd be too young to remember, but when I grew up there used to be silver threepenny pieces.'

'Heard of them,' said Duffy.

'People used to put them in the Christmas pudding. You know, hide them and make a little mark on the side of the pudding so they knew where they were and the kids got them. Well, we didn't have threepenny bits like that in our house. My Dad used to wrap farthings in silver paper. That's what we got. Probably got a dose of metal poisoning as well. And now here I am in a big house. That's England,' said Vic, coming out of what was clearly a set speech with a slurp of grateful patriotism. 'That's England. And look at Belinda. It wouldn't have happened in the old days. You know I dote on her, but she couldn't have done it in the old days. People would have looked down their noses because she took her clothes off for the papers. Now people don't mind that. She goes hunting with people who fifty, no, twenty years ago wouldn't have let her hold their horse. That's England, and bloody good too, I say.'

'Well, maybe I'd like posh people more if I had a big house like this,' said Duffy.

'No need to be chippy, old son. I mean, the house is a good example. Know who I bought it off? Do you remember the Filth?' Duffy nodded. The Filth had been briefly famous in the early sixties: three or four top-ten hits, never quite made Number One, but picked up a good following, who stayed with them for some years. Not as good as the Hollies or the Tremeloes in Duffy's book, but still . . . 'Remember the one who played keyboard?' Duffy vaguely recalled a velveteen elf with a doggy grin, who always performed with a large feather protruding from the back of his trousers. 'Izzy Dunn? Remember? That's who I bought it off. Point is, houses like this are being owned by people like us' – Vic paused, and slightly adjusted his phrase – 'by people like me, anyway, into your second generation. I mean, the house got a bit knocked around when Izzy was here, he was paranoid about people watching him eat, so he boarded up the minstrels' gallery, and he turned the squash court into a recording studio and he put in quite a few picture windows and he even tried out piranha fish in the lake, but it's still a nice piece of house. I get tourists coming past looking at me like I'm the lord of the manor.

Have the Crowthers been in this part of the world for many centuries? I can hear them asking it.' Vic chuckled.

'By the way,' said Duffy. 'Those stone balls you've got on your entrance. What's that ferret doing climbing over one of them?'

'Duffy, you don't deserve to live in a big house like this. It's not a ferret, you wally, it's a salamander.'

'Is that a sort of ferret? Anyway, it's got bits missing.'

'It's a fully weathered salamander, Duffy. Looks like it's been there for ages, doesn't it? I'll let you into a little secret. There's a place you can go where you get them pre-weathered. Like pre-shrunk jeans, you know. Well, saves you the bother, doesn't it? They've got all sorts, bears, pelicans, you can take your pick.'

'Why did you choose a salamander?'

Vic looked a bit sly. 'Well, to be honest, I didn't know it was a salamander either when I first saw it. I mean, I could see it was a lizard or something, and I said to the fellow, "What's with the lizard?" He said it was a salamander, and that in the old days people thought it was special; they believed it could walk through fire without getting burnt. And you know, I said to myself, that's a bit like old Vic Crowther, is that salamander. He can walk through fire without getting burnt, touch wood, so far anyway. So we got it.'

'Why isn't there one on the other ball? Did it fall off?'

'No, it didn't. You only have one. It's heraldry, or something,' said Vic vaguely.

While they were talking, Duffy had been looking round the room and remembering the system he had installed three years previously. He excused himself briefly and went to examine the control box fitted behind a piece of fake panelling in the master bedroom. On his way he passed Mrs Colin, who was trying to take Nikki out for a walk, and getting kicked quite a bit. When he came back he was feeling irritated. He shut the door of the video library. Sunday afternoon, too; bloody hell.

'We talked it all through at the time, Vic. Doors, windows, pressure plates. We decided not to alarm the windows because all you need is a strong wind and the whole system keeps going off. We agreed on alarming the doors and having pressure plates underneath the ground-floor windows. Only you decided not to have a pressure plate in the video library because it was a small room and someone might want to stay up pretty late there and you didn't want them setting everything off when you'd all gone to bed. Obviously the glass isn't alarmed. But if they'd tried to force the window, all hell would have broken loose.'

'So the flaw in this pricey number you fixed me up with is that if people throw dogs through this window I won't know until Mrs Colin does her rounds in the morning?' Vic was smiling at him as he said this.

'Not if you don't hear the crash. I could install a pressure plate if you liked.'

'No, I shouldn't bother.'

Duffy was feeling pissed off. 'While I'm here I'll check the system anyway.'

'Yes, that's a good idea,' said Vic. 'It might take you some time. And on second thoughts maybe you could install a pressure plate. And I expect you haven't brought all the bits and pieces of equipment you need in your van. And, of course, it's a Bank Holiday tomorrow.'

'I don't understand,' said Duffy.

'Even if they'd forced the french windows last night nothing would have happened,' said Vic. 'I didn't turn the alarm on.'

'I don't understand,' Duffy repeated.

'I hope you will, son. I hope you will.'

At that moment the door of the video library opened and a flirtatious Nikki appeared. She looked up at Duffy and said, 'Can I do my dance for you now?'

'Later, sweetheart, later,' said Vic.

'Can I do my dance for Taff when he comes back from the woods?'

'That's a nice idea, sweetheart. Off you go now.'

Vic unlocked the french window with the brown-paper patch in it and stepped out rather heavily on to a flagged terrace. Duffy followed him. Growing between the square stones were little plants – probably herbs or something – which Duffy didn't recognize. A couple of large urns, which may have been pre-weathered or may have been the genuine pound note, contained a bright array of geraniums. A bumble-bee droned slowly past, flying awkwardly as if weighed down by shopping. Hesitantly, Duffy sniffed the air. He felt like someone asked to taste the wine in an expensive restaurant who doesn't reckon his chances on knowing whether the stuff is meant to taste like that or not.

'Smells different,' he announced cautiously.

'Funny, that, isn't it?' said Vic. 'I notice it, too. It's all these years of being in London. Doesn't smell real, does it, the country? Smells like it comes out of a can. Old God up there with his aerosol thinking, "What shall we give them this morning: puff of Spring Flowers, squirt of Autumn Fragrance?" You know, I often come out here and feel like having a smoke, just to put some real smell in the air. And I don't even smoke any more.'

By this time they were leaning over the stone balustrade at the back of the terrace. Duffy's eye was caught by a movement away to his right. A figure had turned the right-hand corner of the terrace and was coming towards them. He was crawling, quite fast, with his elbows stuck out and his toes kicking at the ground. Head down, he passed five feet below them without taking any notice, scuttled towards the far end of the terrace and disappeared from view.

'Looked a bit like a salamander,' said Duffy knowledgeably.

'Jimmy was in the Army,' Vic explained. 'Loved it, always loved it. They said he wasn't bright enough. He's always going on at me to let him build an assault course in the grounds here. He thinks guests might like to try it – you know, squeeze through those big sewer pipes and swing across the lake on ropes – before they earn their gin and tonic.'

'What's he do now?'

'I think it's called being an estate agent,' said Vic sceptically. 'But I don't think I've ever heard him talk about it.'

He led Duffy to a rustic seat which confirmed Duffy's suspicions about the discomforts of the country.

'Spit it out, Vic,' said Duffy.

'It's Angela. We're a bit worried about Angela. Belinda and me.'

'Is she the one with the red hair?' Out of a bottle, Duffy silently added.

'Right. We've known her ever since we moved down here – longer than any of the others. She's best mates with Belinda, and I'm very . . . fond of her.'

'Does that mean what I think it means?'

Vic ignored him. 'I don't know how to put this, but Angela's always been a bit . . . rackety. She's been around a bit, as they say, by anyone's standards. I mean, that sort of thing's more noticeable in the country. No one cares where anyone sticks their chewing-gum in London, but you have to be slightly more careful out here. And she's never been a careful girl. Do anything, try anything, that's always been her motto.'

'So she screws around a lot and takes drugs,' said Duffy, keeping a professional voice on. 'What else?'

Vic shrugged. 'She might look a tough cookie to you at first glance, but she isn't. That's one of the reasons she gets on with Belinda. You know, they both look like they know the way everything runs, but deep down,' Vic's voice shifted register slightly, 'they're just girls at heart. Little girls lost in the wood.' He paused. Duffy didn't exactly feel a torment of sympathy for the two maidens adrift in the bracken.

'Take a squint at her wrists if you get the chance. Looks like Clapham junction with all those lines. That was the second time, about a couple of years ago. The time before that, it was the pills. They pumped her out, tried to cheer her up, told her not to do it again, and she went on exactly as before. Two years ago, as I said, shaving her legs in the bath, takes the blade out of the razor and . . . Someone found her an hour or so later. It was a miracle she wasn't dead.'

No, it wasn't a miracle, thought Duffy; or not exactly a miracle. It sounded more like incompetence. Duffy had come across quite a few attempted suicides in his days as a copper. People always said that if you failed it proved you didn't really want to die. Duffy disagreed. What it usually proved was that you weren't very good at doing it. People thought cutting your wrists was easy, so they just slashed across at right angles, but often the weight of your hands just closed up the cuts again. The people who were really serious cut their wrists diagonally.

'Poor kid. Why did she do it?'

Vic shrugged. 'Said she wanted to be dead. Said no one loved her. You know, the usual stuff. The parents split up when she was a kid, that may have something to do with it. They're dead now.'

'How old is she?'

'Thirty-seven, thirty-eight. Looks younger, doesn't she? They do nowadays. She's a sweet kid underneath it all.'

Duffy grunted. People were always saying things like that. *She's a sweet kid underneath it all.* So why does there have to be all that stuff on top, Duffy always wanted to ask.

'So, you get the picture. Things definitely a bit dodgy.'

'She got money?'

'She got money. Anyway, a bit dodgy, and all the usual things had been tried, doctors and clinics and you know what, and lots of promises, followed by lots of promises being broken. Even if you're fond of them you can get a bit fed up with people like that. So, about a year ago, she meets Henry.'

'Was that the one who said he'd been to see a man about a dog?'

'Check. Henry's been around for a long time. Comes from one of these country families that go way back.'

'Vic,' said Duffy. '*All* families go way back. I've got just as many ancestors as the next man. So've you. So's a ferret.'

'Don't start getting chippy again. You know what I mean. Henry's about forty-five, and everyone had pretty much given up on him. In the marriage stakes, I mean. He's a bit funny, you know, you don't quite suss what makes him tick. Anyway, contrary to all expectations, he went for her. Perhaps because she was different. I mean with Henry, it'd always been girls with headscarves and green wellies whose idea of fun was to pull the shooting-stick out from under him at the point-to-point.'

'So it's wedding bells, is it?'

'Three weeks' time. The church is booked.'

'Well, that's all right, then,' said Duffy, prodding.

'She lives in this cottage, just outside the village. About two months ago things started happening. Just little things. Noises in the garden and you can't tell if it's a dog or something else. One day she finds a dead bird on the step – well, it could have been a cat leaving it there. Knockings in the night. Then one morning a stone comes through the window. That did it. She took a handful of pills to calm herself down and passed out. That's when we told her to move in here.'

'Where does she get all the pills? And the other stuff for that matter.'

'Rich people can always get pills, Duffy. Anyway, the point is, she's really on the edge now. She quietened down a bit when she got here, then she got worried about the cottage and went back, and do you know what she said? She said she thought the whole woodpile had moved about two yards. The whole pile. Just got up and walked. That set her off, and not knowing whether she was imagining it didn't help.'

'What does Henry think about all her . . . activities?'

'We think he's had the cleaned-up version. I mean, I don't think he gets off on that side of her. He probably just thinks girls are like that, one day they're a bit excited and one day they're a bit quiet.'

'So she's on the edge.'

'She's really on the edge. I mean, I don't know what it's about, and I don't know how much she's imagining, but I do know we've got to keep her in one piece for the next three weeks. This is her last chance, Bel and me both think so. Henry's her last chance. Getting her up that altar is her last chance. We just think she'd fall apart if she doesn't make it.'

'So the dog didn't help.'

'The dog did not help. Who'd do a thing like that, Duffy? Poor innocent creature . . .'

'I thought you didn't like dogs.'

'I didn't say I did. I just said they were poor innocent creatures.'

'Right. What else?'

'She says she's being blackmailed.'

'Now he tells me. Who, why, how much?'

'Wouldn't say. Just clammed up. You don't like to push her in case . . .'

'Sure,' said Duffy. 'Call the coppers.'

'She wouldn't talk to the coppers. And I'm not having coppers around if I can help it. Old habits die hard.' Yes, and coppers with sharp noses might arrive bringing big dogs with sharp noses. They stood up. 'So you'll stick around for a few days?'

Duffy nodded. 'I charge higher rates for posh people.'

Vic shook his head sadly. 'You're such a bad businessman, Duffy. I'll pay you your normal rates.'

'All right.'

They walked slowly round the outside of the house, as if inspecting it for possible ways to break in. When they reached the drive Duffy swore. Bloody hell, someone had been fiddling with his van. It was all at a funny angle. He walked across the gravel, half looking across to the house as he did so. His two offside tyres were flat.

●

Minder to a slice of posh, Duffy thought. Well, if that's what they wanted to pay him for . . . In Duffy's view, Braunscombe Hall didn't need Duffy. It needed the coppers, and it needed a psychiatric nurse, and it needed a good spring-clean, one long squirt with some giant aerosol which made selected humans go around for a couple of minutes buzzing like a dentist's drill before falling down with their legs in the air; but it didn't need Duffy. On the other hand, who did you hire if you wanted to make sure someone got married? Were there wedding enforcers in the Yellow Pages? Perhaps they'd ask him to give Angela away, just to make sure he could accompany her all the way to the altar. Would he have to manacle her for the trip? Yes, sir, and with the grey morning suit and the gloves and the topper, we recommend this nice pair of silver-gilt handcuffs. Very discreet, as you can see, sir. No, everyone's getting married in them nowadays. As the bridegroom slips the ring on the bride's finger, the security adviser unlocks the manacles and throws the key to the posse of waiting girls. First one to catch it is next up the aisle.

Still, it was the client who was paying, and forty a day plus expenses (no, he shouldn't have used that line about charging more for posh people – he should just have upped his rate) also bought, for a brief initial period, the benefit of the doubt. And he hadn't really examined this Angela, just seen her bolt from the room at the mention of a dog. He'd obviously have to watch his tongue about the place. Not say 'Woof Woof' at the wrong moment. Customer relations, Duffy, he thought, customer relations. It wasn't his strong point and he knew it.

'Duffy's staying on for a couple of days,' Vic announced casually as dinner began. 'The alarm system's all cocked to hell.'

'Maybe it was a bad installation,' said Belinda sarcastically. Thanks a bunch, Bel, thought Duffy. He tried to imagine the conversation between Bel and Vic when the latter had informed her that Duffy was going to hang around for a bit. He wondered where he'd be sleeping. Probably in some attic with newspaper on the floor and a broken window, if Bel had her way.

'Well, that's very jolly,' said Damian, looking evenly at Duffy. 'You can make up a four at bridge.' He batted his long lashes and gave the tip of his nose what seemed like an intentional waggle.

'I don't play,' said Duffy.

'Then we'll have to make you dummy, won't we?' Damian smirked and Sally, the one with big squiffy eyes who always giggled, giggled. You watch it, my son, Duffy wanted to say, or you'll get your nice velvet suit all muddy. Instead, he looked around the table and said, 'Who's been mucking with my van?'

'Mucking?' replied Damian. 'With your van? I wouldn't muck with somebody else's.'

'Two of my tyres got let down. That's dangerous. And if the rim's gone through the tyre that's criminal damage as well,' he said, trying to sound a bit more authoritative.

'Round up all the usual suspects,' bellowed Jimmy, as if he had just thought of the line. Bald twerp, thought Duffy, and remembered Jimmy scuttling along below the terrace like a salamander. No, like a ferret.

'I thought you were meant to be secure,' said Sally. 'Duffy Security,' she repeated, and grinned at him.

'I'll pump up your poor little tyres if you'll play bridge with us,' said Damian in a tone of mock weariness, as if this really was his last offer and nothing Duffy did would make him improve it.

'Round up all the usual suspects,' repeated Jimmy. Lucretia was silent.

'Put it on the bill if there's any damage,' said Vic, 'and stop messing about if it was any of you kids.' He treated them like an uncle who had too much patience, Duffy thought; as if smacked bottoms and tears before bedtime were bad ideas.

Turning slightly as he ate, Duffy tried to get a squint at Angela's forearms. Wrists like Clapham Junction, Vic had said. Well, Clapham Junction was wrapped in tarpaulin: a beige rollneck sweater also rolled its way all down her arms and covered the first inch or two of her hands. She didn't talk much, this woman he was meant to be minding.

At that moment, the door opened and a short man in a black turtleneck number entered. His neatly cut black beard made him look a bit like a member of a weekend jazz band who played trad at minor festivals; but the shape of his body made this unlikely. His top half was almost triangular: his swelling shoulders embarrassed his head with their size. His upper arms were powerfully developed, but his hands were quite small. His waist was narrow, and he moved delicately.

'Taffy,' said Vic. 'We wondered where you'd got to.' The black-haired man silently raised one of his hands and showed the table three pigeons, their necks tied together with string.

'Pigeon pie,' he said, in a very quiet voice.

Duffy expected some elaborate sally to come from Damian's curvy lips; but all he said was, 'I like pigeon pie.'

It was only when the pigeons had been handed over to Mrs Hardcastle that Duffy remembered. Christ, you're getting slow, he thought; you'd never have been that slow when you were on the beat. But, then, you'd hardly have expected to run into this particular pigeon-slaughterer on the Buckinghamshire/Bedfordshire borders. Taffy was a Welshman, Taffy was a thief, Taffy came to my place and stole a side of beef. Except that, in this case, Taffy was an Englishman, and his name was a shortening of Tafford. Taffy was an Englishman, and a bit more than a thief.

There must have been a time when Taffy was appearing on the front page of the same tabloid in which you could find Belinda aiming her upper storey at you from Page Three. Neither of them much resembled their photographic images. Belinda didn't look at all like the sort of girl who would romp across the room, plant herself wigglingly on your knee and teasingly undo your top button; while Taffy, seated across from her and neatly slicing his roast veal, didn't look at all like what certain headline-writers enthusiastically referred to as Public Enemy Number One. Where was the glazed hunter-killer look which had helped sell so many newspapers?

Taffy's career went way back and began, like most criminal careers, in mediocrity: a little pilfering, a little taking and driving away, a little gentle robbery. He didn't steal much, he wasn't particularly violent, and he got caught quite often. What with the constant interruptions to Taffy's schooling, there was little chance of him getting into university. He was in his middle twenties before he finally broke out of the self-defeating cycle of small theft, small violence and small spells in prison. He worked out that the amount you could steal was often directly related to the amount of violence you were prepared to use. This key discovery led to his career breakthrough: the very nasty roughing-up of a husband-and-wife in Sussex, in return for which he obtained a large quantity of Georgian silver, not all of it on obvious display. Taffy also worked out that if you stole more at one time, then you didn't have to steal so often, and the fewer times you went to work, the less often the lads in blue uniforms had a chance to nab you. As a result, Taffy was for some time able to live a normal social life; though he never did get into university.

What put him on the front page helping Belinda sell copies for the same press proprietor was a touch of over-enthusiasm with an iron bar during a slack period for news. He'd been serving two years in Maidstone for being over-fond of what didn't belong to him when he suddenly went stir-crazy, brained a prison officer with a piece of railing and did a runner. Where he'd got the weapon from nobody found out. The photo of the officer with blood all over his face looked rather fetching to the professional eye of front-page layout men; and it was swiftly followed by a picture of Taffy himself, definitely not looking his best. For a few summer weeks he became a brief celebrity. One newspaper offered a reward for his recapture; another speculated that he had escaped with the intention of making some public protest – perhaps he planned to interfere with the minor royal wedding two weeks hence. The public quickly deduced that Taffy was on the run, eager to inflict maximum violence on anyone who stood in his way, and plotting to blow up the entire royal family. A Welsh reader wrote to *The Times* pointing out that Taffy was not one of his fellow-countrymen.

In fact, Taffy was the opposite of on the run: he was holed up with a bit of female company and a crate of his favourite beer, both of which he'd been badly missing in prison, and like any other loyal citizen he watched the royal wedding on the telly and reckoned we did these things better than anyone else. He guessed he'd get another five for braining the warder, and get beaten up a bit by the other screws, which was fair enough; but, when he turned himself in, he did it cleverly, by claiming the newspaper's reward for his own recapture, and arranging for what the newspaper imagined was a secret rendezvous in a public place to be covered by several other papers, and even by television. He didn't get the reward, of course; but he copped a lot of publicity, some of which hinted that here was a human being who, though evil, might be reclaimable for society. So he went back to prison, and he got beaten up a bit when nobody was looking, and he got the five he'd anticipated; whereupon he began attending chapel regularly, and started taking an Open University course in sociology, both of which activities eventually impressed the parole board. He was released quietly, at dawn, with a damp mist in the air, and he never went to church again.

Taffy was very quiet over dinner, not saying much and laughing at other people's remarks. His neck and shoulders were enormous. Duffy had seen that sort of muscular development before in ex-cons. The ones who didn't go all apathetic in prison often took to furious keep-fit activity; but

since the opportunities for this were usually a bit limited –
especially if you were doing a spell in solitary – it often ended
up with you doing pull-ups and push-ups in your cell. You
could easily get a bit obsessive about this, and the obsession
eventually showed itself in the shape of your body.

'You're a bit of a chancer,' said Duffy when he got Vic on
one side after dinner.

'How do you mean?'

'Taffy.'

'Taffy? Don't you like him?'

'You know who he *is*, Vic?'

'You mean, do I know who he *was*? Of course I know who
he was.' Vic shook his head a little sorrowfully. 'Don't you
believe in rehabilitation, Duffy? Society offering a helping
hand to the offender? "Come unto me, all ye who have done
more than five years inside." Don't you believe in any of that?'

Duffy couldn't tell how far Vic was taking the piss, so he
ducked the question. 'I notice he kills wild animals,' he said
neutrally.

'A pigeon is not an animal, Duffy. It's a bird. You're in the
country now. And if you want to lock up fellows who kill
birds you may as well begin with all the dukes and marquises
and whatsit.'

'That'd make a good start.'

At this moment Mrs Hardcastle came up to them. 'I know
this sounds silly, Mr Crowther, but I thought I should mention it. Some of the cutlery has gone missing.'

4. BILLIARD ROOM

Duffy pushed open the kitchen door and edged cautiously out on to the terrace. He sniffed the air apprehensively. He knew what Vic meant about wanting to light a cigarette to make the place smell proper. Country smells were all a mixture of you didn't know what: flowers and trees and grass and stuff. People in the country put their heads back and gargled with their noses; they stopped beneath trees for a snort of pong; they held blind tastings of roses. Flowers were all right to look at in Duffy's book, but he thought it a bit degenerate to go sniffing them. Already he felt nostalgic for the smells of the city: the dieselly reek of a hot bus engine; a dense noseful of fried onions escaping from a burger bar; the monoxide of stalled traffic.

Vic had told Duffy to give him ten minutes or so and then to join him in the billiard room for a chat with Angela. Duffy wrinkled his nose. That was another thing about the country he didn't like: it was full of dead animals. Someone had put a dead bird on Angela's doorstep; someone had tossed her pet dog through the french windows; a well-known ex-con walks in with three dead pigeons. In Duffy's experience, all work involving dead animals was likely to be messy. There'd been that case of his in Soho some years back, which had started with something very nasty being done to a cat down in Surrey. Something to do with the spit-roast attachment on the cooker. Duffy didn't like to think about it even now.

Braunscombe Hall looked to the distant or ignorant observer as if it might be an Elizabethan manor, but in fact it was built in the 1880s for a banker who didn't quite make it to Lord Mayor of London. In the normal way, one section of the ground floor had been tacitly reserved for men: smoking-room, gun room, billiard room; and beneath all three lay a large vault where the not-quite Lord Mayor cellared vintages which he did not live to enjoy. There was no longer a gun room, only a gun cupboard, to which Vic kept the key; the smoking-room had long since fallen victim to female emancipation; while Vic's idea of cellaring a vintage was to get enough Vinho Verde from the supermarket to see them through the weekend. Only the billiard room retained its original function, and even that had seen some renovation when

Izzy Dunn, who played keyboard in the Filth with a feather sticking out of his bottom, had owned the house. Izzy had got a bit paranoid about a stretch of green baize, twelve feet by six, and he'd got even more paranoid about his inability to get the fucking balls in the fucking holes, man, so he'd swapped it for a pool table; while into the square divisions of the barrel-vaulted white plaster ceiling he'd stuck twelve by eights of his favourite brothers-in-arms of the music business, and that made it all a lot jollier, didn't it? Vic, who had known a time when the temperance billiard hall above Burton the Tailor's was the best place to spend a wet afternoon, had reverted to tradition and got a mate to knock him out a reconditioned table for not much more than four figures, with a set of super-crystallate balls and half a dozen cues thrown in. Belinda had insisted on smartening the room up a bit, so instead of that awful heavy shade coming right down over the table there was a set of spotlights recessed in the ceiling; she put a pink chintzy sofa at one end in case anyone wanted to watch, and she took down Izzy's photos of rock stars and picked out the cross-bars of the barrel-vaulting in a matching pink. But, all in all, and even though they tended to call it the snooker room rather than the billiard room, it was pretty much like old times in there.

Vic yielded his place on the chintzy sofa to Duffy. Angela didn't seem to register the substitution. As Vic headed for the door, casually rolling a ball up the snooker table as he went past, Duffy examined her profile. Squarish jaw, fullish around the cheeks, a little pouchy under the eyes, brown eyes, pale cheeks which emphasized the glow of hennaed hair and made it seem more artificial. She was a good-looking woman in need of a ten-thousand-mile service.

'Vic tells me you've a spot of bother.'

She looked up brightly. In full face her jaw became less square, her nose slimmer, her large brown eyes even larger. A brief crackle of current buzzed through them, and she seemed animated, laughing, sexy; definitely not one of your green-wellies brigade. Then she clouded over again as the question seemed to get through to her. 'Everything's absolutely fine,' she replied in a monotone.

'Sorry about the dog. Who could have done such a thing?'

'There are a lot of perverts around nowadays,' she said vaguely.

'But don't you want to find out who did it?'

Angela shrugged. 'What's the point in finding some pervert who likes to kill dogs?'

'So that he won't do it again. So that he'll be punished.'

'We all punish ourselves, don't we?' said Angela, giving him a lethargic half-smile which may or may not have been intended to appear mysterious.

'Do we? Look, I know it's none of my business . . .'

'No, it isn't any of your business. Everything's fine, I've told you.'

'Someone's blackmailing you.'

'No they're not. Everything's fine. I'm getting married soon. Do you smoke?'

'No. Yes, I heard. Congratulations. Vic told me you were getting blackmailed.'

'Wherever did he get that idea? He is sweet, old Vic. Must have misunderstood something I said.'

'He's not stupid, old Vic.'

'No, he's not stupid, he's sweet. But he doesn't always understand things.'

'But he did understand that you needed looking after? That's why you moved in here, after all.'

Angela continued looking away from him, her hair shimmering a little in the spotlights. 'Well, we all get nerves before the Big Event, don't we? Nerves, that's what I had.'

This isn't getting us anywhere, Duffy thought. At the same time he didn't know how hard he could push her. Going on this way was exhausting; it was like bump-starting a hearse. That first sparkle of animation seemed gone for ever.

'About your dog. It was you that stole him, wasn't it?'

'What do you mean?'

'You stole him out of the cloakroom so that you could take him off and bury him. Properly, you know.'

'That's a very stupid suggestion.'

'Is it?'

'Yes, it's very stupid.' If it was very stupid Duffy would

have expected her to be cross with him. But she didn't seem to be. She was just reacting as if his interest in her life was completely irrelevant, which from her point of view maybe it was. There was a click as the door opened.

'So *there* you are. Little tête-à-tête? *Do* let me play goose-berry.'

'We've finished, Damian,' said Angela, getting up and slowly leaving the room.

'Chatting up brides-to-be,' said Damian. 'Naughty. I'll have to report you to big Henry.'

'Is she all right?'

'Angela? In the pink, don't you find?'

'I don't know her. Where's Henry?'

'At home, I should think. In his *house*,' Damian added, as if Duffy were too dense to understand the term 'home'.

'Where's that?'

'About three miles away.'

'What's he doing?'

'What do you mean, what's he doing? Rogering livestock for all I know. Actually, he's probably playing Scrabble with his mum.'

'No, I mean, why isn't he here with Angela?'

'Old English tradition. Probably doesn't apply where you come from. Husband and wife in the weeks before marriage see less of one another so that their transports of delight may be the fiercer after the nuptials. Fancy a quick frame?'

'I think I see,' said Duffy. Damian was rattling the reds into the triangle; he closed one eye to line them up, then topped off the pyramid with the pink. 'No, I'm a bit tired.'

'Oh well, poor little Damian will have to play with himself. Story of my life,' he added mournfully. If Sally had been there, she would have probably found this the funniest thing she'd heard since the last funniest thing she'd heard. Duffy disappointed Damian by not responding. 'Go on, you break off for me at least.' Duffy placed the white ball in the D and decided to show him some fancy stuff. Off two cushions, miss the black, and roll gently into the back wall of reds. That was the plan, anyway, but something about the cue, or the lighting, or the cloth, or most probably Duffy's state of mind, sent the cue ball scuttling sweetly into the black.

'Seven away,' cried Damian mockingly.

'I think I'm a bit tired,' said Duffy. 'Perhaps tomorrow.'

'Promises, promises,' murmured Damian, pinging the cue ball off the corner of the pack and taking it safely back into baulk.

As Duffy closed the billiard-room door he thought, 'You're the sort who gives my sort a bad name.' Quite what Damian's sexual orientation might be wasn't clear, and there were frequent occasions when Duffy wasn't sure about his own; but he'd seen enough of Damian to know that if he, Duffy, had been just a regular up-and-down bloke he'd have put this velvety fellow with the wiggly nose down for a screaming faggot. Duffy, of course, was far from being a straight up-and-down bloke; indeed, he had enjoyed what Damian archly termed transports of delight on both sides of the street. Still, this very tendency to cover the waterfront meant that he was impatient with coyness, with not saying what you are; and if he'd run into Damian down at the Alligator or even the Caramel Club, and found him sitting on a bar-stool with a laundry-bag of handkerchieves in his back pocket and a car-thief's clump of keys dangling to his groin, he'd still have had the same reaction. Duffy wasn't keen on camp, and when clever fellows who'd been to university were camp, he was even less keen. People who know long words had a duty to be straightforward, that's what Duffy thought.

He strolled along a dark corridor past what had once been the butler's pantry but which was now a garage for various types of Hoover, and felt a bit lost. He'd never been in a house this big, and one of the disorienting things about it was that you never knew where anyone was. Where was Angela? (Gulping down something that was bad for her?) Where was Taffy? (Stripping the lead off the roof?) Where was Belinda? (Practising her accent with a Sony Walkman and a set of Teach Yourself Posh tapes?) You couldn't keep track of them all, and it bothered Duffy. Where he came from, if anyone left the room and they weren't in the kitchen then they must be in the toilet, so there was no problem. Braunscombe Hall had more lavatories, as he'd heard even Vic calling them, than there were rooms in where Duffy came from.

In what the estate agents had designated as the family room, but which Vic tended to call the lounge, Duffy found Lucretia. She was leaning half-sideways on a sofa, smoking and reading a copy of the *Tatler*. A tumbler of watered whisky stood on a small brass table which Belinda might have picked up in Burma but more probably in Marbella.

'Where are the others?'

Lucretia waved a hand in the air, presumably signifying that they were looking after themselves quite happily just as she was.

'What are you doing?'

Lucretia glanced up and gazed at him levelly. She seemed very smart to him, as if a coachload of tailors and crimpers and grooms had left only a moment ago. He still didn't know what she looked like when she smiled. 'I'm reading a fairly good restaurant critic called Basil Seal in a magazine called the *Tatler*. I don't suppose that's part of your regular culture.'

'No.'

'He's writing about a restaurant called L'Escargot. What do you think of the food at L'Escargot?'

Duffy paused. He wondered if it was a catch question. Finally, he said, as casually as he could manage, 'Very nice last time I was there.' Lucretia smiled, just a little. He wondered what she was like when she smiled a lot more.

'Only you see, if in your feeble way you are attempting to chat me up, you ought to be vaguely aware of what field you're operating in.'

'Check. Actually, I think I'll turn in.'

Lucretia returned to Basil Berk writing about the Golden Sausage in the *Wankers' Monthly*. Oh well, thought Duffy. The funny thing was, she was being pretty frosty with him and he didn't mind. At least it was a change after Damian. And if she liked restaurants, why didn't he take her down Sam Widges while they waited for his laundry to get stolen over the road? Double fried bread, Sam. Righty-ho-coming-up.

Duffy retreated to his bedroom. Despite his fears of what Belinda might inflict upon him, it was quite a nice room:

carpet, comfortable bed, curtains, pile of magazines, only about a quarter of a mile to the nearest bathroom. But perhaps this was Belinda's point: she gave him the worst room, and he still thought it was very nice – which confirmed what she thought about him. Oh well, Belinda was probably the least of his worries. He went to the window, which didn't have any broken panes, opened it a few inches and sniffed. No, he'd had enough of that stuff already, he thought, and closed the leaded casement firmly.

He lay down on his bed in the cast-off shortie dressing-gown that Vic had loaned him and read a copy of *Country Life* in about forty-five seconds. He didn't like the smell of that either: a photo of a posh girl in pearls about to undergo Damian's transports of nuptial delight, lots of pictures of posh furniture, then a letters page with people writing in to ask how they could stop their hedgehog running away. The magazine might as well have been written in a foreign language for all that Duffy could understand it.

He lay on his back and tried to work out what he thought of Angela. Apart from the fact that she obviously wasn't tell-ing the truth, he didn't work out much. Why would anyone want to kill her dog? Was it connected with the blackmail she wasn't admitting? But why should the corpse go missing? Was the dog-killer the same person as the body-snatcher? Was it something to do with the illegal substances that were pre-sumably being consumed on the premises, though he hadn't actually seen any direct evidence of this, your Honour, it was only hearsay so far. Why had someone let his tyres down? That was pretty needless, wasn't it; it might even be construed as provocative, as if someone was saying, 'Fuck you, Duffy, with your silly white van and your alarm system that doesn't work.' And now the cutlery was going for a stroll as well.

It was one o'clock on Duffy's digital by the time he decided to call it a day. He'd better hitchhike down to the nearest toilet first. He'd told Vic to isolate the pressure plates and only alarm the external doors so that he could, if he wanted, creep around the house and spy on people; but even so, he walked along the corridor's paisley-patterned carpet as if there were pressure plates every yard. He felt a bit of a wally in his shortie dressing-gown; it was royal-blue silk and flapping its wings on the back was some big gold bird which looked like an eagle, only fancier. He'd have to ask Vic what it was. The dressing-gown was also more obviously short than he'd initially reckoned: if this was where it came down to on him, then where the hell did it come down to on Vic, who was three or four inches taller than Duffy? Perhaps there were some trousers to go with it that he hadn't been loaned.

When he came out of what was obviously a lavatory as it was a lot posher than any of the toilets he'd ever used, he felt wide awake. The house appeared silent, though an occasional light placed here and there meant that you could see your way round if you wanted to. Perhaps they left the lamps on all night as a sign that they were rich. You woke up in the middle of the night, saw a strip of yellow shining underneath your door, thought, well that's a relief we've still got money to burn, and went happily back to sleep. Or perhaps they left the lights on for the convenience of bed-hoppers.

Duffy decided to slip down to the family room and borrow that glossy mag Lucretia had been reading. He obviously needed to put in some homework on restaurants. He crept gently down the stairs. Carpet all the way: no wonder Vic told him he wouldn't need to borrow slippers. Moving quietly, for no particular reason except that it seemed polite, he made his way to the family room or lounge. He picked up the *Tatler* from a low glass-topped coffee table, then paused. You can be a bit smarter than that, he thought, put the magazine down again, looked around for the newspaper trough and went through it until he found an earlier month's issue. Yes, that's a lot less obvious.

He was about to put his foot on the stair when he thought he heard a noise. Yes, muffled, but a noise. He walked along the corridor and past the former butler's pantry where the Hoovers slumbered and entered what had once been the gentlemen's part of the house. As if nodding to this dead tradition, the carpet gave out at this point and was replaced by hessian matting which wasn't so kind to Duffy's bare feet. Ouch! He stood on one foot and rubbed the sole of his left foot against the swell of his right calf. As he did so, the lower halves of his dressing-gown pulled apart and he stood there exposed, like a flashing stork. Should have kept your pants on, Duffy. Yes, the noise was coming from the billiard room, definitely. Gently, he pushed open the heavy door and walked in.

There are many variations to the game of snooker, and Duffy knew a few of them. There were obscurer ones only played in London clubs by men with braying voices, and with these Duffy would have been understandably unfamiliar. But the game being played on the Braunscombe Hall table would not have been found in any snooker manual, however obscure. Immediately in front of Duffy a velvet-trousered figure was bent over the baulk end of the table, lining up on the blue. In the far corner away from him, and from Duffy, Sally was sitting on the table, her coccyx thrust into one of the bottom pockets. Her skirt was a mere frill around her waist; one leg was pressed against the side cushion, another against the end cushion, forming an angle of ninety degrees. This made it apparent, even from Duffy's distance, that she wasn't wearing any knickers. It also made it quite clear where Damian was trying to put the ball. Various previous attempts lay marooned against her thighs. Sally was on a roller-coaster of giggles. She also, Duffy couldn't help noticing, had kept her shoes on, which were digging into the cloth.

Damian played the blue and made it cannon off a red that was close to Sally's thigh. This deflection took it straight to its target. 'In-off,' he shouted.

'Ooh, I wish you'd warmed the balls,' she said.

'Filthy girl,' he said, fetching the white ball back and lining up another shot. '*Filthy* girl.'

It was clear to Duffy that both of them were aware of his presence, and both of them were determinedly ignoring it. He turned to go. Just as he was about to close the door, Duffy heard Damian murmur, '*Hate* the dressing-gown.'

●

Vic's idea had been that Duffy should spend a few days at Braunscombe Hall pretending to repair the alarm system, while all the time keeping an eye and an ear open. The trouble was, if Duffy kept diligently taking up the floorboards to check the wiring and the pressure plates, it made it hard for him to pad round after Angela and see that nobody sand-bagged her. On the other hand, if he nosed around too much, it wouldn't look good professionally, and it would make old Vic look a bit of a wally: first he hires this old chum who installs a faulty system, then when it breaks down he hires him again to mend it, and what does he do? Starts wandering round the house like a tourist; starts enjoying the free break-fasts. Do you know, I caught that maintenance man nicking a copy of the *Tatler* from the family room at one in the morning? What is England coming to?

Duffy reckoned he'd have to spin out the repair dodge for as long as he could get away with it, and then they'd either have to think up another excuse or level with people. Still, it was Bank Holiday Monday, and perhaps the sight of anyone even vaguely working would impress some of those around. When he'd been at school it had always been said that you could stroll through any part of the buildings at any time of the day as long as you were carrying a note in your hand: all the teachers assumed that some other teacher had sent you on an errand, and you never had to explain yourself. Duffy hadn't tried this line before; now he found, rather to his surprise, that if you wandered around looking thoughtful, with a piece of wire in one hand and a pair of pliers in the other, stopping occasionally to examine a wall or a window, people assumed that you were in some unfathomable way hard at work, and tried not to disturb you in case they broke your concentration. Perhaps that's what professional electricians did all the time.

In the billiard room he found Mrs Colin pulling a fat indus-trial Hoover round after her. He looked at the table, wonder-ing if what he'd seen last night had been some sick, chippy dream. '*Hate* the dressing-gown' – the words came back to him. He looked at the small figure of Mrs Colin tugging at the large steel vacuum cleaner, and wondered why they didn't make special ones for houses this size. When he'd been a kid and gone down the recreation ground he'd always been impressed by those motor-mowers which the parkies used to just sit on and drive; none of that sweaty pushing. They ought to make Hoovers like that. He imagined Mrs Colin driving across the rugs and parquet of Braunscombe Hall, occasionally hooting at you to get out of the way.

'Mrs Colin. Do you mind if I ask you a question?' Mrs Colin switched off the Hoover and waited. 'Why are you called Mrs Colin?' She smiled at him, looked away, switched the Hoover on again and went back to work. Perhaps that was a hint. Duffy continued his exploration of the house. He pushed open the cellar door and went down some concrete steps. He expected it to be damp down here, but it wasn't; instead, there was a dry, musty smell. Rows of wine-bins, in which the not-quite Lord Mayor had cellared the vintages he had not lived to drink, stretched away underneath the house. Vic had made an unconfident attempt at emulation: in the two nearest bins there was a case of Vinho Verde and one of pink champagne. Duffy took out a bottle of the latter and examined the label. On the wall nearby hung a very old thermometer, presumably placed there by the not-quite Lord Mayor so that potentially harmful fluctuations of temperature could be monitored. Duffy reckoned that Vic's wines wouldn't be in the cellar long enough for potentially harmful fluctuations of temperature to get at them.

In the kitchen he found Belinda in her well-stocked jodhpurs, and Vic, to whom he suggested a potential modification of the alarm system which could best be discussed if they went out on to the terrace, down across the lawn, well away from the house and out of earshot of everybody else. Before they left, Duffy asked Belinda if she could spare him a word or two later in the day perhaps.

'I'm afraid I leave the wiring to others,' she replied. He looked at her as if to say, come on darling, you know what we're talking about. She looked back at him as if to say, course I know what you're talking about, but I couldn't resist it, could I?

Down on the lawn with Vic, where no one could hear them unless Jimmy had already dug a series of tunnels as part of his assault course and installed listening devices (which was always a possibility), Duffy said, 'You'll have to give me more background.'

'Be my guest.'

'Why do you let all those people sponge off you?'

'Duffy, you watch your tongue, lad, or someone will cut it off and put it in a pie. Those are my friends, my guests.'

'Belinda's friends, your guests.'

'Maybe. So what? I like people round the house. I'm not short of the odd penny. Anyway, we've got Angela to think about.'

'Is that what they're for?'

'Well, no, not all. I mean, that's Damian and Sally, really, they're the ones I got to take her mind off it all.' Duffy wondered where Angela was when Damian and Sally were taking their own minds off things on the snooker table.

'What about Lucretia?'

'She's a friend of Angela's. She's been down quite a lot. I suppose she's helping with the wedding dress . . . or whatever they do.' Vic sounded vague.

'Jimmy?'

'Oh, Jimmy's sort of . . . around. He doesn't always stay here. He's got a camp in the woods.'

'Are you serious?'

'Sure. I mean, he's got a house a couple of villages away, and he stays here a bit, but he's got this sort of camp, you know, hide, up in the woods. He likes it there. Must remind him of the Army or something.'

'Is that where he runs being an estate agent from?'

'I don't think Jimmy sells that many houses, to be perfectly level with you,' said Vic.

'And Taffy?'

'Oh, Taffy's a . . . house guest.' Vic didn't sound as if he was completely accustomed to using the phrase yet.

'Well, it must make a nice change from being a house guest in Maidstone or the Scrubs.'

'You're so unforgiving, Duffy.'

'No, I just think that if you're harbouring a known criminal and the spoons go missing, then you ought to put two and two together.'

'You know, that's a very posh word for you, Duffy, *harbouring*. I've never much liked it myself. And I don't think

Taffy's much interested in nicking my cutlery. Never steal from your own, that's what they say, isn't it?'

'So Taffy's your own, is he?'

'Duffy, I'll be straight with you. I've known Taffy some time. I knew him before he made the front page. And I'll tell you, he's changed. He's a reformed character.'

'Oh yes?'

'Sure. And I'll give you the proof of it. He's got boring.'

'What do you mean?'

'It's that sociology course he did when he was inside. He's always trying to explain things nowadays. He used to just nick things because someone else had them and he wanted them. Now if you showed him a bank with an open vault he'd want to read a history of Wall Street before he made up his mind whether it was OK for him to help himself.'

'It's a good front, anyway.'

'You're too cynical, Duffy, that's your trouble. I always knew coppers were more cynical than villains. I tell you something, I bet villains give a lot more to charity than coppers ever do.'

'That's because villains earn more.'

Vic laughed. 'You see, I couldn't have a chuckle with Taffy about this sort of stuff. He'd always be wanting to prove something or other.'

'How long's he been here?'

'A month or two, I suppose.' Duffy raised an eyebrow. 'It's hard for him to get a job at the moment. You'd be surprised how prejudiced some people get.'

'Well, make sure he doesn't get institutionalized. You know, can't live anywhere except in country houses.'

'That's my problem.'

'And your bank manager's.'

'I'm all right, Duffy. Don't start worrying about me.'

'OK. So tell me what drugs people are on.'

'Nicotine, I'd say. Bit of alcohol, maybe.' Duffy waited. 'I don't know, and I don't ask. I don't ask who's sleeping in whose bed, and I don't ask if they're using funny tobacco.'

'Permitting your premises . . .' Duffy began, as if reciting a charge sheet.

'Oh, fuck off, Duffy. I'm paying you, you're not turning me over, right?'

'Right. Then who's had it off with Angela?'

'Well, Henry I hope. But as I said . . .'

'Come off it, Vic, saying you don't ask doesn't mean you don't end up knowing.'

'Right.'

'So?'

'Well, Jimmy had been very keen on Angela for years.'

'Was he cut up when she got engaged to Henry?'

'Hard to tell.' Duffy snorted in irritation. 'No, it *is* hard to tell with Jimmy. He did spend quite a bit of time in his camp in the woods afterwards, I remember. But . . . you know, it was a nice summer, and perhaps there were a lot of rabbits around.'

'You've really convinced me. Anyone else?'

'She's been around, like I told you.'

'Damian, Taffy?'

'Do you think Damian's that way inclined? Taffy? Not since she got engaged to Henry, I mean, she wouldn't risk it, would she?'

'You?'

'Duffy, what's this, flattery?' Duffy waited. 'Don't you remember the old seaside postcard? When you're twenty to thirty, tri-weekly. Thirty to forty, try weekly. Forty to fifty, try weakly. No? No, you'd have to see the card, I suppose.' Duffy still waited. 'You *are* serious, aren't you? Listen, if you had Belinda, you wouldn't need Angela, I can promise you that.'

'Right,' said Duffy. 'That'll be all for now, sir,' he added, coming over all copper, 'but don't leave the area without informing us, will you? And we'd like you to surrender your passport.'

'Cheers,' said Vic.

'Oh, and just a couple more questions while we're about it. Why is Mrs Colin called Mrs Colin?'

Vic grinned. 'When she was first with us there was a fellow she was keen on, well he was keen on her anyway, and we kept saying to her, "When are we going to be calling you Mrs

Colin?'' and it sort of stuck. She broke up with him – we never knew the details – and we sort of thought we ought to stop calling her that, but when we tried she got cross. Funny, that. She's been Mrs Colin ever since.'

'I see. And the other thing. That dressing-gown you lent me. What's with the eagle on the back?'

'It's not an eagle, it's a phoenix.'

'Is that heraldry again?'

'Yeah.'

'I don't think I'll ever crack heraldry.'

'Well, the phoenix . . .'

'Don't tell me, Vic. I don't want to know.'

Duffy walked back up the lawn, round the side of the house, and crunched across the gravel towards the stable block. The Elizabethan-style half-timbering was a bit skimpier here, but the block still seemed to Duffy about the size of a very large detached house in the London suburbs which was being lived in by posh people. The stables at Braunscombe Hall were occupied by two horses, three cars, plus Mr and Mrs Hardcastle. The horses had the best of the accommodation, and no doubt saw the gentler side of Belinda, such as it was; but the Hardcastles still had two up, two down and as much parking space as they liked. Duffy hadn't yet set eyes on Ron Hardcastle, who apparently functioned as gardener, handyman and stable lad; and he didn't set eyes on him now, either. Mrs Hardcastle answered his knock.

'Oh, I'm going over the alarm system, and Mr Crowther was wondering whether it ought to be extended to the stable block. Do you mind if . . .'

'Poke around,' said Mrs Hardcastle. 'I'm just off over to the house to do the lunch. Ron's off somewhere. I don't think we've got anything worth stealing.'

'Yeah, I don't know, maybe it's the horses . . .' Duffy realized this sounded a bit feeble. Or maybe it didn't: protect the horses against thieves, but not Mr and Mrs Hardcastle. Yes, that would probably be Belinda's line.

He walked round the stable block, steering well clear of the part where the horses were. Horses bit. They had these sort of half-doors on where they lived, and they lurked among their straw until you put your nose in and looked for them, and then Snap! they had your nose off and probably half your face with it. Instead, Duffy looked into the garage, where he saw a cream Range Rover, a red MG and a Datsun Cherry of some purply colour he couldn't put a name to. He continued until he came to the Hardcastles' end of the building. They also had one of those two-part front doors like the horses had. He reached inside and unbolted the bottom half.

It was a neat little house: kitchen and telly room downstairs, bathroom and two small bedrooms upstairs. Duffy poked around in a professional way; that's to say, he didn't enjoy it much. There were some people's places you enjoyed poking round in: these were usually people who were richer than you, or nastier. Oh, so *that*'s what you do with all the money you made by fiddling the books, is it? And you'd pick up some horrible tapestry cushion as if with tongs. But with ordinary people, or poor people, or nice people, you didn't get that sort of pleasure. You felt what it would be like if someone was rifling through your own stuff. Duffy looked briefly into the two bedrooms, then went downstairs and out of the front door. Just in case anyone was watching him from the house, he stepped back a few paces, scanned the upper windows and the roof, then nodded his head. He walked round to the back, past a neat little kitchen garden. Behind the house was a coal bunker, a wood store and a small lean-to shed. Automatically, Duffy put his hand to the door; it was locked. Just as automatically, Duffy looked around for the key. There was always a rule about keys: if they weren't in the obvious place, they were in the second most obvious place. Not under the big stone? Try under the little stone. Or, in the present case, not under the big flowerpot? Try the small flowerpot. Duffy picked up the rusting key and pulled open the shed door. Various forks and spades and diggers and whatsits that people who had gardens needed were arrayed in front of him, but Duffy didn't really look at them. He reached in to the back of the shed and pulled a large piece of sacking off a square mound. Well, well. He hadn't met Ron Hardcastle, yet, of course, and he might indeed turn out to be a man who knew his Asti from his Spumante; but just for the moment Duffy registered the fact that Ron's wine-cellar was twice as big as Vic's. Two cases of Vinho Verde, to be precise, and two cases of the same pink champagne that Vic had a fancy for.

He locked up, and as he did so thought he registered a slight movement at the periphery of his vision. Nonchalantly, he put the key back underneath the small flowerpot, turned and began to saunter towards the end of the Hardcastles' garden. A small path led across a corner of the wood and back towards the lawn. He followed the path, treading as lightly as he could, listening out and wishing he'd been in the Boy Scouts. When he reached the edge of the lawn, he sat on a bench and continued listening. Just at the appropriate moment, he said,

'Jimmy?'

'Damn. Damn, damn, damn.'

Duffy turned, and saw Jimmy flat on his stomach about three yards away. He was wearing a camouflage jacket and a small home-made hat plaited together from ferns. 'Damn. When did you spot me?'

'Oh, only right at the end. I think you must have, er, disturbed a twig or something.'

'Ah. But how did you know it was me?'

'Well, it was either you or the Boston Strangler.'

Jimmy, lying in the bracken at the edge of the wood, appeared to give the alternative possibility some serious thought. 'Well, it couldn't have been *him*,' he said finally and came to sit beside Duffy on the bench. 'Damn,' he repeated.

'Sorry if I spoiled it.'

'No, you were quite right. Tell you what, why don't you try following me now?'

'Maybe not today, Jimmy. I've got to mend the alarm.'

'Oh, right. Did you find what you wanted?'

'What I wanted?'

'Yes.' At the top of his head Jimmy's bald pate fell away, and at the bottom his chin fell away, but in between his slightly popping eyes were fixed firmly on Duffy. Don't assume he's as thick as he's painted, Duffy thought. 'What you wanted. In the shed.'

'Not unless there was a dead dog in there I missed.'

'Oh. Right.'

'Have you been looking for him?'

'Who?'

'Ricky.'

'No. Why?'

'Oh,' said Duffy, 'I just thought that if we could find him, between the two of us, say, we could give him a proper burial. Seems a bit unfair that first he gets killed and then he disappears. I'm sure Angela would appreciate it.'

'See what you mean,' said Jimmy. 'That's something I could get on to. Not much happens in these woods that gets past old Jimmy.'

Duffy nodded conspiratorially, happy that Jimmy had bought the feed so quickly. There was no point Duffy tramping through the woods and looking for freshly moved mounds of earth and getting nettled and bitten and stung when old Jimmy could do it for him. Perhaps being in Vic's house infected you with Vic's philosophy: sub-contract, never do the work if some prat will do it for you, and if it all comes to nothing, well, mugs will be mugs, won't they?

'I suppose Angela's pretty cut up about this business,' said Duffy after a pause.

'She's a grand girl,' Jimmy replied, 'she's a grand girl.' Whether or not this was intended as an answer to the question, Duffy could only guess.

'You've, um, you're obviously, um, fond of her.'

'Loved her for years,' said Jimmy, 'loved her for years. Poor old Jimmy. Nothing doing there. Washing her car, that's all I'm good for. Not bright enough. Not that women mind that,' he commented ruminatively. 'No oil painting, either. Not that women mind that. No money. Not that women mind that. No prospects. Not that women mind that. I suppose what women mind is the combination of all four. Poor old Jimmy.'

'That's tough,' said Duffy. He wondered if washing her car also included other duties. Running up to London for things to keep her merry, for instance.

'Will she be happy with Henry?'

'Got money – doesn't need prospects,' said Jimmy rather bitterly.

'What's Henry like?'

Jimmy considered the question at some length, gazing across the lawn to the distant glint of the lake. 'He's all right if you like people like him,' he said finally.

'Check.'

They sat on the bench for a while longer. Then Duffy had another thought.

'I suppose you can probably swim.'

'Rather.'

'Probably got a snorkel and some flippers.'

'Rather.' Jimmy looked across at Duffy, then followed his gaze towards the lake. 'Right. Yes. Good thinking.' He stood up. 'Enjoyed the chinwag.'

'Oh, and Jimmy?'

'Yes?'

'Mum's the word.'

Jimmy paused in his departure and half-wheeled back towards Duffy. 'You know I often wonder why people say that. My mum talked *all the bloody time.*'

At that moment a gong summoned them in to lunch. Duffy felt uneasy throughout the meal. When he looked at Jimmy, he half-expected him to blurt out their plan of combing the woods and the waters for Ricky's corpse. When he looked at Lucretia, he wondered if last night's plan of reading posh magazines to impress her could possibly have been serious. When he saw Mrs Hardcastle passing another bottle of Vinho Verde to Damian, he wondered if what he'd seen meant what he thought it meant. And when he looked at Damian receiving the bottle, he wasn't sure what he felt. Embarrassment? Disapproval? Nausea? And what, for that matter, did last night's little incident suggest about Damian's sexual preference? Was his little game hetero or homosexual, randy or contemptuous? Perhaps neither; perhaps it was just a moment's sport which laughed at sex, which said it was about as serious as snooker. He could try asking Sally, except she was probably too smashed at the time to notice.

Whatever Damian felt about it all, embarrassment wasn't at the top of the list. When he caught Duffy's eye on him, he looked straight back and said, 'By the way, you won't forget our little game tonight?'

'Game?'

'You promised me a couple of frames.'

'I did?'

'I assumed that was why you were creeping around the house late last night in your frightful dressing-gown. Wanting to get in some practice before the big match.'

'That's my dressing-gown, actually,' said Vic.

'Oh dear,' said Damian brightly. 'Foot in mouth time again for Damian. All I can say is, I bet it looks *much* more fetching on you, my dear Vic.'

'You could talk your way out of a roped sack,' said Vic.

'I'd just *thcream*,' said Damian. 'Thcream and thcream.'

After lunch Duffy was working in the video library fixing the new pressure plate – well, at least some part of the overhaul could be authentic – when he heard the door open. He looked up and saw Sally. She was either still pissed from lunch or starting her aperitifs early for dinner; or perhaps she'd mixed some private cocktail of her own.

'Thought I'd find you in here,' she said, half falling on to the sofa. 'Got an apology, you know.' She giggled as if apologies were almost as funny as jokes. 'Let down your tyres.'

'You?'

'Yeah. Sorry, right? Well, it wasn't my idea. Damian said why don't we let down his tyres, you do the ones on that side I'll do the ones on this side, but by the time I'd done mine he'd buggered back into the house. Said he thought he heard someone coming.'

'Why did you do it?'

'Seemed like a good idea. Fun. Sorry, right?' She turned her head to one side and her heavy black curls flopped round the side of her face. Clearly, she was bored with apology now.

'By the way,' said Duffy, trying to keep his voice in neutral, 'I should take your shoes off next time.'

'Next time? I wouldn't do it again. It wouldn't be worth it. Anyway, you'd guess it was us.'

'Not the van. The snooker table. Heels are bad for the cloth.'

She paused, thought, and remembered the previous night as if it had been a month ago. 'Oh, right.' Now that she was clear what they were talking about, she began to laugh again. 'I'll take them off next time. Ooh, those balls were cold.'

'You shouldn't do things like that,' said Duffy. He hadn't meant to say it, he'd wanted to stay cool. It had just slipped out. Anyway, he meant it.

'Do what I like,' she replied sulkily.

'You shouldn't let . . . *him* do things like that to you.'

'Oh, you mean, like he won't respect me?' Duffy grunted. 'You're neolithic, you know that, neolithic. Anyway, what makes you think I want to be respected?' Duffy hadn't quite meant that, but he couldn't find the words for exactly what he did mean. 'It's fun,' she added listlessly.

Duffy thought it didn't matter too much what he said to this girl; she probably wouldn't remember anyway. 'You shouldn't drink so much.'

'It's fun,' she replied.

'It's not fun for others.'

'You're the first to complain, Mr Neolithic.'

'And you shouldn't take whatever it is you're taking.'

'It's fun,' Sally said, 'it's fun, it's fun, it's *fun*. It's not fun here any more. No fun with you. How old are you anyway?'

'Old enough to be your brother.'

'Then don't come on like my fucking father, right?' She screamed this last part.

'Right.'

Sally stomped off, and Duffy carried on wiring up the pressure plate. He felt depressed. It was always the same problem. The same problem whether you were at Braunscombe Hall or in the back alleys behind some South London comprehensive where the crime figures were higher than the national average. Duffy had still been a copper when the first scares about glue-sniffing had started up. Kids putting their heads in plastic bags and sniffing away at solvents. It sounded like a really dumb thing to do. Duffy had read all the reports in the papers. Glue-sniffing gave you headaches, it gave you sores round your nose, it made you apathetic. It made you do badly at school and it screwed up your home life because all you were thinking about was getting outside with the plastic bag and the aerosol. And that was just the start. The end was that you OD'd on solvent. You died. Kids of ten, twelve, thirteen dead on the streets, and all their own work. Duffy couldn't fathom it. You blame the parents, you blame the teachers, you blame the shopkeepers who ought to know better than to sell the stuff to users, and you blame the kids themselves. But after all this blaming, you still don't understand.

Duffy had wanted to understand, and one day he'd found a couple of kids in an alley who hadn't run away from him. He wasn't a teacher, he wasn't a social worker, and they weren't old enough or canny enough yet to smell a copper. He got round to asking them why they did it. Fun, they said. What sort of fun? Different sorts of fun, they said. Fun looking forward to it, for a start: you never knew what was going to come out of that bag when you sniffed. And what did? All sorts of things, they said. Sometimes you saw things, like giant frogs jumping over the houses, that was magic. And you hear great winds rushing around you but you're not cold, and you see colours, fantastic colours, and you feel good, you feel good. It's fun. What's it like after? It's not so good after. You come down, and it's not so good. But there's always the next time. It's fun.

That's what you don't want to accept, thought Duffy, but that's what you've got to. They do it because it's fun, whether it's behind some railings with a plastic bag in the rain or whether it's in a comfortable toilet, sorry lavatory, on the Buckinghamshire/Bedfordshire borders. It seems to you that the fun they get can't be worth it, you can see that it can't be worth it. To them it is worth it. You can call it addiction if you like, but you mustn't duck the other truth: they do it because it's fun.

●

'Belinda.'
 'Just hold her a minute.'
 '*Hold* her? Where?'

'Not by the tail, you berk. *There.*'

Duffy got hold of one of the metal bits with leather attached which in his view were altogether too close to the horse's mouth and held on. Christ, they were big, horses. Much bigger than on the telly. A huge eye bulged at him; a colossal vein ran down the snout; lips like sofa cushions pulled back to reveal vast yellow teeth. Why did they need such big teeth if all they ate was grass?

'Thanks,' said Belinda. Duffy nearly shook his head to clear his ears. Had she said thanks? Had he done something right at last?

She had slipped to the ground while he held the horse – or rather, while he stood there and the horse very decently decided not to run away – then took charge of it. She led the way into a stable and indicated that they could talk while she gave the horse a rub-down, or a shampoo, or whatever people did after riding. Duffy stood apprehensively just inside the horse's two-part front door. That was the other thing about stables: they reeked of horse-shit.

'How's Angela?'

'Fine.'

'How's Angela?'

'She's taking rather too many anti-depressants. She's up and down all the time. Most nights she comes in and sleeps with us. She's very apathetic. And she doesn't take any bloody exercise at all.'

'She sleeps with you?'

'Not the way your perverted mind assumes. There's a bed – well, it's a sort of large cot, really, in our room, and when she's feeling bad she just comes in, doesn't even wake us usually, and climbs into it. Find her in the morning sleeping like a child.'

'Do you think she's . . .'

'. . . a danger to herself, as the doctors put it? I can't say. Got it wrong twice before, didn't we? She's my oldest mate – well, my oldest mate down here – but I don't know what's going on inside her.'

'Who do you think's trying to tip her over?'

'No idea.'

'But you think someone is?'

'Could be.'

'Does she have anyone – I dunno, anyone who's mad at her?'

'Not that I've heard.'

'Old boyfriends? Someone she's jilted?'

Belinda stopped rubbing down the horse and laughed. '*Jilt*? I haven't heard that word in years. You mean, someone she's stopped screwing?'

'Well, it's a bit more than that, I suppose.'

'What, gave him back his engagement ring, that stuff?' She laughed again. 'No, Angela hasn't *jilted* anyone.'

'Is she OK for money?'

'As far as I know she's still comfortable.'

'And what about Henry?' Duffy had only glimpsed him briefly so far, a large, square-faced county fellow with clothes Duffy wouldn't have been seen dead in.

'What about him?'

'Well, for instance, is she in love with him?'

'I hope you're better at fixing alarm systems than you are at asking questions. Jilted? In love? Look, Duffy, if you're a girl, and you're thirty . . . thirty something, shall we say, and you're falling apart at the seams, and you've never even had an engagement ring on your finger before, and the chap is presentable and he's got a farm and he comes from an old family, then you're in love.'

'Is that what it is? And what's it like for the chap?'

'See what you mean. Crafty little girl and all that. Well, what it's like for the chap is this. If you're a chap, and you're forty-three, and you're still living at home with your mum who isn't very keen on being left alone, and you don't have the greatest track record with the girls in green wellies and headscarves, and you don't really have any friends that anyone knows about, and all of a sudden you meet this sexy girl who isn't married to someone else, who's got a bit of money and actually doesn't mind moving in and living with your old mum after you're married, and she knows how to drive a car, then you're in love.'

'I think I get it,' said Duffy. 'And then they'll have babies and live happily ever after?'

'I don't know if they'll have babies,' said Belinda. 'They'll have to get a move on if they're going to. And they'll live as happily ever after as anyone else.'

'Meaning?'

'Meaning you can't tell beforehand. After a while it's not a question of love, as you like to put it, but stamina.'

'Like the three-day event?'

Belinda looked up across the horse's back in surprise. 'Very good, Duffy. Where did you get to hear about three-day eventing?'

'I must have seen it on the telly.' He remembered a big country house somewhere and lots of men with flat caps and shooting-sticks. There'd been Land Rovers everywhere, riders falling off at the water-jump, and a commentator whose tongue sounded as if it was wearing a flat cap and was supported in his mouth by a shooting-stick.

'There's nothing wrong with my alarm system, anyway,' he said suddenly. He didn't want people passing the news on.

'No. Right. Vic told me.'

'So don't go around saying so.'

'I thought that's what we had to pretend?'

'Well, don't say it like it wasn't a big surprise to you when it went wrong.'

'OK.'

At that moment they heard a loud and regular noise on the gravel, a sort of thumping, not like the sound of someone walking. Belinda came across the stable and stood at the half-door with Duffy. Someone was marching across the driveway. Someone, what's more, in a wet suit, with flippers on his feet and a mask on his face. Someone carrying a snorkel under his left arm like a swagger stick. Jimmy. He noticed Duffy and Belinda standing at the stable door but didn't break step. Instead he yelled, 'Special Boat Squadron . . . Eyeyes . . . *right*' and snapped his head across on his neck. When he had passed them he eyes-fronted again and disappeared on to the quiet grass in the direction of the lake. Duffy wanted to laugh but Belinda looked serious. No, perhaps it wasn't funny. And perhaps poor old Jimmy had really thought about it. If you want to dive in the lake secretly, how do you do it? By diving in the lake obviously. Maybe he's been reading Sherlock Holmes.

'And Taffy?'

'What about Taffy? He's a house guest.' She said it with considerably more ease than Vic did.

'Mrs Hardcastle says the cutlery's going missing.'

'Duffy, number one, Taffy is our friend, number two, Taffy is a reformed character, number three, if Taffy was still into nicking, he'd go for the Range Rover or the house or something, not the spoons.'

'Right.' Unless he couldn't get it out of his system. Unless he was just keeping his hand in. No, that wasn't very likely.

Duffy left Belinda, thinking she wasn't necessarily as bad as he'd imagined, in fact quite a bit less bad, and went in search of Vic. When he'd been given the directions he needed, he set off round the back of the house, dodged behind a hedge, and slowly worked his way towards the wood. As he tiptoed cautiously up the path, expecting everything that wasn't obviously a nettle to be a camouflaged nettle, he wondered about Taffy. Just a house guest. Quiet, polite, a bit boring, liked to talk about the individual's relationship to society, looked like a weekend jazz-player. Fine, except that he had a habit of beating people up and braining screws with iron bars. This, of course, was precisely what gave him his social pull. It was well known that London café society welcomed major criminals, so why shouldn't country society welcome minor villains who'd once made the front page for a couple of weeks? In the words of his host, England had become a place where your Vics could mix with your Damians, and your Damians could hob-nob with your Hugos. Why shouldn't your Taffys rub shoulders with your Vics, your Damians and your Hugos? Besides, it wasn't just about social mobility. Crime was sexy. This was another truth that Duffy, as an ex-copper, found it difficult but necessary to accept. Drugs were fun and crime was sexy; not always, but often enough. You read about East End villains splashing around in pink champagne at those restaurants written up by Basil Berk in the *Tatler*. You read about

– you'd even seen – ex-cons (as long as they were really violent ex-cons who'd really scared people) pulling girls as easy as shelling peas. It wasn't fair, Duffy thought. Why weren't coppers sexy?

What a way to spend a Bank Holiday Monday afternoon. The path had got steeper suddenly, and the bracken thicker. Vic had said there was a bit where the path seemed to go straight on but there was a little nick in a beech tree and a track you normally wouldn't notice off to the left. Was that a beech tree? Was that a nick? Was that a track? If only he'd been in the Boy Scouts. He'd probably need to know a few posh knots before the week was out, and how to light a fire by rubbing two Girl Guides together.

This seemed to be the place. Vic had said you had to go past and then look back, otherwise you'd never notice it. Yes, there it was. Even Duffy could appreciate that Jimmy's camp, though only ten minutes from the house, was well hidden. The leaves on the ground gave way beneath him like posh carpet, and he approached the hide with caution. He had a sudden memory from a kids' book, or maybe the cinema, of the sort of traps Red Indians or Africans or whoever used: all of a sudden the ground gave way, you fell ten feet and got a sharpened stake up the bum. You lay there like a piece of meat on a kebab stick until the locals turned up, piled lots of wood around you, and had you for dinner. Duffy! Duffy! That's enough. Even so, he half-wondered, as he approached Jimmy's camp, whether he shouldn't have a long stick with him, and be poking at the leaves as he walked.

It wasn't exactly a camp, more a sort of hide from which you watched birds, or a place thrown up for the night by a particularly tidy soldier in a war film. A large piece of tarpaulin had been stretched over stakes at a point where the ground shelved away; bracken and stuff had been piled on the roof. It didn't at the moment look particularly concealed – there was even a patch of burnt earth by the front door where a fire had presumably been – but it looked as if it could be very concealed if necessary. Duffy dodged sideways down the slope for a closer examination.

The hide was about eight feet long and consisted of two

rooms. Not that there was a division between them; it was just that six feet of the space was clearly the bedroom, and the other two the kitchen and bathroom. At one end was a bedroll wrapped in a sheet of polythene and staked to the ground. At the other Duffy found a small primus stove, various square green tins and a mirror. He opened the tins: shaving equipment, canned food, a few bits of biltong wrapped in foil, and some cutlery. Not, however, the cutlery that had taken a walk from Braunscombe Hall; only one of those knife-fork-and-spoon sets with a screw through the middle to hold it all together.

In a corner of the sleeping section, by the bedroll, was another row of green tins. Bedside reading, thought Duffy facetiously. In the first tin he found a small paraffin lamp; in the second a large jar of presumably paraffin plus a small jar of what smelt like methylated spirits; in the next three copies of *Playboy* wrapped in a polythene bag. He looked at the date: they were several years old. The fourth tin he nearly put the lid back on as soon as he'd flipped it open: what business was it of his? Well, you could never tell what might turn out to be business. On top lay a photograph of a small boy with a receding chin; he was dressed in some uniform, maybe Boys' Brigade. Next came proof that the child hadn't changed much fifteen or twenty years later, by which time he was in a grown-up uniform, that of the Army. Then a much older photo of someone's wedding: a smiling bride, a severe groom, looking from their lapels and hairstyles as if it were just after the war. Jimmy's parents, presumably. Underneath was a picture which Duffy had no trouble in identifying: Angela, with large eyes looking away from the camera, and what smelt like a bit of touching-up around the jaw. Clearly a studio job; Duffy flipped it over, but the photographer hadn't bothered to stamp the print. Finally, a clipping from a newspaper which puzzled Duffy until he read the caption: only then did he realize that it was a story from the local *Mail & Advertiser* about Henry and Angela's engagement. He hadn't been able to grasp this at first because the clipping was punctured by several dozen circular burns. The sort of burns you make with a cigarette at the end of an evening when you've only a four-year-old copy of *Playboy* to tuck up with. Duffy stared at the tortured photo and found an extra reason why it worried him: the burns obliterated not only Henry's face, but also Angela's.

When he emerged from the wood, having miraculously managed to avoid the bear-traps, the killer spiders and the Iroquois, he wandered to the lake's edge. A gesture brought Jimmy swimming over to the bank. He stood up, water streaming from his wetsuit, and raised his mask. He was better-looking with his head all swathed in rubber.

'Any sign of Ricky?'

Jimmy shook his head. 'Nothing.'

'Must be lying doggo,' said Duffy.

'I don't think that's funny.' Jimmy pulled down his mask, adjusted his snorkel, turned and trudged back into the lake.

'No, maybe it isn't,' Duffy muttered to himself.

He lay on his bed waiting for the dinner gong with a copy of the *Tatler* open at the society pages. Miss Olivia Fartface marrying the Hon. Peregrine Pokerupthebum, the couple to take over the ancestral home at Much Gelding, where he will live off inherited wealth and she will bear a royal flush of laughing children fit only for the finest schools. Duffy wondered idly about the joke he'd made to Belinda: marriage as a three-day event. Maybe it wasn't a bad comparison. It started with that section where the horses were all got up to look their best. What was it? Dressage, that's right. They skittered around on tiptoe, all primped and shiny, doing very formal manoeuvres ever so tidily. That was like the courtship part. Then there was the main bit, the cross-country. None of that pointing the toe and looking good, you just ran, or cantered if that's what they called it, out across the open country, and that was fun and a release, except that every so often there'd be these hurdles you had to get over, some of which were pretty steep, and there were great muddy banks with water at the bottom of them, and you might be inclined, if you'd had enough, to throw your rider. What's more, it went on and on, this cross-country bit, miles and miles of it. Finally, it was over, and they took you back to your stable and you had your dinner, and thought you'd done pretty well – or if not well, at least you'd done your duty. Then the next day, just when you were thinking about putting your four legs up, they took you out again and made you jump all these obstacles, even though you were really knackered. And all you did in the show-jumping was lose points. You never gained points at this stage, you only lost them.

Was it like that? It looked a bit like it from the outside. Duffy had never tried marriage, never been tempted by the three-day event. Of course, having quite a spell of being queer hadn't improved his chances. Or, if not being entirely queer, at least walking both sides of the street. Had he ever been in love? He wasn't sure. Well, if he wasn't sure, he couldn't have been, could he? He remembered how he'd felt about Carol when they'd first started going around together; he'd felt as if he was beginning to understand things, and as if there'd always be something for dinner. Was that love? Maybe you called it this because you reckoned it was the best you were going to get. Maybe Belinda had been right to laugh at him. In the real world you married not for love but because someone else would have you, because there was someone out there who could bear to be with you, and because if you didn't you were lost. Perhaps he ought to phone Carol.

Instead of phoning Carol, he flipped back a few pages in the *Tatler* until he got to the restaurant column. What was Basil Berk writing about this month? Duffy read the page with rising incredulity. Call this a job? You went along to some wallies' rendezvous – in the present case one of three fish restaurants in Chelsea – had a jolly good nosh-up, took Lady Berk along with you, copied down the menu, made up some joke or other and pretended Lady Berk had said it to you across the fish-knives and went on to the next restaurant. And the prices . . . You could get seven good dinners at Sam Widges for the price of a single fish snack in Chelsea.

He threw down the magazine and yomped to the nearest lavatory. Then he went downstairs and into the family room. Lucretia was in her accustomed position on the sofa, blonde hair cascading down the back of it, cigarette and watered whisky on the go. She nodded expressionlessly at Duffy. He sat in a chair opposite her and found himself, rather to his surprise, clearing his throat. He was almost as surprised by what he said next.

'I find the sauce is very good at the Poison d'Or.'

'What?'

'I find the sauce is very good at the Poison d'Or.'

'The what?'

'The sauce. The way they put saffron in it.' (Had he got that right?) 'It's very nice.'

'Where's this?'

'The Poison d'Or.'

'Now,' said Lucretia briskly, 'after me. *Poisson. Poisson.*' As she said the words her lips parted and then came together in a way that was really very, well, nice, Duffy thought.

'Poison.'

'*Poisson. Poisson.*'

'Poison.'

Lucretia gave him that half-smile which made him wish he could somehow get her to give him the full version. 'Promise me one thing. Don't ever go into a French restaurant and ask for the fish, all right?'

'Promise.' He looked at her. 'How did I do?'

'You're funny, you know that? You are funny.'

Was that good in her book? Either way, Duffy felt a little less out of his league with this girl. He was about to turn the conversation suavely on to topics of wider interest – like whether she enjoyed horses and had she ever been for a ride in a Sherpa van – when there was a commotion at the door. Jimmy ran into the room, with dripping hair, though fortunately no longer in his wet suit, and stood between the two of them, his back to Lucretia, and winking furiously at Duffy.

After about a dozen of these facial contortions Duffy finally got the message.

'Oh, er, excuse me, Lucretia.' Silent, she waved a hand at him in dismissal.

Excitedly, Jimmy led him round the house to a bit of undergrowth by the lake. There, by a discarded wet suit and a pair of flippers, lay a blue plastic laundry-bag with a tail sticking out of it. The handles were tied together.

'Had to cut the string,' said Jimmy. 'Probably tied round a stone or something. Couldn't bring that up as well, though.'

'Great stuff,' said Duffy, and clapped Jimmy firmly on the shoulder. It wasn't at all the sort of phrase or gesture that came naturally to Duffy, but he supposed he ought to speak Jimmy's language. The snorkeller beamed, and began to explain in more detail than was necessary how he'd divided the lake up into sections with markers on the bank and removed each marker as he cleared each section. Duffy heard him out and at the end repeated, 'Great stuff.'

'Ange will be pleased, won't she?'

'I'm sure she will, Jimmy. But perhaps we won't tell her immediately.'

'Oh.' His face fell, which was easy given its shape.

'You see, I've been thinking.'

'Right.' Jimmy seemed to fall in with Duffy's idea even before it was explained to him, as if anyone who had been thinking automatically deserved respect and obedience.

'The point is, someone threw Ricky into the lake because they didn't want Angela to bury him. Maybe they didn't want us to have a good look at him. And whoever did it can't be that far away. So, if we just tell everyone about it, the same thing could happen all over again. Ricky would go for walkies. Permanently, this time.

Jimmy was nodding slowly. 'So?'

'Well, I suggest we put him in a safe place for a bit. Until we can think about what to do.' Duffy had already thought about what to do.

'Where's a safe place?'

'Well, my van, for instance.'

'Is that safe?'

'Well, it says DUFFY SECURITY on the side, it ought to be.'

'Is it alarmed?'

'No, it isn't as a matter of fact.'

'Righty-ho, well, I'll leave it in your capables.'

Jimmy picked up the wet suit and flippers. Duffy belted him on the shoulder in congratulation once again, and he headed off towards the house. Duffy, the laundry-bag in one hand, worked his way stealthily round Braunscombe Hall until he crossed the driveway at a point two-thirds of the way to the stone balls with the salamander on top. There he left Ricky in a ditch. He jogged back to the house, climbed into his van, and set off down the drive. He returned after ten minutes, which was longer than necessary. Ricky was safe; but Ricky was not in the back of his van.

The gong had gone by the time he returned, and everyone was seated round the refectory table.

'Been putting in some practice?' asked Damian.

'Eh?'

'Been making pretty patterns on the green baize in anticipation of our nocturnal showdown?'

'No. I've been checking the van.'

'You know,' said Damian, again managing his trick of addressing the whole table while excluding Duffy, 'it always amazes me that the lower classes have taken to snooker with such ferocity.'

'Why's that?' asked Vic. He could tell when Damian needed to be stoked up with the obvious question.

'Glad you asked. Because it's so élitist. I mean, can you imagine, some of the balls are actually more valuable than others. The black's always worth seven, the pink's always worth six, and the poor little reds are only worth one point each. It's like people having more money than one another, not just for a bit but for always. I bet if this was *Russia*,' he said emphatically, '*all* the balls would be red, and *all* of them would be worth one point each. You'd probably prefer that, wouldn't you, Duffy?'

'It wouldn't be such a good game,' he replied. Don't let him rile you, he thought; don't let him rile you now, and don't let him do it on the table either.

'But it would be more democratic, wouldn't it?'

'I don't think that's relevant,' said Duffy.

'He isn't going to rise,' put in Lucretia.

'That's your problem, sweetie, not mine,' said Damian. Sally giggled violently at this, and Jimmy looked blank.

Henry was at dinner that night, and Duffy was able to get his first good look at him. He was large, square-headed and fleshy, with big red hands and a mouth that turned down at the corners; he looked straight at you when you addressed him, but still seemed to keep something in reserve. He wore a farmer's jacket with a check big enough for even a myopic noughts-and-crosses player to be able to manage, and a yellow silk handkerchief cascaded out of his top pocket; the same spotted bow-tie continued to clash with the same Viyella shirt. He didn't say much, not even to Angela, though when she addressed him he would turn slowly towards her and beam in a benign sort of way. Duffy thought he looked just right for the green-wellies brigade; which was perhaps why Angela had come as such a bright surprise to him. Angela, for her part, seemed calmer in his presence; neither hyped-up nor apathetic, but more or less normal, which was probably as normal as she got.

Occasionally, Damian would address the odd remark to Henry, as if trying to bring him into the conversation. 'Dipped many sheep today, Henry?' he would ask brightly, whereupon Henry would reply, 'It's not the time of year for that. You dip sheep . . .' but before he could tell Damian when you dipped sheep, his interlocutor had gone on with, 'Well, you must have shot some pheasant then?' And as Henry started up again explaining that no, he hadn't done that either, Damian danced off to another topic.

Duffy thought this a bit unfair, and at one point turned to Henry and did his best with, 'Have you got a large farm, Henry?' but Henry wasn't allowed to answer. ' "How many acres have you got?" is the better way to phrase it, Duffy,' cut in Damian, 'but that's a boring question anyway, because everyone but you knows the answer to it already, so why don't you stick it down your jumper until you're alone with Henry and ask him then. I do think conversation over dinner ought to involve as many people as possible.'

'Are you always like this?' asked Duffy.

'Like what, like what?' Damian was expectant.

'Do you always go on like a prat?'

'Ah, aaah,' Damian moaned. 'Stabbed. A poniard in the vitals. Such a turn of phrase, such a pretty turn of phrase.'

'Knock it off, kids,' said Vic.

After dinner Damian tried to get everyone to watch the

Braunscombe Hall snooker final, but something about his jocular over-enthusiasm – 'Roll up, girls, and listen to the clicking of balls' – seemed to put people off. Vic and Belinda went to bed; so did Angela; Taffy went off to watch a television programme hosted by a female rabbi about whether or not we choose to do evil; and Lucretia disappeared without explanation. Duffy was a bit disappointed by this. Still, maybe when she was next in town she'd like to watch him play in goal for the Western Sunday Reliables; she probably enjoyed football.

So it was only Henry and Sally, sitting at opposite ends of the pink chintz sofa, who watched Duffy break off – none of this fancy stuff, just a normal prod with a touch of right-hand side – in the best-of-five Braunscombe Hall snooker final. When Damian offered a little bet, Duffy replied, 'I should have thought the satisfaction of winning was enough.' When Damian started chatting to Sally, Duffy suggested that such conversation as there might be should only be about the frame in progress and not about whether Petronella Pipedream's Pimms Party was on Tuesday or Wednesday. When Damian left his cube of blue cue chalk on the rail, Duffy pointed this out as a breach of etiquette and asked him to remove it before his next shot. Duffy played it very cool, and he also played it carefully, suspecting that Damian was one of these players who might auto-destruct when under the cosh.

Sally retired to bed, or so she said, but maybe it was just for more supplies, when Damian was leading two frames to one. Despite the fact that Angela must now have been alone between the sheets for almost an hour and a half, Henry stuck solidly on the pink chintz. Duffy pulled back the fourth frame with the help of a canny bout of snookering, but was always behind in the fifth. By the end, he needed blue, pink and black to win, and his attempted safety shot on the blue sent the white rolling gently into the middle pocket. 'In–off,' cried Damian for the second successive evening in Duffy's hearing. Duffy racked his cue as an admission of defeat. '*Must* tell Sally,' said Damian. 'Excuse me for a little gloat.'

All through the match Henry had sat silently. You couldn't tell from his expression whether he could follow what was going on in front of him or not. Now he rose, picked the longest cue from the rack, put the white back on the table, and said, 'I think you're not staying down on the shot long enough.' He mimed the little head-jerk which Duffy knew was an all-too-frequent feature of his cue action; indeed, he played the same shot twice for Duffy's benefit, missing the pot on the blue by a couple of inches when using the special Duffy head-twitch, and rolling it home without touching the sides of the pocket while using his own personal set-in-concrete head-positioning. Then he potted a long and difficult pink, and followed it by doubling the black the length of the table into the top pocket.

'You're very good,' said Duffy. 'You must play a lot.'

'Billiards. Billiards with Daddy from an early age. Never really played snooker. Daddy thought snooker was a degenerate game.'

'Played by yobs,' suggested Duffy.

'No, not that. It was more that the game itself decided how long it went on. Daddy thought billiards was a gentleman's game because the players decided how long it lasted. More subtle, too, of course.'

'Anything else apart from the head?' asked Duffy.

'I think you're holding the cue too far back. Small chaps often do. The forearm isn't hanging vertically enough.'

'Anything else?'

'I think you should have gone for the first frame more. The first frame's vital.'

'I know. I was going for it.'

'Oh, well.'

They sat on the sofa, Duffy still wondering what Henry was doing downstairs. It must be nearly half-past eleven.

'How's Angela?'

'She's fine.'

Why did everyone keep saying that to him. 'She's fine.' Did they think he was an idiot? Or were they just telling him to mind his own business?

'The Ricky thing must have upset her.'

'Ricky was a lovely dog,' said Henry, not quite answering the question.

'Was he Angela's or yours, or both of yours?'

'No, he was hers. Mind you, he was everybody's around here. They all loved him. Sally loved him, too.'

'Sally?'

'Yes, I should think she took him for walks as often as Ange did. Probably more often.'

'Damian?'

'I don't see Damian as a dog-walker.'

'Check.' There was a pause. The evening was coming to its end. 'Well,' said Duffy, turning to Henry in what he hoped would sound like a jolly male stag-night tone, 'Only a couple more weeks before you tie the old knot. Can't be too soon, I shouldn't think.' Duffy wondered if he should elaborate his new theory of marriage as three-day eventing, but thought it might not be appropriate, or at any rate might take too long.

Henry didn't react for a while, then smiled distantly and got up. 'Oh well, Mother calls.' He clapped Duffy on the shoulder for no obvious reason, then shook his hand, grinning all the while. Duffy was left alone in the snooker room, practising a few shots and supposing it was normal that Henry went home to his mother instead of staying with his girlfriend.

The next morning, over breakfast, Duffy made the noises he and Vic had planned about how he had to go down to London to get some pieces of equipment for the alarm system which were obviously unobtainable on the Buckinghamshire/ Bedfordshire borders. He might be back that night or he might not. One thing he'd make sure to bring with him, he thought as he crossed the gravel, was his own dressing-gown. Not that he worried about Damian. In fact, if he had any sense he'd forget about Damian altogether. Three—two. Damn. If only he hadn't been over-ambitious on that long red in the final frame and let old Waggly-Nose in for a break of twenty-two. Perhaps he should get some practice. That was a thought. Maybe when he got back to London he'd call the local hustler and get himself seriously beaten.

He walked casually round his white Sherpa van, inspecting it with care. At least Sally hadn't retired early last night in order to let down his other two tyres. He examined the locks and the join of the rear doors to see if anyone had tried inserting a metal instrument and wrenching. No sign of anything. Well, this proved one negative at least: that Jimmy had kept quiet about finding Ricky. The Sherpa started at the second touch, and Duffy drove off taking a deep breath. Perhaps he'd wind the window down, swear a lot, play some junky music on the radio, and stop off at a motorway caff for some real food of the sort that would make Basil Berk throw up all over Lady Berk.

First, though, he had to retrieve Ricky. Duffy turned off the road a couple of minutes east of Braunscombe Hall, and went up a quiet track still marked by his tyres from last night. Blue plastic was quite a vivid colour, so he'd carefully piled a few branches and lots of bracken on top. Such a brilliant piece of camouflage he almost missed it. Go on like this, Duffy, and you'll get your woodcraft badge. He picked up the laundry-bag and put it in the back of his van. Ricky was already beginning to pong a bit and some of the hair had fallen out of his tail. Duffy wondered if he'd better stop and grab himself a hamburger with lots of extra onions just to make the van smell nice.

When he got back to the flat he made a few telephone calls. There wasn't anywhere obvious you could go – Yellow Pages weren't any help – but eventually he tracked down someone from his past, someone from forensics who'd always done a bit of freelancing. Then he drove to an address in Kensington near the Natural History Museum and handed over the laundry-bag. He recognized Jim Pringle at once, while noting that he was losing his hair almost as fast as Ricky.

'Sorry about the smell,' said Duffy.

'You should take something for that, you know. Might start interfering with your social life otherwise.'

'Check.' Jim was always like that. Didn't mind who he said what to, either. Perhaps that was why he hadn't had the promotion he deserved. Still taking in laundry after all these years.

Duffy explained what he wanted, asked Jim not to make too much of a mess, in case Ricky had to be returned to the grieving widow, and left a couple of telephone numbers. As he turned to go, Jim said, 'Do you want him stuffed as well?'

'Eh?'

'Stuffed. Stuffed and mounted. I could do you an all-in price. The thing is, if you've got to cut him open anyway . . .'

'Jim, I'll get back to you.'

'It'd be cheaper if I knew now.'

Back at the flat, he opened the freezer to see if Carol had eaten the fish with the low-calorie sauce. No. She must have eaten the pizzas, then. No. What had she been eating? Where? Who with? She'd been seeing that Robert Redford again and that Paul Newman and that Steve McQueen . . . No, he was dead, she wouldn't have been eating at the Poison d'Or with Steve McQueen. Duffy's brain skedaddled off on its usual track of mild paranoia. Look, if he had rights, she had rights . . . Sure, sure. And if you don't have to tell, she doesn't have to tell . . . Sure, sure. And if it doesn't mean anything serious for you and doesn't affect the relationship, it's the same for her, too . . . Sure, sure. I just want to know why she didn't eat the fish in the low-calorie sauce.

'You didn't eat the fish,' he said rather sharply when Carol walked in.

'Been having an affair with Paul Newman, haven't I?'

'Why didn't you eat the fish?'

Carol was tired. It had been a long shift, and there'd been that midday alkie. You'd have thought daytime drunks would have had less of a skinful than evening drunks; that they'd be less belligerent. But they weren't, and she'd had to radio for assistance. She didn't like having to do that, not in a crowded street, anyway. She kicked off her shoes and fell on to the sofa. 'They're your rules, Duffy,' was all she said. 'Kiss?'

Sure, kiss. And they were his rules after all. Perhaps they ought to discuss things again. They hadn't done so for years, it seemed to him. But that's what they'd agreed. In the old days there'd been explanations and openness and No-you-just-go-ahead, but that hadn't worked. Then there'd been discussions and rules – the main rule being No Discussions. Had that worked better? Duffy kissed Carol again and she yawned, but politely, and he went to transfer some chicken Kiev from the freezer to the microwave.

'So how's old Vic doing?'

'Vic's doing all right for himself. Bum in the butter. Don't know where he gets the money from.'

'No one ever did. And how's Little Miss Tits?'

'Belinda. Very horsey. She'd be all hoity-toity if you called her that. You could say she's putting her front behind her.'

Carol laughed. 'Bet you thought that one up in the van on the way down.'

He had, too. 'You know me too well,' he said.

'It's not bad, knowing you too well, Duffy.'

He kept his head down and picked at his dinner. It tasted a bit funny to him. 'Do you think the sauce needs a touch more seasoning?'

'You what?'

'Do you think the sauce needs a touch more seasoning?'

This time Carol really laughed. Much louder than at his joke. She got up, went to the fridge and came back with a bottle of Heinz. 'Here, have some red stuff in it. That'll make it taste different.'

'Do you ever want to go to a really pricey restaurant?'

'If you'll take me, I'll go.'

'There are some nice fish restaurants in Chelsea.'

'Duffy, I think you've been mixing with too many Hooray Henries.'

He grunted. 'More like Hooray Nigels. Bit of a mixed bunch, really. Mind you, what's going on is a bit of a mixed bunch. We've got dead dogs, stolen spoons, blackmail except everyone's denying it, a bit of drugging except everyone's denying it. My main job is to see that someone gets married.'

'Don't they want to get married?'

'Sure.'

'Then what's the problem? Can't afford the ring?'

'No. Well . . . no.' That was another rule. Not to bring too much work home with you. Carol always obeyed that particular rule. Duffy was less good at it. 'Got beaten at snooker last night. Three–two. On the blue. I had this problem with my head . . .' Carol smiled, but Duffy didn't notice. Without specifically – or even generally – being asked, he talked her through each frame, describing the key shots, characterizing his opponent's style of game, discussing aloud where he might have gone wrong. At one point she murmured, 'Sounds as if you deserved to win,' but the irony was lost on him, and he explained, again with vivid detail, how that was indeed more or less the case.

He packed a holdall, twice checking that he'd included his towelling gown that came down to well below the knee, and put it by the front door for the morning. As things turned out, this was a sensible move. They went to bed early, but Carol's encounter with the drunk had taken it out of her, as perhaps too had Duffy's extended account of his snooker match with Damian. She lay turned away from him, a heap of dark curls on a pillow, all just visible in the orange burn of a street light filtered through a curtain. Duffy was propped on one elbow, smiling at her in the dark, when the telephone rang.

'Get your arse up here, Duffy, and pronto.' It was Vic.

'What's happened?'

'Angela's disappeared.'

5.•GROUNDS

Which did he prefer, the daytime drivers on the M1 or the night-time ones? It was like asking Carol whether she preferred tangling with an aggressive drunk in a crowded shopping street or in a deserted alley lit only by a smudge of sodium. There wasn't really much in it. Duffy joined the other half of the Le Mans 24-hour race, with the maniacs driving just as fast and just as close, yawning away as the radio disgorged some disc jockey with a voice as smooth as yoghurt, and only shaking themselves awake again when their heads hit the steering wheel. He kept to a steady fifty-five, the same as in the daytime, but now found himself being shunted across into the slow lane. That told you something.

Vic was standing in the porch when Duffy arrived. 'Where've you been?' he grunted, adding wearily, 'Look what you've done to my gravel.'

'Have you found her?'

'No.'

'When did she go missing?'

'Don't know.'

'What do you mean you don't know?'

'We don't know when she went missing. No one *saw* her go missing.'

'When did you last see her?'

'Lunch.'

'When didn't she turn up?'

'Dinner.'

'Have you called anyone?'

'Only Henry. To see if she was there. She wasn't. He's here.'

'Who saw her last?'

'Everyone. At lunch.'

'Called the coppers?'

'You know me.'

'Right, we'll search the house.'

'We've searched it.'

'We'll search it again.'

They left Sally, Damian and Belinda having stiff drinks together in the kitchen. Vic, Henry, Jimmy, Taffy and Lucretia started in the not-quite Lord Mayor's wine-cellar. They looked in all the spaces large enough to contain Angela, then in all the spaces large enough to contain half of her. Duffy directed the other five and together they lifted sofas, turned over beds, climbed up to look on top of wardrobes, moved large industrial Hoovers, even – you had to be logical, however silly – opened the doors of grandfather clocks. By four o'clock they had established that Angela was not in the house – not unless she'd been dodging round them all the time. The others wanted to call it a day, but Duffy insisted that they carry on and clear the outbuildings. Partly they had to do it, and the sooner the better; partly, this was something he knew about, and doing it with Lucretia's eye on him wasn't entirely displeasing.

They shifted the horses to one side and poked around among their bedding. They looked through the garage and opened the boot of each car. They knocked up Mr and Mrs Hardcastle, who were awake anyhow, and apologetically rummaged through their cottage. In a criss-cross of flashlights they examined the coal bunker and the wood store. They got to the garden shed.

'This open?' asked Duffy rather gruffly. He hadn't told Vic about Ron Hardcastle having exactly the same taste in wine as his employer, and he wasn't sure that now was the time, but there was no avoiding it.

'The key's under that flowerpot there,' said Ron. 'No, the little one.'

Duffy opened the shed and pointed his flashlight round it. Spades and forks as usual, and a square mound covered by some sacking. Vic was beside him as he pulled the sacking away. Piled neatly underneath were six slatted boxes of freshly picked apples.

By a quarter to five the sky was getting light and they had found no sign of Angela. As they walked across the gravel Duffy said to Vic, 'Call the coppers.'

'Suppose there's no other way,' Vic replied.

Everyone assembled in the kitchen, where Sally and Belinda were still patronizing the whisky bottle. Vic's speech was short and to the point. 'We haven't found her. I'm going to call the coppers. The coppers will have to search the house again. If any of you have got anything you think it might be a bad idea for the coppers to see, I suggest you get rid of it now. I also suggest that if we all leave the room at the same time, then none of us will start thinking naughty things about the others.'

There was a shuffle of chairs. Belinda asked, 'You didn't find anything?'

'Not really,' said Vic. 'Oh, we found the cutlery.'

'The cutlery?'

'Yeah. It was under Mrs Colin's bed.'

Duffy caught Vic by the elbow as the others were leaving. 'When you call the coppers, better tell them they might need a diver.'

●

Detective-Sergeant Vine had not had a good Bank Holiday weekend. The roses had needed pruning, the grass seemed to have grown a foot, the kids wanted to be taken to the public baths, and the one-day cricket final, which was about the only thing he'd actually been looking forward to, was rained off. He was glad to get back to work, and there were worse ways of doing so than dealing with a disappearing female. They said they'd searched the house, in fact they said they'd searched it twice, but they were only amateurs, so he got Constable Willey to do it in a professional manner.

Whether or not they yet had a missing female on their hands was a matter on which D/S Vine was currently suspending judgement. People went off on long walks sometimes, and just forgot what time it was. People had rows. People played hard to get. People played that old game of Miss Me, Miss Me. This particular female didn't even live at this particular address, and the inhabitants of this particular address – who looked a pretty strange crew, not just because they'd been up all night – hadn't even checked Miss Angela Bruton's home address. Well, they said they'd telephoned, but there was no reply, and since her car was still at the Hall and she wasn't known as a walker, they'd assumed . . . That was the trouble with the public, they always did assume. So Detective-Sergeant Vine and Constable Willey and the lady in question's fiancé drove round to the cottage. They knocked a bit, then quizzed the neighbours and finally pushed in a back window. No, after you, Constable. Constables and children first, I always say.

But she wasn't there and by late morning it had been established securely enough in D/S Vine's mind that the woman in question was, as they said, of a nervous disposition, which translated into normal language meant that she was barking mad and liable to top herself at any minute. So at about half-past eleven on an otherwise very pleasant morning the police frogman lowered himself into the lake and D/S Vine began the boring task of taking statements from the household; statements which, he knew from experience, would express either complete surprise at the fact that Miss Angela Bruton had gone missing, or else complete surprise that she hadn't gone missing a lot earlier.

It was while he was interviewing the Filipino woman, who kept clutching at her throat and going on about some spoons or other which the Detective-Sergeant wasn't the slightest bit interested in, that a short fellow with a broad face and a grown-out brush-cut came into the room.

'Later, sir, if you don't mind.'

'Duffy, West End Central. Used to be, anyway. Freelance.'

'Put in your six-penn'orth.'

The intruder nodded at the Filipino woman, who was dismissed. Duffy was cross with himself for not having thought of it earlier. He hadn't because it was a possibility which implied a gloomy view of human nature. But that was exactly the view he had been trained to take – which was why he was now cross with himself.

D/S Vine put his head round the door and told Constable Willey, who was standing outside, to make sure everyone waited their turn in the family room, and not to let anyone into the video library, where he was conducting his interviews. Then he and Duffy slipped out through the french windows, one of which was still to be mended, and crossed the terrace.

Vine, a plumpish young man with sandy hair and a dark moustache, was obviously much more at home in the woods than Duffy was ever likely to be. Silently, they followed the path as it rose through the thickening bracken. This time, Duffy knew where the nick in the beech would be and instantly turned left. He didn't need to walk past the hide before turning back to spot it. This time he simply cut his way firmly down a nettled slope until he and D/S Vine came out opposite the low entrance to the camp. What they saw made them break into a run.

She was lying on her front on a piece of tarpaulin with a brown-paper bag over her head. Her wrists were tied together behind her back and her ankles were roped as well. To ensure that she couldn't turn over, each elbow was lashed to a short stake like a tent peg which had been hammered into the ground. She made a noise in her throat as they approached, which at least allayed their most obvious fear. Their next most obvious fear was not allayed: her skirt had been pulled up over her back, and her tights pulled down to her knees, leaving her naked from waist to lower thigh.

'It's all right. You're all right, we've found you. It's OK. It's Duffy. We've found you.' It didn't matter much what you said, you just have to say it in the right tone. Duffy babbled, and alongside him D/S Vine also babbled, two streams of meaningless comfort as they undid the loose piece of string holding the brown-paper bag in place, then unfastened the gag and the blindfold and cut away the ropes. She sat blinking for some time, and the two men rubbed at her wrists, then she sat up, which made her skirt fall back into place, and when Duffy whispered, 'Pull your tights up, love,' she did as she was told. But she didn't look at either of them, and she didn't reply when D/S Vine asked her gently if she knew who'd done this to her.

They helped her to her feet and she stood there wobbling like some new-born animal. Then after the detective-sergeant had taken a good first look round Jimmy's camp the three of them set off down the path. At first Duffy tried holding Angela round the waist, but she didn't want that; then he tried taking her arm, but even this amount of physical contact seemed unacceptable; so they came through the wood in single file, with Angela silent between the two men. At one point she began shivering, but as soon as D/S Vine touched her shoulder from behind, she stopped.

They came out of the light bracken and made their way across the lawn towards the house. There was at first only one face at the large picture window in the family room, then there were several. One of these suddenly broke away, and a few seconds later the kitchen door was thrown open. Duffy and D/S Vine, more baffled than curious, watched as Jimmy ran across the terrace, down the steps, across the lawn and hurled himself straight into the lake. As there was a police frogman on duty there at the time, it proved easy enough to arrest him.

Duffy joined the others in the family room. They would all now have to wait longer to be interviewed. Priorities had changed. D/S Vine would be back probably the following day, but in the meantime no one was to leave, right? 'What about calls of nature, Sergeant,' asked Damian. 'I don't think this is a time for levity, sir,' replied Vine.

They let Jimmy change into some dry clothes, but he still looked damp and wretched as they took him away. Angela followed in Mrs Vic Crowther's red MG, driven by Belinda. Going off to be interviewed about kidnapping and rape in a red MG with the hood down, driven by former model Belinda Blessing, didn't look or sound quite right to Duffy. He knew who it would sound pretty good to: the tabloids.

'We're going to have a problem with the papers,' said Duffy. 'They're going to love this one.' Big house in the country, missing girl, posh people, ex-Page-Three girl, rape, the old villain – sorry, local businessman – Vic, the young villain Taffy; all they needed was sex and drugs, which they could probably find without even needing to use a telephoto lens, and they were well away. Every neighbour interviewed, every speculation indulged. It would keep all those what-is-the-country-coming-to? columnists happy for weeks.

'Yeah, well, I might be able to hold it off for a day or two,' said Vic, and left the room.

There was a silence. Somehow, Duffy expected the first direct question to come from Lucretia. He was right. 'How did you know where to go?'

'What, the camp?' It was easier to lie with Vic out of the room. 'Oh, Jimmy told me about it. Roughly. It wasn't too hard to find.'

'No, I don't mean that. Why did you think it was Jimmy?'

'I wasn't particularly thinking it was Jimmy. I was just thinking of places she might be. I suppose you could call it a hunch,' he added, using the professional term.

'Do you think Jimmy did it?'

'Well,' said Duffy. He wasn't sure whether it was tactically better to be fair or unfair to Jimmy. 'We don't know what anyone "did" yet. Angela didn't say anything on the way down, so we're just assuming. I mean, it looked like something had happened, I have to admit that.' It could only have looked more like something had happened, Duffy admitted to himself, if they'd actually caught the fellow still zipping up his fly. 'And Vine did have a poke around when we were up there. Jimmy had these tins. With things in.' He looked at Henry as he said the next bit. 'There was an engagement photo of you and Angela, from the paper. It had burns all over it. Like it had been done with a cigarette.'

Henry didn't reply. Duffy went on. 'The funny thing was, he hadn't just put burns all over your face, he'd done it to Angela's as well.'

Henry wafted his hand from side to side in disbelief. 'I don't understand any of it.'

'Come on, Henry,' said Lucretia. 'It's called jealousy.'

'He never told me he was jealous of me.' Henry made this sound like a full answer to the problem. He took his floppy handkerchief out of his breast pocket and blew his nose loudly.

'They don't,' Lucretia explained. 'They don't. That's the point about it.'

'But I didn't steal her from him. He's a . . . he's a . . . friend.' There obviously wasn't a nearer word Henry could lay his hands on.

'Henry, *everyone* stole her from him.' Lucretia's emphasis made Damian chuckle; a response which irritated her. 'No, I don't mean *that*. I mean everyone had more chance with her than Jimmy. The milkman had more chance with her.'

'The milkman has more chance with everybody, I'd say,' smirked Damian.

'So I just happened to be the one at the time? But why didn't he do something to *me* if he was soft on Ange?'

'Maybe that's the point,' said Lucretia. 'It could have been you, it could have been anyone, if not quite the milkman. But it was always going to be her. There was always going to be Ange around. I suppose poor old Jimmy couldn't take it any more.'

'Poor old Jimmy,' Sally mimicked crossly. 'What about poor old bloody Ange?'

'He had been behaving a bit oddly lately, I suppose,' said Henry.

Lucretia demurred. 'No odder than usual I'd have thought.'

'What was he doing in that frogman's suit yesterday? Everyone saw him, but from what you say he was going on as if he was the Invisible Man.'

'He was looking for Ricky,' said Duffy.

'Looking for Ricky? That was a bit potty, wasn't it?'

Duffy shrugged. He didn't feel he'd confess who'd put Jimmy up to it. 'Well, it doesn't seem so strange to me. If you're soft on someone, you probably think their dog needs a decent burial.'

'Yes, old Jimmy would be just like that,' Damian spotted a chance to annoy. 'I can just see him saluting on some rain-swept hillside with the Last Post on a bugle and a damp little headstone. Ricky: He Barked His Last.'

Henry cleared his throat. 'One of these days, Damian, someone's going to thump you.'

'If only they would,' sighed Damian, 'if only they would.' Henry moved approximately a foot closer to Damian, where-upon the latter yelped and jumped over the back of the sofa. 'I didn't mean it. Nice dog. Nice doggie. Woof, woof.' Sally giggled, and Vic's return to the room was fortunately timed.

'They'll do what they can,' he said, making Duffy wonder if the local papers up here also described Vic as a 'local busi-nessman', and if so what they thought his business was. 'At the moment the coppers can say there's no story because they don't know that any offence has been committed.' Sure, thought Duffy, long-term open-air bondage is all the rage among posh people nowadays.

'What about a couple of frames before lunch?' Damian suggested.

'I think I've been up all night,' said Duffy.

'About those cigarette burns on the photo,' said Lucretia. 'Jimmy doesn't smoke. And another thing I don't understand.' Duffy rather wished Lucretia would shut up. No one else seemed to be thinking at the moment, which suited him fine. 'If Jimmy killed Ricky, why was he looking for the body?'

'Because he's potty.' This was Henry's suggestion.

'No, no, my dear Watson,' said Damian. 'Don't you see, he did it to throw suspicion off himself. Who would ever suspect he was the murderer if he was the one that found the body?'

'Brill,' sighed Sally in genuine admiration.

'Only one thing wrong.' It was Lucretia with another correction. 'He didn't find it. The body. If he'd hidden it, you'd think even Jimmy would know where to look.'

'Maybe it's not helping anyone, going over things like this,' Vic suggested. 'Why don't we break it up and have a spot of lunch?'

The women and Damian led the way. Duffy turned to Henry. 'Have you still got your Dad's billiard table?'

'Of course.'

'Look, say if you think this is a bit silly, but if I'm stuck down here for a couple of days, what about you giving me a couple of lessons, secret, you know. Then I could really take that Damian apart.'

Henry grinned, looked serious for a bit, then grinned again. 'Well, I suppose it depends on Mother a bit. And Ange. But I'd like to.'

'Then you wouldn't have to thump him.'

'But I quite want to thump him.'

'So do I. But I wouldn't mind thumping him with a side-bet.'

Despite Vic's suggestion that going over it all wouldn't help things, there seemed nothing else to talk about. Henry's presence inhibited some of the preciser speculations on what might have been done to his fiancée, but the character and career of her assailant were thoroughly examined. Jimmy's professional reputation as an estate agent was confirmed as not being of the highest; in fact, no one had ever known him sell a house. His less than moderate success with women was apparently known through two counties. His mother had died young, and his father had pushed him hard. He'd really enjoyed the Army, but the Army hadn't enjoyed him. He was a loser, a wimp–out, and at thirty-five it had all just got too much for him.

'There's something else I don't understand,' said Lucretia. Shut up, shut up. 'If Jimmy was clever enough to start fishing for Ricky's body to put us all off the scent, why was he so stupid as to run away when the police brought Ange down from his camp?'

'Because he's potty,' said Henry.

'Ah.' Lucretia had aimed the question at Damian, who briefly got going. 'The psyche of the criminal is indeed a Hampton Court maze. But perhaps . . . My dear Taffy?' Damian lobbed the question on to the man in black with the triangular torso.

'Well,' Taffy began. 'He looked as if he was running away, didn't he?'

'Yes,' various people replied with various emphases.

'I've been reading up on this, you see. Sometimes, the psychologists say, running away isn't what it looks like. Running away isn't running away, you see. Running away is really wanting to be caught.'

'Isn't it easier to stay where you are if you want to be caught?' Lucretia swept her blonde hair off the side of her face in a manner which implied polite scepticism, if not that Taffy was the biggest fucking fool she'd listened to for some time.

'No, not necessarily. There has to be a moment of symbolic fugue followed by symbolic reintegration into society.'

'You mean running away and getting arrested?'

'If you want to use the layman's terms. You see, the offender isn't any different from most of us round this table.'

Well, he isn't any different from *you*, thought Duffy. 'The offender is always seeking his place in society. It's just that he sometimes uses unusual methods.' Like hitting people with iron bars. 'But what he's seeking is reintegration, or rather the integration he never had in the first place.' Duffy looked across at Vic; he wondered if Vic's move to the Buckinghamshire/Bedfordshire borders had been a symbolic fugue in quest of a symbolic or actual reintegration.

'So Jimmy ran into the lake,' Lucretia said slowly, as if only just following Taffy, 'because it was a sort of public gesture which would provoke a forceful reaction which he might not knowingly want but which would bring him what all his life – since his rejection as a child – he'd secretly been looking for.'

'More or less,' nodded Taffy.

'I think he did it because he's potty,' Henry repeated stolidly.

After lunch Duffy and Vic were on the terrace, sniffing the dangerous air.

'I like those red flowers,' said Duffy politely.

'Yes, they're nice those red flowers,' replied Vic, 'but I don't know what they're called either. They're full of those great hornet things, though.'

'Bumblebees,' stated Duffy authoritatively.

'Bees.'

'Wasps? Bluebottles?'

'You have to have the odd chuckle, don't you, with all this going on?'

'What are you going to do about Mrs Colin?'

'Mrs Colin? Hadn't thought. It's up to Belinda, I expect. I should think she'll have to go. I mean, that's the first rule of employing people, isn't it?'

'I wouldn't know.' And if it were, Vic might have to let the Hardcastles go as well. Duffy wondered when to mention the matter of Ron's taste for pink champagne; he also wondered where Ron had shifted the stuff. He couldn't have drunk it all in the time. 'Maybe you could give me a day or two on that one?'

Vic grinned. 'Are you sure you're up to it? The case of the

missing spoons which have turned up anyway in the possession of the culprit who has given a fortnight's notice. I mean, I'm not sure this isn't out of your league.'

'I thought I might be able to pin it on Jimmy.'

'Yeah. Get him a parking ticket at the same time. Actually, I'm not sure why you're still here, Duffy.'

'Detective-Sergeant Vine told us all to stay, didn't he? And you're paying me daily rates.'

'Am I?'

'A gentleman's word is his bond.'

'Do you think those red things are called salvias?'

'Bound to be. Unless they're not, of course.'

'Yeah.'

Mrs Colin's attic room looked very bare; though whether it was always like this, or whether Mrs Colin had already started putting things away in her case, Duffy couldn't tell. There was a small crucifix above the bed, a mirror on one wall, a pile of magazines which Mrs Colin had saved from the waste-paper baskets downstairs, and a framed colour print of people in Davao drinking San Miguel beer on somebody's birthday.

'Is it . . .?' Duffy hovered by the door. Mrs Colin had been crying, but she waved him in and pointed at a small Lloyd Loom chair. Duffy didn't know whether or not she would think it proper for him to shut the door; he hesitated, then firmly did so. Yes, that was probably the right approach. 'Mrs Colin,' he began, and it was a statement not a question, 'you didn't steal those spoons.' She didn't reply. 'I don't think you stole those spoons.' Not unless it was a symbolic gesture aimed at achieving social reintegration, in which case Duffy would just climb into his van and drive away. 'I'll tell you why you didn't do it,' said Duffy. 'Because you wouldn't do so. Because you don't do things like that. And because anyone who did anything like that would be daft to leave them under their bed.'

'They found them,' said Mrs Colin. 'You found them. I have to go.'

'Are you happy here?'

'Yes. Happy here.'

'How do you get on with Mr and Mrs Hardcastle?'

'Oh, very nice.'

'They aren't . . . I don't know, jealous of you?'

'Jealous?'

'Jealous, sure.' Well, why not, it seemed to be the flavour of the day. 'They don't think you work too hard? They don't think you're too popular with Mrs Crowther?'

'No. They are normal. Mrs Crowther, she is nice.'

'What was that run-in you were having with Nikki? What was she shouting at you about ?'

'Oh, she's a bit spoiled, Miss Nikki. No, that's normal. I just caught her in the video room watching something she shouldn't be watching, so I send her off. That was a few days ago, but she's still cross with me.

'What about Jimmy?' Well, he'd promised Vic he'd try and pin it on Jimmy.

'Mr Jimmy, what's he done?'

'We don't know yet.'

'Mr Jimmy, he's a *gentleman*,' she said forcefully. 'He helps with things.' Maybe Jimmy could go into business designing Hoovers you drove around on, Duffy thought, and Mrs Colin could do the advertisements. Maybe he could; when he gets out in six or seven years.

'Mrs Colin, if I did something for you, would you do something for me?'

'I do something for you anyway. What you want done? These shoes don't look too clean.'

'No, well, that's how I like them. Look, don't just go off or anything. I mean, the police will want to talk to us all, I expect.'

At the mention of the police Mrs Colin reached for her handkerchief. 'No, no, Mrs Colin. About Jimmy. They'll want to talk to you about Mr Jimmy.'

'Mr Jimmy, he's a gentleman,' said Mrs Colin.

'Sure.'

Whether or not Mr Jimmy was a gentleman was a matter much discussed over dinner, and speculation became the freer because Henry, after telephoning Detective-Sergeant Vine, had obtained permission to go home and look after his aged mother. Angela and Belinda had returned at about six o'clock; Angela had been put to bed with a large drink, a meal on a tray, a portable television and a bell to ring if she wanted company; now Belinda's report of what had emerged at the station gave things a new impetus.

The first point was that Angela hadn't seen who had attacked her. She'd been walking at the edge of the woods, sometime in the middle of the afternoon, she couldn't say when, and had been attacked from behind. A hand was over her mouth, a knife which she didn't see and couldn't describe was at her throat. She didn't resist as she was dragged, blind-folded, and gagged. Strong, that was all she could say about the man, he was strong. She didn't see his hands, might have glimpsed some bit of greeny-buff sleeve but she couldn't swear to it. No, she absolutely didn't recognize the man who'd made her walk to Jimmy's camp. That's what she said. How did she know it was a man, then? Well, it would have had to have been an incredibly strong woman. And a woman couldn't have done what happened at the camp.

That was the second point, the one that led to the main part of the discussion. Angela hadn't been raped. There was a genuine exhalation of relief when Belinda revealed this piece of information; and Duffy heard Mrs Colin's voice in his head – 'Mr Jimmy, he's a gentleman.' Angela had been dragged the last few yards, then thrown down on to what didn't feel like the ground and turned out to have been a tarpaulin. She heard a hammering noise quite close. She didn't try and kick, or stand up, or do anything, because she realized how hopeless things were; and she also thought that this was perhaps what the fellow wanted her to do. After a minute or two she found her elbows being roped tightly to whatever had been banged into the ground. Something extra was put over her head. Her ankles were tied together – she did try to kick out against that – and her tights pulled down. When her skirt was hauled up round her waist she lay there and expected the worst. She expected worse than the worst. Then nothing happened for a while, though she thought she heard some distant noises, some scrabbling, perhaps. After a few minutes she felt some-thing, perhaps a knee, against the outside of her right thigh, and shortly afterwards something wet began to fall across her buttocks. It wasn't rain. After that, there had been waiting, and feeling cold, and thinking about suffocation, and wondering if anyone would find her, and wondering what would happen if someone else, someone who didn't want to rescue her, found her instead.

There was a silence around the table. 'The thing I couldn't get over,' said Belinda, 'was that this fucking policeman kept asking her about her knickers.'

'I thought they got policewomen to do the questioning.' Another nasty job for WPC Carol Lucas, thought Duffy.

'Yeah, well, we're a bit backward in the provinces.' Belinda didn't hold back on the sarcasm. 'They got in some trainee girl, I don't know, she had the uniform but I shouldn't think she was more than seventeen, and obviously Ange didn't want to talk to her, 'cause she knew she'd have to go through it again with the detective fellow, so she just asked for him.'

'Bloody plucky.' Damian for once was looking subdued.

'But what he seemed to be most interested in was where her knickers were. "He pulled down your tights. Can you tell me what happened about your knickers?" She said she didn't wear knickers, just tights. He was incredible, I thought he was getting off on it. "What happened about your knickers?" – he came back to it later. Like either Jimmy had stolen her knickers and if they went through his pockets and found them they'd have him all locked up, or else she was a tart because she went around only wearing tights, and so she got everything she deserved.'

No, it wasn't like that, Duffy thought; but he didn't say anything. You had to ask, and you had to repeat the question. Stealing knickers was a completely normal thing to do – given that you were the completely abnormal person who'd already done everything else to Angela.

'They're all perves, coppers,' observed Sally.

'Now, now,' said Damian, 'I bet there are some really sweet ones somewhere.'

'Why did he do that?' Lucretia asked suddenly. 'Why did he just wank off on her? Why didn't he rape her?'

No one answered for a bit. Duffy remembered the

four-year-old copies of *Playboy* in the green tin. Maybe that was what he liked doing best, and doing it with a real person was even better than doing it with magazines. Maybe, for all the brutality leading up to it, he just didn't have the guts to go ahead and rape her. Maybe, in a funny sort of way, he thought it showed he loved her. A very funny sort of way, admittedly.

'Perhaps Taffy can give us a line on this one,' said Damian mischievously.

'Never did understand sex offenders,' Taffy shook his head gravely. 'They're not like your ordinary offender. They always keep themselves to themselves when they're inside.' Duffy thought this the understatement of the decade. If sex offenders didn't keep to themselves in prison, they lived a very short life. They got it from the screws, and they got it from the other inmates. Everyone thinking, that could have been my girlfriend, my daughter, my little boy. It wasn't, but it might have been. Thump. Filthy pervert.

'Perhaps it's all about humiliation,' Lucretia tried answering her own question. 'That's what they say, isn't it? Maybe he reckoned it was more humiliating this way. Sort of, I could have raped you but you aren't even worth doing that to. Does that sound likely?'

'Sounds likely,' said Belinda. 'The only thing is, can you see old Jimmy thinking like that?'

'Who knows what went on in old Jimmy's head.' Vic was rueful. 'I was wondering. Maybe I should have let him build his assault course. Work it all off, sort of.'

'Did she actually ever, you know, go out with him?' Duffy asked.

Damian chuckled, and his face shone. 'Isn't it funny how people say "go out with" when what they really mean is "stay in with".'

'No,' said Belinda. 'She never teased him or anything. He was always around, sort of useful, could you shift that, Jimmy, please, and so on, but she never showed him any leg or anything.' Not like an experienced Page-Three girl might have done.

'So he knew it was hopeless all along?' This was what Duffy

had been told by Jimmy, but you never took people's word on things like love and sex.

'Suppose so. No one ever thought, "If Ange breaks up with So-and-so, there's always Jimmy." No one got anywhere near thinking that.'

'Perhaps that was the trouble,' said Vic.

'Hey, look, what about Ange, all right?' It was Sally, almost violent. 'I mean, fuck Jimmy, that's what I say. What about Ange?'

Ange, it seemed, had made her statement to Detective-Sergeant Vine in the presence of Belinda and the woman police constable who wasn't meant to be old enough, then said they could talk to her again tomorrow if they wanted to, and asked Belinda to take her home. By home she presumably meant Braunscombe Hall. She didn't speak on the journey there, nor did she weep.

'Christ.' Belinda suddenly got up from the table and ran upstairs. Everyone else must have been thinking roughly the same; they didn't look at one another, and just waited. A door banged, and they heard Belinda swear. Then there was silence, and no one knew quite what to do. After a minute or so, Belinda could be heard coming slowly downstairs again. The silence continued; people began wondering whose fault it might be.

'Christ,' she said. 'It's all right. Christ, I got a shock, though. She wasn't in her room. She's in the cot. Fast asleep.' She turned to her husband. 'Early night, Vic? She might need us.'

'Sure, Bel.' Vic threw his napkin down on the table in a lordly way, a mannerism recently learnt.

Duffy caught Lucretia's eye as the others politely rose and followed the example of their hosts. When they were alone, she said, 'I hope you don't want to discuss restaurants.'

He grinned briefly. 'Where's Henry?'

'At home. With Mum.'

'I don't get it. Your girlfriend's been missing and nearly raped and he's at home with Mum. Does it make sense to you?'

'Oh yes,' said Lucretia. 'You haven't met Mum.'

'Bad as that?'

'And you don't know Angela.'

'What is there that I don't know about Angela?'

'Well, that Ange's USP is understanding about Mum.'

'What's a USP?'

'Sorry. Unique Selling Point. Worked in advertising once,' she explained.

'So it's apron strings all round?'

'Tied in a double bow.'

'And Angela will put up with that after they get married? No, don't tell me, I've already had the lecture about love from Belinda.'

'Which one's that?'

'About how love means just about being able to put up with the other person.'

'Do I detect a Romantic?' She was teasing him now; he could guess that.

'Dunno. I'm no good with flowers and things.'

'That's not what it's about,' said Lucretia firmly.

'Oh, well, maybe I am, then. I'm not good at candlelit dinners, though.'

'Is that a back-handed way of asking me out?' This time she sounded less teasing. Was she serious, or was she just trying to draw him out so she could have a good laugh at him?

'Dunno.' He couldn't really ask her out to dinner, not when he almost never took Carol out for a meal, could he? Or could he? Why hadn't Carol eaten that fish with the low-calorie sauce? This running joke they had about her going out with Paul Newman and Robert Redford: you didn't have running jokes that meant nothing, did you? And she hadn't explained about the fish. Maybe . . . maybe . . . Then he realized that Lucretia's eyes were on him. He wondered how much of all that she could read.

She didn't let on. Instead, she lit a cigarette and said, 'But anyway, the matter in hand.'

'They aren't seeing so much of one another before they're married because it's an old posh custom.'

'Who told you that?'

'Damian.'

Lucretia laughed. 'Well, for once, Damian's giving you the censored version. Which is probably only because he doesn't know the uncensored one.'

'Which is?'

'You know that thing that people do?'

'Sorry?'

'That thing that people do. When they're alone. People of opposite sexes. Two of them. The thing they do.'

Did he blush? He cleared his throat and said, 'Gotcha.'

'They haven't done it.'

'*What?*'

'That's right. They haven't done it. Angela told Belinda and Belinda told me. Girls' talk. You know, it goes on, while we're waiting for you and Taffy to finish your port and tell the one about the nun with big tits.'

'But . . . but . . .' But Angela's meant to be a right little goer is what he wanted to say; in the circumstances it didn't seem the proper phrase.

'Yup. Henry,' she said, with a lecturer's emphasis, 'is saving himself for marriage.' Something about the way she pronounced the phrase suggested that it had been used originally by Henry and dutifully transmitted down the female line.

'Christ.'

'Yup. You're a pretty weird bunch, you men, I'll tell you that for nothing.'

'How long have they been going out together?'

'Which in this case does not mean staying in together. About a year.'

'Hmm. Still, if it takes two to tango, it takes two not to tango as well.'

'That's a funny way of putting things but I suppose I see what you mean.'

There was a pause. Duffy wasn't sure if he was on dangerous ground or not. 'Do you know,' said Lucretia, 'with horses, really top horses, the ones that race, they don't get any sex. They aren't allowed it. Then if they turn out to be good at racing and they're worth breeding from, they're sold to stud. By that time they've usually forgotten what they never learnt. Have to be helped to do it.'

Well, if Henry's like that, Duffy thought, Angela will certainly be the right girl to know how to help him, by all accounts. He coughed. 'Do you think that Basil Berk's a good writer about restaurants?'

'He's not bad.'

'It looks a bloody easy job to me.'

'Just say there's saffron in everything.'

'That's right. Well . . . goodnight.'

Lucretia waved an arm in dismissal. If you could wave an arm in dismissal and not seem unfriendly, she managed it. Or maybe Duffy was fooling himself. He wondered what the joke about the nun with big tits was. He'd have to ask Taffy.

He lay on his bed thinking over the events of the last twenty-four hours. It didn't make sense, except on the psychopath theory. This was a very common phenomenon in American detective series on television, but less frequently encountered in real life. It was useful because it explained everything: Jimmy, for instance, left a dead bird on Angela's doorstep, killed her dog, planted some spoons on Mrs Colin, stashed four cases of wine in the Hardcastles' shed, hid the dog, found the dog, kidnapped Angela, tied her up, wanked over her, and when the police came ran off into the lake. He also let down Duffy's tyres, and Sally's confession was bogus. Why did old Jimmy do all these things? Because he's a psychopath. What's the definition of a psychopath? Someone who does all these things. Perfect.

There were times, of course, in police work, when you longed for the odd psychopath – especially one with a willingness to confess to any old crime you shoved in front of him. Compliant psychopaths would certainly help tidy up the crime figures. Though there were simpler ways of cooking the books if that's what you were after.

The next morning, while they were still in theory housebound and awaiting the return of D/S Vine, Duffy decided it was time to make a very small start. He was pretending without much sincerity to examine a bit of wiring in the alarm system when he saw Nikki coming along the corridor. She stopped, looked up at him, and before she could open her mouth, he said, 'I'd love to see your dance, Nikki.'

'I thought you didn't. Taffy doesn't want to. Taffy always says he's got things to do.'

'I'd love to see it. Can you do it anywhere?' She looked dubious. 'Can I choose where I'd like you to do it for me?'

'All right.'

'The summerhouse. Now I've chosen that, you can have the second choice: either I can sit on the verandah and you can dance on the grass, or you can dance on the verandah and I'll sit on the grass.'

She thought it over as they crossed the lawn to the pagoda-like building that had been painted white in the days of the not-quite Lord Mayor and in psychedelic stripes under the tenancy of Izzy Dunn, but had now been toned down under the Crowthers to a mere bright Chinese red. Nikki took to this as a location and walked the length of the verandah as if pacing out her jumps. While Duffy lolled on the grass, she explained rather sombrely that she didn't yet go to ballet class, so what he was about to see wasn't a 'proper' dance, but rather something she'd invented. The music was also something she'd invented; at least, Duffy hoped no one had ever been paid for writing down the whoops and wails and little tra-la-las with which she accompanied her dance. As for the ballet itself, it didn't look bad to Duffy, who admitted he knew absolutely nothing at all about dance. She seemed to hop and twirl rather gracefully, he thought; even if he couldn't be said to be concentrating.

When silence and stillness from the verandah indicated that Nikki had finished her performance, he got off his haunches and gave her a standing ovation. She did the prima ballerina bit, bowing and all that; whereupon Duffy quickly pulled a few dandelions and daisies out of the grass, shuffled them together into a bouquet, and shyly edged forward to present them. Mademoiselle gave him a curtsey of thanks. He stepped up on to the verandah.

'Very nice, Nikki, very nice. I don't think you'll have any trouble with your ballet classes.'

As he was talking he crossed behind her to the window. He leaned back and pressed his palm against the glass. Then he stood away and acted the big surprise. 'Hey, look at this,

Nikki.' She turned round and, at his bidding, examined the full set of fingerprints left on the dirty glass. 'I wonder who left them there?' Nikki shrugged, then laughed as Duffy took her hand and pretended to match it to the broad spread of the marks.

'I used to be a policeman, you know,' he said. 'If someone had broken into this summerhouse we'd have come along and a fellow with a brush and some special sort of dust would have gone over all the door-frames and window-frames. Now, say those weren't here' – he rubbed away his own prints with a wetted corner of handkerchief – 'they'd still be able to catch the fellow.'

'How?'

'Well, you leave prints even if you can't see them. You leave prints all the time, on everything you touch. Your knife and fork, that sort of thing. You may not see them but they're there right enough.'

'How long do they last?'

'Weeks,' said Duffy. 'Weeks and weeks.' There was a silence. Nikki held her bouquet of dandelions and daisies. Duffy timed the next bit carefully. 'Mrs Colin's very upset. She's very fond of you, Nikki. She won't be cross. Just tell your Dad.'

He could see the child's lips push forward, then came a bit of a frown. 'She shouldn't have stopped me watching video. It's not her house.'

'No, it's not her house. But would your mum have done any different if she'd found you in there?'

She didn't reply. They set off across the lawn. After a dozen or so paces, Nikki, still carefully holding her bouquet, slipped her hand up and into Duffy's. 'Next time I'll wear gloves,' she said crossly. In spite of himself, Duffy burst out laughing. He was still smiling when the explosion occurred.

The estate agents acting for Izzy Dunn had not gone into much detail about the construction of the stable block. In fact, it was an architectural hotch-potch. The two stables themselves dated back to the time of the not-quite Lord Mayor; the Hardcastles' cottage, at the other end of the block, had been put up ten years later with no particular regard for stylistic harmony; and the central section, which not surprisingly had given its designer a number of problems, had been completed only a few years before Izzy Dunn moved in. As it was modern, and flimsily built – merely a horizontal and vertical skin designed to protect three cars from the rain – the force of the explosion did not initially damage either the Hardcastles' cottage or the stabling proper. The danger to them was from fire, not blast.

When Duffy arrived people just seemed to be staring: at the blown-out garage door, the hole in the roof, the blazing car. Mrs Hardcastle, who had telephoned the fire brigade, stood on the gravel clutching her handbag and her wedding album. Vic, who had also called the fire brigade after a long wrangle with Damian, who wouldn't get off the phone, was shaking his head. Taffy and Damian looked as if they were waiting for someone to start setting off the fireworks. Only Belinda, trying to calm two hysterical horses, was actually doing anything.

'Anyone in there?' asked Duffy. They nodded a negative. The middle car of the three was still burning hard. If the Range Rover on the left caught fire, then the stable proper would go; if the MG caught, then the Hardcastles would join the list of the nation's homeless. Duffy ran to his van and backed it across twenty yards of gravel towards the fire. He stopped about fifteen feet away, got out, opened the back and took out his towrope.

'Taffy,' he shouted as he started crawling under the Sherpa to fix one end of the rope. 'Taffy,' he shouted again. There was a pause, then the sound of feet sprinting across gravel. From under his van, Duffy thrust the clamp on the other end of the rope out towards his tardy helper. 'The axle, not the bumper,' he shouted. 'I know,' came the testy reply. Perhaps Taffy's voice had broken slightly with the excitement; and perhaps he'd also slipped into a pair of velvet trousers which hadn't previously been on display; but this seemed unlikely. Duffy jumped into the van, pulled the protesting Range Rover clear, backed up hard to the MG, saw Damian clamp the axle, and towed that to safety. Then they all watched the purply Datsun Cherry burn. After ten minutes or so, when the flames were beginning to die down, the fire brigade, clanging a needless bell, tanked up the drive and swirled to a stop in front of the porch. Vic shook his head. 'Look what they've done to my bloody gravel.'

6 • BEDROOMS

The last person out of the house to see the fire brigade douse the wreckage of the purply Datsun was its owner, Sally. She looked from Duffy to Vic, from Vic to Taffy, as if seeking permission to giggle. It wasn't forthcoming. Finally, Damian, brushing at some singe marks on his velvet jacket, murmured, 'Frightfully unstable, these foreign motors,' and that did the trick. Sally was back to her usual irritating self, and Damian, his surprise moment of heroism over, was also reverting as fast as possible.

'I'll have to buy a new set of maps,' giggled Sally, the funniest thing she'd said since the last funniest thing she'd said.

'It's my bloody garage,' said Vic, who wasn't at all entertained, 'and it nearly took my bloody stables.'

'Sorry,' said Sally. 'Sorry. It's just . . . it's just . . .' she wasn't even sure she could contain herself long enough to get the sentence out, 'It's just that these foreign motors are so frightfully unstable.'

'Well done,' said Duffy to Damian.

'I didn't need to be told about the axle,' he replied huffily. 'I've seen enough films where the bumper just gets pulled off.'

'Check. I thought you were going to be Taffy.'

There was a pause which invited the ex-con to explain himself. 'Always had this fear of fire, see. Two-bar electric fell on me when I was just out of my pram. Had this phobia ever since.'

And Moscow's the capital of America, thought Duffy. Strange how everyone had phobias these days. Nobody had phobias where he came from. Nowadays, if there was anything you didn't want to do you had a phobia which stopped you doing it. I've got a phobia about sitting on the top deck of a bus. I've got a phobia about cigarette smoke. I've got a phobia about wearing a seat belt. What they meant was they didn't like it. Duffy didn't care for aeroplanes, but he wouldn't say he had a phobia about them. He'd just say they made him bloody frightened; he just knew that if one of them took off with him on board he'd be shitting himself all the time until it crashed, which it inevitably would. That didn't seem to be a grand enough feeling to call a phobia. Maybe Taffy also had a phobia which led to him thieving and hitting people with iron bars. Oh, it's not that my client is a criminal, your Honour; it's just that he has this phobia about going straight. Oh well, in that case, three months' probation. And then there was this new posh word Duffy had seen around called homophobia. In the old days there had been people who were prejudiced against homosexuals, or gays, or queers, or whatever people who were prejudiced against them called them. Nowadays these people didn't have prejudice, they had homophobia. Duffy disapproved. It sounded too much like a clinical condition, too much like something you couldn't help. So after kicking him in the groin and stealing his wallet you also stamped on his spectacles? Yes, officer, you see I got this attack of my homophobia. Shocking, it always comes on at this time of year, nuffink I can do about it, must be the east wind or something. Oh, I've also got this phobia about being arrested and charged and sent to prison. Well, in that case, on your bike, son, and watch the weather forecast more carefully next time.

'I suppose this means the boys in blue crawling all over the place again,' said Vic, who clearly suffered from an advanced case of copperphobia. 'What about a spot of lunch while we're waiting?'

That's another thing about posh people, thought Duffy as they moved inside. They eat a lot. Even someone like old Vic, who had only acquired the trappings of poshness recently, while remaining awesomely unposh in his own person, went on about his dinners. They drank a lot, and they ate a lot. What's more, they thought about it before they did it. They didn't just go out for meals, they read up in magazines first about where to go out for a meal. They didn't merely eat when they were hungry, or when it fitted in, they had thumping great dinner-hours which were always observed. If you wanted to torture any of this lot, all you'd have to say was, 'We don't know what time lunch is,' and they'd blab anything you needed to find out.

For the first ten minutes or so, Duffy looked rather hard across the table at Nikki. It was probably a psychological tactic which the European Court of Human Rights would have deemed illegal, but at least it worked. She slid from her chair, went and sat on Vic's knee, and whispered in his ear. Vic frowned at first, then nodded, muttered 'Good girl,' and pushed her off towards the kitchen, presumably to find Mrs Colin.

Since this tactic had worked so well on Nikki, he transferred it now to Sally, frowning at her across the table in a way that might look vaguely menacing. After a while she noticed this and said, 'You all right?'

'Fine,' said Duffy.

'Only you've got a funny expression on your face.'

'What do you think happened?'

'Happened?'

'To your car.'

'Dunno. Expect I left the ignition on or something,' she said rather airily. Then she caught Damian's eye and they chorused through giggles, 'It's just that these foreign motors are so frightfully unstable.'

'Knock it off, kids,' said Vic.

'Electrical fault?' Taffy suggested. Well, at least he wasn't blaming the car's combustion on society's malice.

'When it isn't running?' said Duffy.

'Could happen.' Taffy was determined to back up his hypothesis, even if only because it had been attacked. 'F'rinstance, something like a squirrel could have got inside and chewed through a cable, you never know.'

'Round up all the usual squirrels,' bellowed Damian.

'Gypsies?' suggested Belinda.

'Could it have been . . . summer lightning?' This from Lucretia.

Christ, thought Duffy. Talk about another world. Or maybe they didn't want to think about it until they'd finished lunch. Well, he'd had enough to eat already. 'Christ,' he said forcefully. 'Squirrels? Summer lightning? Gypsies? If it was squirrels, why aren't cars blowing up all over the place? I mean, it took the roof off, didn't it?'

'So what do you think happened?' Lucretia didn't seem too dismayed by the rejection of her thesis.

'I think someone put a bomb under it.'

'Hang on, this isn't Northern Ireland,' said Vic.

'Or someone set light to it, which isn't all that easy unless you know what you're doing, and the explosion was the petrol tank going up. The coppers are quite good at finding out. They get a lot of practice nowadays.'

Duffy's suggestion was not very well received. He wondered why Sally wasn't asking more questions. He tried his questing look on her again.

'Who'd do something like that to my car?' she said, rather as if prompted, which indeed she had been.

'You tell us?'

'No idea. Maybe someone's in love with me,' she laughed. There was a tricky silence. Yeah, like Jimmy was in love with Angela, most people were thinking.

The fire brigade went away, and the police arrived. Perhaps we'll get the ambulance as well before the day's out, Duffy thought. Actually, the padded van would be more like it as far as some of those around here are concerned. They could take Taffy away and see if they could do something for his phobia about two-bar electric fires and anything upwards. They could take off Damian and find out why such a lazy, irritating prat didn't mind singeing his velvets when he hadn't even been asked. They could certainly put Sally under the lens and see if all her grey matter had dribbled out of her ears while she was asleep one night; perhaps a squirrel had climbed up her nose and chewed through a few cables inside her head – that might be the reason. And while they were about it, Duffy thought, they could examine Lucretia and tell him if she would by any chance be willing to go to bed with him.

They were told to stay within hailing distance of the house and await Detective-Sergeant Vine's summons. After turning down Damian's offer of some blindfold snooker, Duffy wandered out into the garden, vaguely hoping to find Lucretia. All he turned up was Taffy sitting on a bench with a thick volume over his knee. Duffy coughed a lot as he approached, knowing that cons – even incredibly reformed ex-cons who wouldn't steal the dandruff from your collar – don't like being crept up on. It makes them jumpy, and where they jump can end up being painful.

Taffy glanced up from his book like an Oxford don disturbed by a window cleaner. Hey, Duffy thought, don't *you* try putting me down as well. You haven't come up the slimy ladder that fast. Pointedly, he sat down on the bench beside Taffy; pointedly, Taffy carried on with his book. Duffy squinted across at the running title. Taffy was reading *Theories of Social Revolt*. He was doing it, Duffy also noted, without moving his lips or tracking his forefinger along each line like a wriggling salamander.

'Good, is it?' he asked, after a tactful wait until Taffy got to the end of the chapter.

'Bit simplistic. You wouldn't think he'd ever looked at Laing.'

'Surprising the gaps in some people's reading. By the way, what's the one about the nun with big tits?'

'Eh?' Taffy turned towards him for the first time, shifting his hulky shoulders all the way round as he did. They made the head look laughably small, but you didn't grin because of the still way the eyes rested on you.

'Lucretia said you like to tell it with the port and nuts.'

'Sounds like she's having you on.' Taffy started to swivel his torso back towards his book, as if he could only read when chest-on to the page.

'You still keep in shape?' Taffy arrested his movement. 'Got some weights myself,' Duffy went on, referring to the dusty bar-bells which skulked in his fitted cupboard. 'They sort of wear you out, though, don't they?'

'Not if you're fit. Got to go through the pain barrier, that's all.'

'I guess I never came out the other side. I'm a goalkeeper myself.'

'You look a bit small for a goalkeeper.'

Duffy rattled on. He kept throwing out hooks, but none of them would catch. 'I suppose I'd get more exercise if I moved upfield. Snooker doesn't exactly keep the muscles in trim, either. Not even if you play it the way Damian and Sally do.' Taffy didn't respond. 'Have you seen the way they do it?'

'No.'

'She takes her knickers off and sits in a corner pocket and he tries to pot the balls you know where.'

'Well, as long as it doesn't frighten the horses, eh?' Taffy went back to *Theories of Social Revolt*. Duffy wondered what it took to get a rise out of him. Quite a lot, obviously. That was another thing about ex-cons. After years of being cooped up you either came out with a hair-trigger temper, in which case you found yourself back inside again pretty soon; or else you learned to keep the lid on it. Taffy kept the lid on it so securely that you didn't even see a puff of steam. This took a lot of practice. Duffy imagined him in Maidstone or wherever: pull-ups and push-ups every day in the cell, thoughtful visits to the chapel and the library, a new line in politeness to the screws – all to make the parole board believe he'd really calmed down and got all that pus out of his system. Sometimes it was for real, of course, but mostly the cons would just be faking their new-found serenity.

One of the things that helped them fake it was fancy tobacco. Every so often, when there wasn't a royal wedding or garrulous star-fucker to fill the front page, the tabloids would wheel out the old story about drug-pushing in Her Majesty's prisons; how shocking it was that criminals were still able to go on committing crimes even when locked up, how the heroic Police Sniffer Dog Freddie (photo above) had located a milligram of hash in some lifer's bum, how if there wasn't law and order in our jails what hope was there for society, and by the way if you're exhausted by all these words just turn the page and you'll find this week's descendant of Belinda Blessing with her tits snouting out of the paper at you. Every such investigation would duly conclude with a stern statement from the Home Office that it was fully committed to stamping out the use of illegal substances in Britain's jails. What Duffy knew, and what the Home Office was thick if it didn't, was that the drug searches in Her Majesty's prisons could often get a bit perfunctory. The screws were well aware that if a con was smoking a nice fat home-made roll-up, then the chances of him getting off his bunk and teeing off with an iron bed-post weren't very great. In the old days they used to put things in the prisoners' tea to calm them down. Now, if the prisoners chose to put things in their own tea, or in their own cigarettes for that matter, who would bust a gut to restrain them? The habit was hardly surprising, what with all the overcrowding and the boredom. The screws could also work out that if they pretended not to notice that the tobacco smelt a bit funny, and the cons realized that the screws knew but did nothing, then this could turn into a handy extra means of control. I'm on to your little game, my son, but the Big Boss doesn't get to hear of it as long as you don't give me any trouble. Any naughtiness and before you know where you are I'll have Sniffer Dog Freddie so far up you that only his back paws and the tip of his tail will be showing. Do you read me, my son?

'So you're out on licence?' Duffy asked quietly. Taffy closed *Theories of Social Revolt* and turned to him. 'You know, you may drive that poxy van and put in alarm systems that don't work, but you still stink of copper.'

'Normal, isn't it?' said Duffy, getting up. 'And what makes you think I can't smell the con on you?'

D/S Barry Vine, who couldn't have cared a monkey's whether or not he stank of copper, hadn't expected to return to Braunscombe Hall until later in the afternoon, but he didn't mind arriving early. At least it meant a break from going round in circles with Jimmy Beckford. Most of it had been easy – except for the difficult part. Yes, that was his camp in the woods. Yes, everything in it did belong to him. Yes, he had known the woman in question for some time. Yes, he did have feelings for her. No, those feelings weren't reciprocated. Would it be an exaggeration, sir, to suggest that you were in love with her and she did not care for your attentions? No, that wouldn't be too much of an exaggeration. It was just, he said, that he hadn't done it. Where had he been between lunch and dinner? Well, he'd been around the grounds, but not up near his camp; in fact in the woods and the fields on the other side of the house. He'd been playing Army games. I see, sir, and while you were playing these Army games did you see anyone? Oh yes, he'd seen Taffy and Vic and Belinda and Lucretia. They could vouch for these meetings, could they? Oh no, they weren't meetings, I saw them. But they didn't see you? That's right, that's the point of Army games. Stealth, concealment, that sort of thing.

Look, put it this way, sir, if you were me, would you believe what I'm hearing? Jimmy Beckford, who had been arrested but not yet charged, thought for a long time over this question, and his reply, when it came, had rather impressed D/S Vine. If you believed how I loved Angela, he said, you'd know I couldn't have done it. Barry Vine was a family man of some years' standing, and he was also a copper; but he found himself curiously affected by Jimmy's words.

'It's just a thought,' said Duffy.

'Yes?' Detective-Sergeant Vine wasn't prejudiced against ex-coppers, though he was well-aware that some of the means by which they acquired that 'ex-' were a bit naughty. He hadn't properly talked to this chap who'd directed him to Jimmy Beckford's camp; but that action put him in credit so far.

'You'll have looked in Jimmy's tins. You'll have found that newspaper photo with bits burnt out of it.'

'When did you see it?'

'Oh, I was poking around. I came to mend the alarm system.'

'What, has Jimmy got a bell on his camp?'

'Not exactly. Look, I thought you ought to know Jimmy doesn't smoke.'

'I know. I asked him.'

'Ah.'

'But he admits burning the photo. With a piece of stick from his fire, he said. So it's not what you think.'

'Right.'

'I'll talk to you in a bit.'

Duffy went out on to the terrace with Vic. A clean, fresh breeze, lightly scented with roses, made them both cough.

'Wish I smoked,' said Vic.

'It keeps the wasps away as well.'

'Yeah. Right.'

'You miss the old days, Vic?' He didn't just mean the old days: also the old places, the old smells, the old rackets, the old racketeers. Duffy had known quite a few villains, and most of them, even when they'd made it to the big house and had the cabin cruiser moored down at the marina, even when they were big enough to bribe a junior cabinet minister and develop a taste for vintage claret, still felt attached to some particular square mile of territory. Some anonymous patch of a sprawling city sparkled in their memory like a little village – with its friendly vicar (sent down for his friendliness with juveniles), its beaming butcher (caught with his thumb on the scales) and its picturesque green (where the grass was carpet-bombed with dog turds). But this 'village' was where they first grew up, where they first learned to nick things and it made them tearfully sentimental. Perhaps their mum still lived in the same street, and some of their mates, whose careers hadn't prospered quite so well, could still be found in the council flats, except for when they were doing spells with Her Majesty. Vic's particular patch had been a little corner of Catford backing on to the railway line and the dog stadium. Of course, this was going back all the way: before he'd finally made the big jump to the Buckinghamshire/Bedfordshire borders he'd had a few years in Lewisham; and by the time he met Belinda he was up in ritzy Blackheath, which apart from anything else was handier for the offices of Laski & Lejeune.

'Thing about the old days,' said Vic philosophically, 'is that at the time they didn't seem like the old days.'

'They wouldn't, would they?'

'But you don't think that at the time, do you? You don't think, one day these are gonna be the old days. I mean, today for instance, you'll look back on today at some point in the future and say that was the old days. It gives the brain a bit of a spin, doesn't it?'

'You're a deep one and no mistake,' said Duffy. He gazed across at Vic: a stocky, red-faced man settling into late middle-age who didn't dress as if he'd ever been to the country, let alone lived there. Duffy wondered if Belinda had had a go at him about his clothes. You'd still take him for a mildly sucessful street trader, a barrow boy who'd made it big and could now afford to pay someone to run his stall on Saturday afternoons while he went down the football. 'See much of the first Mrs Crowther?'

'I keep in touch. Don't let on to Bel, though.' Duffy nodded a promise. 'Well, you can't just tear up your life like that, can you? And she's got these legs now, you know.'

'Sorry to hear that, Vic.' Didn't she have legs before? Duffy remembered Bessie Crowther as having pretty vigorous legs, with one of which she'd attempted to separate his wedding tackle from the rest of his body one evening in the old days when he'd popped round and tried to arrest Vic.

'Something to do with the circulation, they say. Anyway, she has to have these check-ups. She's back in that little house we had when we were first married. I sort of never got rid of it, you know, and when we broke up I said she could live in it if she wanted to.'

'Bel doesn't know that either?'

'That I've still got the house? No, she'd hit the roof if she knew. See, it's a bit complicated. I mean, Bel's always believed that when we met my marriage was on the rocks. Well it was, but only because the rocks, if you get my drift, was Bel. Otherwise I suppose Bessie and me would still be together now. I was gone potty on Bel from the moment I clapped eyes on her. But I'm only flesh and blood; I couldn't just throw Bessie over like that. Every so often, when I'm down in London, I take her out like in the old days. Schooner of sherry, scampi and chips, that's what she likes, that's what she gets.'

Must make a nice change from all the posh scoff he gets around here, Duffy thought. And it all sounded just like Vic: walking both sides of the street, even in his marriages. Perhaps it gave him a funny sort of thrill, to kiss his second wife goodbye and go off for an illicit night out with his first wife. Made him feel like a salamander walking through fire or something.

Apart from how he juggled his marriages, how did he juggle his finances? Two establishments, the horses, all those house guests, the servants. 'Do you still have the launderettes?' Duffy asked suddenly.

'Why? You got any complaints?'

'No. Well, now you mention it . . . No, forget it.' That was hardly central to the current business. 'And the video shops?'

'I'm on social security, Duffy, what do you think?'

'What about the others, do they have jobs?'

'You mean, do they pay rent here or are they squatters?' Vic was beginning to get testy.

'No, just curiosity. That Sally, for instance, what does she do for a living? She an estate agent as well?'

'Those are real copper's questions, you know. Or maybe they're just London questions. We don't ask things like that down in the country. Do you want to marry her or something?'

'Maybe,' said Duffy. Then she wouldn't have so far to go whenever she wanted to have a whole load of fun and let his van tyres down.

'Her dad's got a spot of cash. She was married when she was about twenty and picked up something from that. She does some of that art. She sells the odd drawing, if you must know. Don't ask me how much she gets, I haven't bought one.'

'I'm surprised she can draw straight.' Surprised she can find the crayons to start with.

'Well, she doesn't as a matter of fact. It's got a name.'

'What has?'

'Not drawing straight. You know, paint a dog and it comes out looking like a monkey. It's got a posh name in the right circles, that has.'

'Check. And what about Bel?'

'What about her? You want to see her bank statements?'

'No. Just wondering if she missed the old days as well.'

'Oh. What, the modelling? Don't think so. She's all horsey nowadays. And mumsy as well, of course, with little Nikki. By the way, Duffy, congratulations.'

'Come again.'

'You did good with the spoons. Real good. Nothing like hiring a minder to look after one of your house guests and after she's got kidnapped and nearly raped he manages to screw a confession out of your own daughter that she's planted a few worthless spoons on one of your servants. I mean, how did you manage it, Duffy? Rubber hoses, water treatment, sensory deprivation?'

'See what you mean. Told her that her dabs were all over them.'

'That old lie?'

'It still works.'

'It never worked with me.'

Duffy thought back to the days of threatening calls from Laski & Lejeune. 'No, it didn't. By the way, if Nikki starts asking for a pair of gloves, I should lock your stuff away.'

'So what have we got now, Duffy? Moving up a league or two from Toytown crime.'

'Well, the car proves we haven't just got Jimmy, doesn't it?'

'Assuming it wasn't a squirrel.'

'Which we assume. So if we go along with Jimmy being rightly locked up, we've got one other something. If we don't go along with the Jimmy line, we might still have one other something. Or we could, of course, have two different somethings which happen to have coincided.'

'I like a bit of clear thinking,' said Vic ironically. 'You could put that in writing and start charging guineas.'

'With headed notepaper. I've thought of it, but I couldn't handle the V A T. The point is, who's being naughty around here? Are we dealing with strangers or are we dealing with your distinguished house guests? For instance, what about Angela and Taffy as a number?'

'Eh? I shouldn't think so. Poor old Taff. All these aspersions.'

'For instance, it was you who threw Ricky in the lake, wasn't it?'

This was perfectly timed. Vic was starting to say 'No' when he realized that only the person who'd thrown him in and the person who'd fished him out would know Ricky had spent some time under water, so he stopped, changed gear, and said, 'What, you mean they've found Ricky?'

Duffy laughed. 'I think you're about as unconvinced by yourself as I am, Vic.'

'Why on earth should I want to do a thing like that?' Vic demanded, all honest-citizen, all get-me-Laski-&-Lejeune.

'The dog's one of the main problems in this whole business.

I think I've worked out a bit of the dog, but I haven't worked out the whole dog.'

'Where is Ricky?'

'Up in London with his guts on a slab.'

'So Jimmy found him?'

'Jimmy found him. The problem was, who killed him and who threw him in the water? Why should anyone want to do first one and then the other? Why not just throw him in the water to start off with if that's what you wanted? So, the only sensible conclusion is, it was two different people, not connected with one another. Someone who we presume wanted to fuck up Angela, and then you.'

'Me.' It wasn't a question, or a protestation of innocence; it was more of a prompt.

'No body, no crime. No crime, no coppers. Sensible, really. The other side of it goes: no body, no criminal; no criminal, no justice. But it's all a matter of priorities.'

'So if I'm number two, who's number one?'

'I don't know. I really don't know.'

'Telephone, Mr Duffy.' It was Mrs Colin, beaming at him. She continued beaming as he followed her into the house and along a corridor. She didn't say a word, but then she didn't need to.

When Duffy emerged again into the unhealthy air, he was shaking his head. 'I think I've had enough for the moment,' he said to Vic. 'The old brain's racing. I'm going to have a snooker lesson. Give my regards to the Detective-Sergeant if he needs me.'

'Who was the call from?'

'And can I borrow a tie? Preferably without too much heraldry on it.'

Duffy took the five miles to Winterton House at a conservative speed. Off the M1 things were just as dangerous. There was a lot of inbreeding in the countryside, he knew, and everyone drove like lunatics whether they were or not. Carefully, he turned into the driveway of Winterton House, past some entrance pillars of genuinely weathered stone. He made the gentlest of rustles on the gravel, in case Henry's mother was taking an afternoon nap. As he got out of his van, Duffy adjusted the brown kipper tie Vic had lent him. This sartorial touch wasn't just a matter of courtesy; it was also to help with his cueing. Brush the knot lightly as you slide through on the shot: that was one of the things he had to remember.

A woman of indeterminate age and status answered the door, and after a brief discussion agreed not to send him round to the back despite his appearance. Henry seemed pleased to see him, and offered a large hand.

'Glad you telephoned. Mother says we are both to join her after our lesson. Tea is at four-thirty in the conservatory.'

'Did you hear about Sally's car?'

'Mmm. Ange telephoned. Dreadful. Didn't come over as Mother had a slight turn and . . . anyway, I wouldn't have been any help.'

Winterton House went back to 1730; it had been inhabited at one time by a fully paid-up, long-lasting Lord Mayor of London; it had a wine-cellar with properly dusty bottles; it had never been lived in by a rock musician who played with a feather up his bum; and its billiard room, though post-dating 1730 by at least a century, remained as it had been originally designed – a quiet enclave of mahogany and old leather, with a tang of yesterday's cigar smoke in the air. Duffy sniffed, and pretended to be reminded of something.

'Henry, tell me, is there a lot of drugging over at the Hall?'

'Drugging?'

'Yes. Taking drugs. You know what I mean.'

'Yes, I know what you mean. I'm just not sure that I . . . I . . . how can one tell? I don't think I'd be very good at telling. Who are you thinking of?'

'Well, I don't know them very well.'

'I don't think Ange would do anything like that,' said Henry. He drew the heavy plum curtains, pulled the cover off the table and, while folding it, pointed to the cue rack. Duffy put a white on the table and played it firmly round the cushions. Then he did so again, in the opposite direction. Compared to this, the table at Braunscombe Hall was like a ploughed field.

'Lovely and true, Henry.'

'It's an 1866 Thurston. Looked after by them ever since.

Can't get slate like that nowadays. There's a real chunk of Wales under there.'

'New cloth?'

'Five years ago, actually. Mother thought the old one was quite good enough because it was still green, so I had it done on the sly. Bit of a row and all that. Didn't tell her I had new cushions at the same time.'

Henry was a fine player; indeed, he looked much more relaxed leaning over a snooker table than he did standing up and being normal. He was also a good teacher, patient yet firm. It was a revision course as much as anything; Duffy in theory knew all about not coming up on the shot, about follow-through, about matching your tactics to your capabilities; he just had to be constantly reminded about them. Henry was particularly keen on getting Duffy's stance right. 'If you don't stand right, you don't cue right, and if you don't cue right, you can't control the ball.' He demonstrated; Duffy tried to copy. 'Doesn't matter about the feet not being parallel as long as you're comfortable. What makes the difference is locking the hips.' Duffy was slow to get this bit. 'Look, get in position, and, excuse me, keep your feet exactly where they are, now, sorry about this bit.' In the crepuscular atmosphere of this Victorian gentlemen's room, Henry put his hands on Duffy's hips and tugged at him gently, like a sweet-palmed osteopath. Duffy's hips swivelled and locked. Henry took his hands away. Be my guest, murmured Duffy under his breath.

At four twenty-five the lesson stopped, and Henry went away to brush his hair before tea with Mother. Duffy didn't need to brush his hair. Instead, he adjusted Vic's kipper tie.

'How do you do, young man. What a very unattractive tie,' said Henry's mother. She was sitting on a wicker chair in the conservatory, surrounded by plants which Duffy might just have been able to identify if he'd done a ten-year course at Kew Gardens.

'It's not mine, actually.'

'Then why on earth do you wear it?' She was about eighty, an erect, bony figure, with sharp blue eyes and white hair cut short; she wore a pale green silk dress which Duffy reckoned had been very expensive about ten years before he was born, and pink running-shoes. 'So you're my son's new billiards partner?'

'He's giving me lessons. It's very useful.'

'I'm glad to hear he's good at something. He's always seemed to me singularly useless at most things.' Duffy glanced up at Henry, who wasn't reacting. He'd obviously had this for years. 'And you're staying over at the Hall with that crook, what's his name?'

'Vic Crowther. It's his tie, actually.'

'That doesn't surprise me in the least. The only interesting question is whether he paid for it with his own money.'

'Mother!'

'Well, of course he's a crook. Someone like him doesn't end up owning the Hall unless he's a crook, stands to reason.'

Duffy couldn't work out whether Henry's mother was as rude as this because she was posh, or because she was old, or a combination of both. Or maybe it wasn't to do with either: she was just rude, and that's all there was to it.

'So you will have examined the gel who is shortly to make Henry the happiest man in the world?'

'Angela. Yes.'

'And what do you make of her?'

What did Duffy make of her? 'I haven't really seen much of her.'

'How very diplomatic of you, particularly in front of your billiards tutor. She's obviously neurotic.'

'Mother!'

'The only thing I couldn't make out, because she was wearing such extraordinary clothes on the occasion I was permitted to meet her, was whether or not she has good child-bearing hips. Have you examined her hips?'

Duffy tried to remember. 'I think they'll do the business,' he suggested cautiously.

'Do the business? Do the business? I see what you mean. But will Henry be able to do the business?'

'Mother, really.'

'Perhaps it would be best if the line were just allowed to die out. Oh well,' she said, re-crossing her pink running-shoes, 'perhaps the gel will have her menopause before she gets to the altar. You definitely want another cup of tea.'

'I need one,' said Duffy.

'I hear she had some kind of bad turn the other day?'

Look, what's going on, Duffy thought. He couldn't follow this mixture of over-statement and under-statement. 'That's right, she had a bit of a turn. Someone tried to rape her.'

'Tried? What are the men coming to nowadays? When I was a gel they would have succeeded. It's just another name for marriage, anyway, isn't it?'

'I don't know. I've never tried it.'

'What, rape or marriage?'

'Either.'

'Mmm. Does that mean you're a bachelor boy like my Henry?'

'Uh-huh.'

'You're not one of those homosexuals, are you?' She pronounced the word with no apparent distaste, though using the old-fashioned long *o* on the first syllable.

Duffy thought it was too complicated to explain, so he nodded and said, 'That's right.'

'How fascinating. You know I've never met one who said he was. You must come to tea again and tell me what it is you do. I've always wondered what went where. Of course, that is, if you survive.'

'Oh, I'll survive.'

'But you're all dropping like flies, aren't you? They tell me there's this new disease which is going to purge the world of shirt-lifters, as my late husband used to refer to them. I hope you don't find the term offensive.'

'I think it's a bit of an exaggeration.'

'That's what it says in the newspaper.'

'The newspapers are full of homophobia,' said Duffy. Well, why not? She thinks I'm just a common shirt-lifter in a nasty tie. Why not show her I know a few long words as well?

'Never heard that term before,' said Henry's mum. 'I suppose it's a polite way of saying you don't like fairies.' Henry stood up and put his cup on the tray. 'You will bring your friend back again, won't you?' was the parting line from the wicker chair. 'I'm so looking forward to finding out what goes where after all these years.'

The gravel outside Winterton House seemed ever so slightly posher than the gravel over at the Hall. Perhaps you could even get upper-class gravel. Perhaps Vic's had fallen off the back of a lorry. 'She's a real character, your mum.'

'I don't know how to apologize . . .' Henry seemed to be almost blushing.

'Forget it. She's like a breath of fresh air compared to some I could mention. But if you want to apologize, you can give me another lesson. I don't think I'm confident of thumping Damian yet.'

'It'd be a pleasure.'

●

Back at the Hall D/S Vine had left for the day. He either had to charge Jimmy or release him in the next twelve hours or so – not that the fellow seemed particularly interested in his rights – and he might as well get on with it. The remains of Sally's Datsun Cherry were cordoned off with a rope which wouldn't have deterred a squirrel. As Duffy opened the front door he ran into Damian, who shook a finger at him. 'Naughty boy. Naughty boy.'

'Eh?'

'The rozzers. Not very content, the rozzers. A policeman's lot is not a happy one. Skipping off and leaving the scene of the crime. Had to tell them about rescuing the cars all by myself. Pulled them free with my bare teeth while thousands quailed.'

'I bet he believed you.'

'That was the trouble. He didn't even believe me when I told him the truth. Just because I'm pretty that beastly Detective-Sergeant thought I didn't know what an axle was. Said I'd get you to corroborate my deeds of heroism. And where were you? Skipped the country for all we knew.'

'I was having . . .' Duffy stopped. 'Actually, I was having tea with Henry's mum.'

'And you survived? You must have been wearing asbestos close to the skin.'

'No, I liked her. Not sure I could be married to her.'
Damian peered at Duffy as if to say, But who would have you
anyway? 'Incidentally, what happened to Henry's dad?'

'Keeled over from a punctured eardrum, I should imagine.
No idea – it was all long before Damian's time.'

Duffy chuckled. Thinking of Henry's mum made him
understand a bit more why posh people's architects set aside
certain parts of the house for gentlemen only. They were running away, that's what the men were doing. And the Henry's
mums of this world were all kitted out in pink running-shoes
so that they could chase after them and find out what goes
where. 'She seemed to be putting Henry down quite a bit.'

'I don't think he notices any more. Just gives that look of
his – you know, like a fairly intelligent Aberdeen Angus – and
occasionally a little smile, but he's probably leagues away.'

'You're not a writer, by any chance, are you, Damian?'

'Why do you ask?'

'Well, you use these words nobody else uses.'

'I do a bit of this and that,' said Damian, in a manner worthy
of his host. 'I have . . . ambitions.'

'Glad to hear it. No, cheers, mate.' Duffy was almost not
being ironic; it was a nice change for someone in this place to
mention, however vaguely, that they might want to, well,
have a job or something at some time in the future. 'What
does she think about Henry? About him getting married?'

'*His* getting married. Well, she's changed, of course. Spent
at least forty years telling Henry it was his duty as an only son
to keep the flag flying, and then as soon, or as late, as he brings
a girl home and says this is the one for me, she starts taking
the opposite line.'

'Doesn't she like Angela?'

'Nothing much to do with Ange, I don't think. She just
likes keeping Henry on the run. I suppose the fact that Ange
isn't a teenager gives her something to go on about though.
Says what's the point of marrying someone you can't breed
from. Says Henry might as well shack up with some ewe in a
stone barn.'

'She said that?'

'So Henry reported. Mind you, he seemed almost amused by it.'

'Can't Angela have children?'

'No reason why not. Not as far as anyone knows. She'll probably get a couple in before the old drawbridge comes up.'

'I'm surprised Henry hasn't killed his mum,' said Duffy. 'Or at least left home.'

'They tried that once, apparently. Shipped him out to Argentina, or "the Argentine" as they tend to refer to it. Some family connection with corned beef, I should think. He lasted three weeks. Took the next plane home.'

'Things must be bad in Argentina.'

'Couple of frames before dinner?' suggested Damian.

'Got a few things to do,' Duffy replied. 'Perhaps in a day or two.'

'I'll be waiting for you.'

Damian went off towards the ploughed-field snooker table. Duffy wandered into the family room, where he found Belinda reading *Horse and Hound*; beside her, Vic was bent over a copy of *Exchange and Mart*. 'Just looking up a good breakers' for the Datsun.'

'Breakers'? Is there anything left to break?'

'There's always something. Anyway, Sally says she's a bit strapped for cash at the moment, so I said I'd see what I could do.'

'She doesn't behave as if she's strapped for cash.'

'No, she doesn't.'

'There are those funny old-fashioned things called jobs,' said Duffy.

'You know, it's odd. Those kids don't seem to have heard of them.'

Belinda laughed. 'You two sound like you've got big grey beards.'

'Come on, Bel, you say it yourself. About when you were working. How it changed in the few years you were in it.'

'Sure,' said Belinda cautiously, not sure if the analogy was fair.

'How d'you mean?' asked Duffy.

'When I went into modelling, back in the Seventies' –

Belinda made it sound as if Queen Victoria had been on the throne at the time — 'I did all the training. Paid out a lot of cash. How to walk, how to hold yourself, how to show the clothes to the best advantage.' And how best to show the bits of you that burst out of the clothes like trains from a tunnel, thought Duffy. 'You know, the whole bit. Model school. Even taught you how to speak proper. *Ly*,' she added with a grin. 'Anyway, you went along to your first job, you knew more or less what you were in for, what was expected. And even then you sometimes got treated like a pushy tart.'

'Really?' Duffy tried to sound as straight-voiced as possible.

'Christ, yes. I mean, I was one of the new wave of models. I was sort of real. There were one or two others around at the same time, sure, I don't take any credit away from them, but it was mainly me. Before, the glamour models were sort of artificial, like packet custard. Wanting to have it both ways — taking off their clothes and pretending they weren't. And then they tried putting me down. Used to look down their nose-jobs at me and say I didn't have the "classic chassis". That was their phrase. All 'cause they had little ones. Bitches.' Her tone was friendly, though, as if she'd won by ending up in the big house.

'I quite like packet custard,' said Vic. Belinda slapped him playfully.

'And now?'

'Now? Christ, you get everyone thinking they can do it now. Girls of sixteen off the train from Leeds and Bradford, all squidgy with puppy-fat, dropping their blouses as soon as their foot touches the platform. They don't think it takes work. They think anyone can do it.'

'Maybe the country's going to the dogs,' suggested Duffy.

There was a ruminative silence. Belinda put down *Horse and Hound* with a sigh and headed off towards the kitchen. Vic turned confidingly to Duffy. 'By the way, our Detective-Sergeant is cross with you.'

'I heard. Still, he's bound to be back, isn't he?'

'Yeah, I think he went off to charge Jimmy.'

'Well, I'll wash behind my ears for him tomorrow.'

'I suppose,' said Vic musingly, 'I suppose it's just possible that Ricky died a natural death and that some yobbo who happened to be passing chucked him through the window.'

'You get many yobbos around here?'

'There are yobbos everywhere, Duffy. State of the country.' Of course, if they were around, your yobbos could mix with your Vics who were cuddling up with your Damians who were brown-nosing your Hugos, and everyone could join hands and sing 'Auld Lang Syne'.

'Bit of an outside runner, I'd say, Vic.'

Duffy could see Vic's line of thought, and it was natural in someone with Vic's background. Close down as much of this business as possible, that was his instinct. We've got a near-rape and we've got an exploding car and the coppers are crawling all over the place, why throw them a dead dog as well? Natural causes, a passing yobbo, and no body to show for it, that would sort things out. Vic was ever so quietly suggesting that Duffy didn't mention the dog business to the coppers when it came to his turn with the thumbscrews. Perhaps he was also fishing a bit, and wondering about the phone-call Duffy had had that afternoon.

But if Vic had kept quiet about dumping Ricky in the lake, Duffy felt he could reply with a bit of hush on his own account; even if Vic was paying him. So he merely repeated, 'Bit of an outside runner, I'd say,' and let Vic go back to his *Exchange and Mart*. The phone-call had changed things; had changed things quite a bit, and Duffy had to think carefully. He liked old Vic, but he wasn't sure he'd be able to go on confiding in him. If you showed Vic a knife with blood on it, he'd put it in the dishwasher and turn the knob. If you showed Vic a dismembered corpse left in brown-paper parcels in six different luggage lockers, he'd say it was shocking how people kept thinking up new ways to kill themselves. Duffy understood this instinct, but it wasn't always entirely helpful, except in giving Vic a quiet time. So he thought that for the moment he'd keep a few things to himself; especially the thing Jim Pringle had told him on the telephone.

It had all begun with the dog. The dog was in two parts (well, it was probably in even more parts now after featuring on Jim Pringle's slab). Duffy had solved the second part of the dog; solving the first part of the dog might be the key to the whole business. And just as there were two parts to the dog, there might turn out to be two parts to the business. One domestic, say, and one professional. Or two domestics that didn't know about one another. Or two professionals . . . The riddling combinations made Duffy realize how far he currently was from solving anything. He needed help. Of two kinds, in fact: domestic and professional.

The domestic help might be obtained from . . . well, the domestic help. Mrs Colin attributed her recent salvation in the matter of the missing cutlery to two causes: the power of prayer and the intervention of the man from London in the white van. It was, indeed, the power of prayer which had brought the man in the white van down to the Buckinghamshire/Bedfordshire borders to help her. If someone had pointed out to Mrs Colin that Nikki had in fact planted the spoons on her only after Duffy's arrival, this would have disturbed neither her faith nor her sense of logic. The Lord knew in advance the wickedness in little Nikki's mind, and Duffy was the temporal answer to it; the fact that he got to Braunscombe Hall before the sin was perpetrated was neither here nor there. This did not cast doubt on the efficacy of prayer; all it cast doubt on was the reliability of the man in the white van.

Mrs Colin's room was as bare as it had been on Duffy's previous visit. The process of packing, and soon afterwards unpacking again, hadn't affected the look of the place; not that these operations could have taken much time. Mrs Colin smiled broadly as Duffy knocked on the half-open door, came in, and sat down on the bed. There had been opportunities for Mrs Colin to thank Duffy verbally for her salvation, but she had not yet mentioned the matter, and she didn't do so now; she merely beamed at him. Perhaps she thought that a gesture, a smile, a series of smiles, was a truer way of showing gratitude than a few words in a foreign and untrustworthy language; or perhaps she thought that Duffy was merely an agent of help: spoken words of gratitude should all be divided between Our Lord and the holy sisters at the Church of Our

Lady of Penitence, who prayed for the moral safety of those in service overseas.

'Mrs Colin,' Duffy began, 'we're in a spot of trouble.'

'We?' Mrs Colin, sitting erect on a hard chair in front of one of Belinda's cast-off dressing-tables, was alarmed. Not more trouble already?

'No, not *us*. Not you, not me.'

'Ah.' But if it wasn't him and her, why had he said 'we'? Mrs Colin was confirmed in her belief that most of the time the face can speak more truly than the tongue.

'No, I mean the trouble at the Hall, here.'

'Trouble here?' More trouble, did he mean?

'The trouble about the dog, Mrs Colin. The trouble about Miss Angela in the woods. The trouble about Miss Sally's car.' Mrs Colin nodded. She knew all about *that* trouble. Why was he telling her what she knew already? Why did he come to her room, sit on her bed, smile at her, and tell her things that were familiar to both of them? An interesting thought crossed Mrs Colin's mind, and she smiled back at Duffy, though a little more shyly this time. He was short with darkish hair and quite powerfully built. He was much more the physical type she was used to in her own country; here this strange damp climate sprouted tall blond men with pot-bellies and dripping noses. That, at any rate, was Mrs Colin's generalized impression of the race she worked amongst. Perhaps this man in the white van . . .

'The point is, Mrs Colin, that Mr Crowther has asked me to help him. To help him find out what happened.'

'The policeman . . .'

'Mr Crowther is very grateful for the help the policemen are giving, and he is of course co-operating in every way with them, but he feels that any help I might be able to give them, with, well, the specialist knowledge I might be able to bring . . .' Duffy was waffling, and he knew it.

'Mr Crowther, he pays you for this?' It was not the question that Duffy had expected. Mrs Colin was looking sharply at him. One of the side-mirrors of Belinda's cast-off dressing-table gave Duffy a simultaneous view of her profile. She was looking just as sharply at him in profile.

'Well, sort of, I suppose.'

'And you want me to help you, to tell you things?'

'Mmm. Well, I was hoping . . .'

'So you will pay me, then.'

'Sorry?'

Mrs Colin suddenly laughed. She pulled open the bottom left-hand drawer of her dressing-table and fished out a small buff envelope, which she handed to Duffy. 'This is a manilla envelope,' she said, repeating one of Mr Colin's old jokes, 'It is for sending to the Philippines.' Then she turned her back on him.

Duffy looked at the address printed in red; it was that of a church, presumably in Mrs Colin's home town. He took out his wallet, stuffed a tenner into the envelope, paused, wondered if bribing Vic's domestic staff could be claimed back from Vic as legitimate expenses, and put in another tenner. As he licked the gum on the envelope, he realized that Mrs Colin, with an oblique glance in the side-mirror, had monitored the extent of Duffy's charitable impulse. She seemed to approve, and smiled shyly as she returned the envelope to her bottom drawer.

'Mrs Colin, you've been with Mr and Mrs Crowther for . . .'

'Five years. Two in London, three in the country.'

'And you're happy working for them?'

'Very happy.'

'No trouble?'

'No. No trouble.' This was just like talking to the policeman. Perhaps she should also have invited the Detective-Sergeant to assist the holy sisters at the Church of Our Lady of Penitence.

'Mr Crowther said to tell you that he wants you to answer my questions as truthfully as possible.' Mrs Colin nodded. Who did they think she was, these English policemen? She laid her hand gently against the bump of Our Saviour at her throat. Unlike the Detective-Sergeant, the stocky fellow with the white van didn't have a notebook. Perhaps he remembered all the answers. 'Did you see anyone near Miss Sally's car at any time before it caught fire?'

'No.'

'Have there been any quarrels?'

'Quarrels?'

'In the house. Anyone been cross with anyone?'

'Miss Blessing, she's cross.'

'Who with?'

'No, I mean, she's cross. That's what she's like. She's often cross.' Well, Mr Crowther had asked her to tell the truth. 'And Mr Damian, he's often cheeky. Very cheeky.'

'But no quarrels.'

'No quarrels.'

'And while you've been down here, in the country, have you seen anything . . . naughty. I mean, anything wrong?'

'Mr Hardcastle steals Mr Crowther's wine.' She said it as if it were a perfectly normal and regular occurrence, which perhaps it was.

'How does he do that?' Duffy felt slightly disappointed that he wasn't alone in having made this discovery.

'Oh, he waits until everybody is out and then he goes and takes it from the cellar.'

Subtle ploy, that, thought Duffy. The touch of a master criminal. 'You mean, a whole box of it?'

'Sometimes. Sometimes just a few bottles. Depends whether Mr and Mrs Hardcastle are running short or not.'

'Do they say anything to you about it?'

'Yes, they say do I want a bottle? But I do not drink.'

'Did they say anything else?'

'Yes, they say it is an old British custom in the big houses.'

'And you didn't tell anyone about this?'

'Who am I to question the old British customs?' said Mrs Colin. She gave one of those smiles that were handy for all occasions.

'And what about some of the newer British customs, Mrs Colin?'

'Which you mean?'

'Well, like, Look who's sleeping in my bed.'

'Who's sleeping in your bed?' Mrs Colin looked alarmed, as if something had gone wrong with the domestic arrangements at Braunscombe Hall and it might be her fault. At the same time, she wondered if this rather nice . . .

'No, I mean, you're delivering the breakfast trays, for instance, or you go in to turn the beds down, or to open a window. Or you just . . . notice things.' Monogrammed knickers, for instance; lingerie with a giveaway salamander or a tell-tale phoenix.

'You mean what Mr Damian calls fucky-fuck?' Mrs Colin wasn't to know that Mr Damian only used this expression when he knew that she was within earshot. He had several dozen other expressions for normal wear.

'What Mr Damian calls fucky-fuck, yes.'

Sally, it seemed, was the principal fucky-fuck artiste in the house; a fact which didn't greatly surprise Duffy, given the view he'd had the other night in the billiard room. Damian liked fucky-fuck too, though it had apparently struck Mrs Colin that Damian often seemed to prefer staying up late talking about fucky-fuck to actually doing fucky-fuck. Lucretia liked a certain amount of fucky-fuck, though not as much as Sally. Taffy had asked Mrs Colin for fucky-fuck on a couple of occasions; though he had been very polite about it, and completely understood when she had declined.

'Jimmy?'

Mrs Colin giggled. 'He likes fucky-fuck with girls in magazines,' she said, remembering an occasion when she had gone to change the flowers in Jimmy's room. She didn't think Duffy would need to know the details of what she had seen.

'Miss Angela?'

'Miss Angela's getting married. We're all going to the wedding.'

'So . . . Miss Angela and Mr Henry?'

Suddenly, Mrs Colin giggled. Duffy repeated his question and Mrs Colin silently shook her head, though whether in ignorance or denial of the engaged couple's sexual habits Duffy could not tell.

'So . . . Miss Angela.'

Mrs Colin shook her head again, more violently this time. Duffy noted this reaction. Then he dutifully checked the marital fidelity of Vic and Belinda with Mrs Colin, and moved on.

'What about drugs?'

'There are many drugs.' That was the thing about the British. Their bars looked like chemists' shops, and so did their bathroom cabinets. They were very worried about their health, the British. Perhaps they did not believe in God enough.

'But . . . naughty drugs.'

'You mean like the Beecham's?'

Duffy just about managed to look puzzled. 'What's the Beecham's?'

'The Beecham's. You put it up your nose for the hay fever.'

'Ah. And who has the hay fever?'

Damian had the hay fever; he also, Duffy realized, had a teasing vocabulary with which he had infected Mrs Colin. The other person to have the hay fever was Sally. In fact Sally had the hay fever all the year round, even when there was snow on the ground, and she needed a lot of Beecham's to cure it. Damian's hay fever wasn't half as bad as Sally's. Mrs Colin wasn't sure if there were any other sufferers in the household. Perhaps Lucretia, or Taffy? Perhaps; but she couldn't tell. She hadn't seen. Angela? No, she really couldn't tell.

The other thing that had to be kept at bay was the wasps. Damian had a special tobacco which he smoked to ward them off. It also worked, he said, for gnats, mosquitoes, midges, bees, tsetse flies and ladybirds. Unsurprisingly, Sally liked shooing away the wasps; Lucretia and Taffy didn't mind distracting them, either. There had even been an occasion, Mrs Colin revealed, when they persuaded Jimmy to try. It had been on the terrace, after dinner, when Mr and Mrs Crowther had been out. Jimmy had coughed a lot, and the others had laughed. Miss Angela had laughed as well. Miss Angela also seemed to enjoy special tobacco.

'Anything else?'

'Like what?'

'Like the Beecham's or the wasp tobacco?' Mrs Colin looked doubtful. Duffy wondered what Damian's euphemism for shooting up might be. 'Has anyone got anything like diabetes?'

'What's that?'

'It's a sort of illness. What you have to do if you've got it is take a little syringe and inject something into your arm. You have to do that for lots of other illnesses as well,' Duffy added hopefully.

'Maybe you look in the medicine cabinets,' said Mrs Colin. Really, the British were an odd people. Injecting themselves for all sorts of illnesses. In Davao only the doctor did that to you. Perhaps the doctors over here weren't as good as everyone said. That was why everybody drank so much – 'What's your medicine?' – and had to inject themselves.

Duffy didn't think he'd bother with the medicine cabinets; though it might be worth pulling open a few bottom drawers. Or rather – on the principle that people hide things not in the most obvious place but the next most obvious place – a few drawers up. He wondered whether Mrs Colin was quite as naïve as she made out. Perhaps she understood everything; perhaps she was finding a way to obey Mr Crowther's instruction (which Duffy in any case had invented) while seeming not to betray his guests.

'What about the dog?'

'What do you mean?'

'Did anyone . . . not like the dog?'

'Everyone liked the dog. No, that's not true.' Mrs Colin paused. She had been instructed to tell the truth, and so she would. Duffy was expectant. 'Everyone liked the dog except for one person. Me. I didn't like the dog. I was bitten by a dog in Davao when I was a girl. It was a dog that looked like Ricky.'

It seemed unnecessary to check with Mrs Colin whether Ricky's death was indeed a long-term Filipino canine revenge killing. He thanked her and left. He'd got . . . what? Confirmation rather than anything else. Bed-hopping, drugging – he'd more or less had that from Vic to start off with; Mrs Colin had just brought it more into focus, filled in who and what, relayed Damian's jaunty euphemisms. There'd been something about Angela and fucky-fuck – some hesitation on Mrs Colin's part – which might be worth pursuing. And he had, of course, received confirmation of Ron Hardcastle's enthusiasm for the Vinho Verde and the pink champagne. Would Vic be pleased with the news? Look, Vic, I bribed one of your servants with twenty quid I'd like you to refund me, and she said that one of your other servants was nicking from you. How would Vic react? Perhaps he might suggest that Duffy wasn't exactly concentrating on essentials.

One of the essentials was the dog, even though Vic had tried to dispose of all the evidence. Duffy sat on an uncomfortable rustic bench looking back at the terrace and the french windows, which still had a papered hole in them. A bumblebee droned slowly past, and Duffy clamped his lips together in case the insect flew into his mouth and stung him on his windpipe which would immediately swell up and stop him breathing and kill him unless he had a swift tracheotomy which could of course be an amateur job performed with a penknife but probably the only person around Braunscombe Hall who knew that sort of stuff was Jimmy because he'd been in the Army and probably received emergency medical training but Jimmy was all locked up so Duffy would simply have to die a horrible suffocating death on the bench. Oooff. The bumblebee passed on, and Duffy, who had been using his teeth as well to clamp his lips shut, briefly relaxed. Perhaps he needed some of that special tobacco which drove the insects away. And what if you kept your mouth shut but the bumblebee flew up your nose?

The dog, Duffy, the dog. What did the dog mean? Who was the dog aimed at? It was Angela's dog, so the obvious deduction was that Ricky's death was aimed at Angela. Someone, it seemed, had been trying to get at Angela, drive her potty, or whatever, and killing her dog was an intermediate stage between throwing a stone through her cottage window and kidnapping her in the wood. Was the same person responsible for all these actions? And was that person Jimmy? The police, who were looking as if they'd charge him quite soon, presumably thought so. Duffy was dubious. For a start, he instinctively distrusted the psycho theory – the one put forward by Henry and much loved by television script-writers. And what finally knocked it on the head for Duffy was the thing Jim Pringle had told him on the telephone. He hadn't heard of that being done to a dog before. Not the chucking through the window – anyone might come up with that – but the thing they'd done before, the way Ricky had actually died. To Duffy's mind, this ruled out Jimmy – poor old Jimmy, who in Mrs Colin's account was so unfamiliar even with ordinary funny tobacco that he'd spluttered and coughed on the terrace one night. No, Jimmy might still have done that thing to Angela in the wood; but he wouldn't have done the dog.

And was it, in any case, aimed at Angela? That was another loose aspect to the case. Perhaps the target was someone else. Vic, for instance: a warning over some contract or other. Or even a warning to the whole house? The whole house – apart from Mrs Colin – had liked Ricky; and the whole house – apart from Damian – had taken him for walks. Sally used to exercise him a lot, apparently. Hmmm. It was time, he decided, for a bit of professional help.

'I've never heard of that before,' said Detective-Sergeant Vine.

'Nor have I. Nasty.'

'Very nasty. Sick, in fact. London?'

'Could be.' Duffy was non-committal.

'London, definitely.' D/S Vine didn't have a whisper of evidence for this statement apart from somehow wanting it to be true. Country policemen tended to see the big cities as the source of all corruption. This wasn't sentimentality about their own patch – they knew vice could flourish just as well among the bluebells as among the council flats – but observation. The criminal psyche always did seem to spawn its sickest novelties up in London or Glasgow or wherever. D/S Vine had a wife and kids – a dog, too, for that matter; and when you heard about some nasty new trick you always imagined it invading your own village. It tended to make you a little conservative; which was only normal.

'You realize . . .' he began, but Duffy cut him off with a nod and a grunt before he got going. He was about to mention freelancing, and cowboys, and the illegal removing of evidence in a criminal case. But on the other hand it had been this ex-copper who had led him to the camp in the woods, and if this ex-copper had removed evidence from the scene of the crime and taken it to London for examination, he had also found that evidence after it had disappeared in the first place. Or rather, caused it to be found. Jimmy in his frogman suit had done the diving. Jimmy, who had only been charged with assault to be going on with, just to hold him. They were taking advice on the merits of gross indecency versus attempted rape versus something even tastier; and there would be a kidnapping charge as well in due course.

But for the moment Vine saw there was too much going on around Braunscombe Hall for him not to need all the inside help he could get. When the case had merely been a question of a disappearing female he had not been struck by the helpfulness of the Hall's inhabitants and house guests. Some of them were unconcerned, some of them downright cheeky. And when that car had gone up, they didn't seem much more bothered. When he'd asked the owner to describe what had happened, she'd giggled and replied, 'I'm afraid these foreign motors are frightfully unstable.' Now there was the dog as well.

'I shall have to ask you . . .'

'Sure. I'll go down and fetch it. Probably tomorrow, if that's all right.' One thing about being an ex-copper was that it made you guess what coppers were going to ask.

D/S Vine was a fair man; and feeling a touch unhappy about a case made you perhaps even fairer. 'Look, I'm grateful . . .'

'Sure,' said Duffy. 'But this is a police investigation into a serious offence and you're not going to start trading information with a freelance, and on the other hand it is of course my duty to turn over to you immediately anything I do discover.'

'Something like that.' Vine grinned. 'Don't know why you ever left the Force.' Duffy didn't return the smile. 'But what I will say is I'm not going to tell you to keep your nose out of things. That's strictly off the record, of course.'

'Of course,' said Duffy. 'And when I bring you the dog back I'm sure I wouldn't like to overhear you talking to yourself about what made that car explode. I mean, some of the locals have this theory that a squirrel might have bitten through an electric cable or something.'

'Strictly off the record,' said Vine, 'I think I can let you know that there was a shortage of electrocuted squirrel bodies found at the scene of the incident. And I have been known to start talking to myself occasionally. But only when I'm under stress.'

'This looks a pretty stressful case to me,' said Duffy.

'Could be. By the way, I can't work out why Vic Crowther doesn't have a record.'

Duffy grinned. 'Nor could we. We did our best when he was down in our manor. Still, Taffy more than makes up for it.'

'He told me. Not that I didn't know already. Sometimes I think I'd rather talk to a straightforward villain who's lying through his teeth than to a reformed ex-con with a degree in sociology or whatever he's got.'

'Did he tell you the one about getting nicked being a symbolic reintegration into society?'

'Sounds a laugh a minute,' said Vine. 'Perhaps I could pay him not to tell me.'

'First you'd have to listen to him thinking aloud about whether or not to take the money. He's got this phobia about not boring you.'

D/S Vine nodded at Duffy. 'I'll be in touch.'

'Ditto.'

It felt like a reasonable arrangement to Duffy. In fact, it felt like the best arrangement he could hope for. Vine was using him as a sniffer dog. Nothing wrong in that, as long as the collar wasn't too tight and the choke-chain wasn't pulled on him whenever he found something naughty going on under his nose. At the same time, Duffy hadn't made any promises to Vine. The detective-sergeant hadn't overtly rebuked him for his freelance treatment of Ricky's body, and Duffy took this as a wink of permission in case he wanted to forget about the small print of legality on a similar occasion. Provided things worked out right, of course. If they didn't . . . well, he'd only come to mend the burglar alarm, Chief Inspector, honest.

It was plain to Duffy that the case needed a bit of forcing. The coppers were concentrating on Jimmy at the moment – quite right, too, it was the most serious part of the business so far – and were waiting for the report on the car and then the delivery of Ricky. It gave Duffy a day or two in which to press. The obvious place to press was Angela. She was where it all started.

He was supposed to have been minding her, of course, but somehow that bit of the job had got blown off course. Well, maybe he'd better go and mind her for a while. Only earning his money, after all. He didn't actually like Angela, which was one reason why he probably hadn't minded her as much as he should have done. Another reason was the size of Brauns-combe Hall: maybe he should have tied a beeper to her at the start of the job. Yet another reason was that she obviously didn't much care for Duffy. It wasn't that she was frosty with him – which he could have handled, or reacted to; it was just that he seemed not to exist for her. He was a sort of delivery boy who had strayed into the house and somehow kept turning up to meals, a consequence of Vic's puzzlingly generous open-door policy. Duffy remembered that at no point had she thanked him for finding her up at Jimmy's camp.

He tried saying poor kid to himself as he hitchhiked round the Hall looking for her; but he wasn't really convinced. Poor kid for what happened up in the woods, sure. Poor kid for the life she led, sorry, nothing doing. Duffy didn't soften at the sufferings of the rich. He'd heard about them often enough, he'd seen them all the time in American soap operas on the telly; but he didn't buy the package. People with money didn't have the right to whinge, that's what Duffy thought. He'd known a lot of people with no money, most of whom frequently imagined that the solution to everything would be to have some; so it was up to rich people not to disillusion them. They had what everyone else wanted: shut up and enjoy it, that was Duffy's line. Vic Crowther would probably have called it chippy, but Duffy didn't care.

'Do you mind if I show you something?' He had found her in the family room, looking out of the picture window up towards the wood. A couple of upturned magazines lay on the floor; a cigarette busily smoked itself in the ashtray. She turned. Duffy could tell that when she was looking at you, when she dropped her lethargic profile and gave you the big brown eyes and the shiny red hair, she was in theory attractive; but he didn't fancy her. No doubt that was chippy, too; he probably suffered from physical chippiness as well as social chippiness. Still, if he were to be tempted by upward sexual mobility, Lucretia would be the one to get the nod.

'What?'

'Do you mind if I show you something? It's not far.'

'Can't you tell me what it is?'

'I'd rather show you.'

Reluctantly, she accompanied him through the kitchen, out across the lawn and into the long grass at the edge of the lake.

'We've found Ricky.'

'Oh yes.' Her expression, as she stared over his shoulder and took another puff of her cigarette, didn't change. What had Vic said? *She's a sweet kid underneath it all.* So why was there all that stuff on top?

'Don't you want to know where we found him?' Don't you want to know who I mean by 'we' anyway?

'You're going to tell me, aren't you?'

'I thought you might be pleased that we found him, so that you can bury him properly now.'

'Is that why you found him, because you thought I'd be pleased? I don't remember you asking. Did you ask me if I'd be pleased?' Her tone was neutral and unimpressed; as if she couldn't even get around to faking irritation.

'Jimmy found him.'

'Jimmy's always good for useless things.'

'Jimmy found him in the lake.'

'Do you want to bury him now? Is that why you've brought me out here? Put flowers on his grave?'

'Ricky had a rope round his neck when he was found. It was attached to a brick or something. Jimmy had to cut it away.'

'I don't think it matters what happens to people after they die. I only think it matters what happens to them while they're alive. I don't know why you didn't just leave him in the lake.'

Right, my girl, thought Duffy, and grabbed her by the elbow. She tried to shake him free but her movements were as listless as her speech, and in any case Duffy had marched her several yards before she appreciated what was happening. He took her over to a bench and shoved her down on it. He remained standing, and faced her, leaning over.

'Right,' he said. 'You don't think it matters what happened to your dog after it died. So I'll tell you. Jimmy fished it out of the lake, I took it to London and a bloke I know cut it up. He cut it up because I asked him to find out how it had died. Are you any more interested in knowing what happened to your dog before it died than after it died?' Duffy's tone was deliberately insulting, but she avoided his eye and let him go on. 'Your dog died of an overdose of heroin. A huge overdose. Enough to kill a cow.'

Duffy watched her face as she took another draw on her cigarette. She showed no anger, either at the event or at the bringer of the news. He put one foot up on the bench and leaned over. He became sarcastic as well as aggressive. 'Now I think we can rule out the possibility that Ricky was an addict who got his sums wrong. I don't think his paw slipped on the plunger. I don't think he suddenly started using with pure stuff because he forgot to cut it with something else. I don't think that happened. Someone took your dog,' he leaned more closely towards her, 'and shot enough heroin into it to kill a cow.'

'I'd have had to get rid of Ricky anyway,' she finally said. 'Henry's mother drew the line at him. Perhaps it was providential.'

'Jesus,' said Duffy, and slumped down on the bench beside her. 'Jesus. You mean you're tabbing Henry's mum for this job? Came creeping round in her pink running-shoes and snaffled Ricky? Got some other old-age pensioner to help her chuck him through the window?'

'It'll never happen,' said Angela. Her voice wasn't lethargic now, but sharply sad. 'It'll never happen.' She threw her half-smoked cigarette out into the grass and immediately lit another.

'What'll never happen?' asked Duffy, as gently as he could.

'I'll never get married,' she said. 'I'm going to come to a bad end, I know it.'

'Course you're getting married. I'll see you up the aisle myself, if you like.'

'Hah.' Angela laughed, the first sign of animation since Duffy had taken her outside. 'Why do they always say that, up the *aisle*? You don't go up the *aisle*. You go up the bloody nave. The aisle's the bloody side thing. Do you see,' she turned to Duffy and was shouting now, 'it's up the nave not up the bloody aisle.'

Duffy, who had got the point fairly early on in this outburst, said, 'I'm not married myself.'

'It's not going to happen,' Angela repeated. 'I'm going to come to a bad end.'

'No you're not,' said Duffy quietly. He was suddenly sorry for her. He didn't like her, but he was sorry for her. He knew terror when he heard it.

'Anyway I haven't been a user for ages.'

'But you were?'

'Who wasn't?' she said, her voice regaining its original apathy. 'They sent me away a couple of times. I beat it, I really did. I haven't used for about five years. I sometimes think it's the only thing I've done in my life, stopping, I mean. But then again, I sometimes think I might as well have gone on, because I'm going to come to a bad end anyway.'

'But you take . . . other stuff.'

'Not really. It's pills mainly. They keep you going.'

'What about the tobacco that keeps the wasps away?'

'You've been talking to Mrs Colin,' she said suddenly. Damn, thought Duffy, damn. But her neutral tone was swiftly resumed. 'Well, who doesn't? Anyway, it's only a puff. But I haven't used for years. I really, really haven't.'

'I believe you,' said Duffy. 'And I'll get you up the nave or whatever you like to call it.' Even if Henry's mum was lurking behind a pillar in her pink running-shoes with a syringeful of smack in her handbag.

'It's not that I didn't care about Ricky when he was alive. It's just that caring about him seems pointless after he's dead.

I don't want people caring for me after I'm dead. It wouldn't be worth it.'

Christ, thought Duffy, she really could be on the edge. She needs minding not just because of what someone else might do to her. There was a silence as they both gazed across towards the lake for a minute or two. Finally, Duffy said, 'Do you know who it is that's blackmailing you?'

'Some foreigner,' she replied wearily. It seemed not to matter any more, now that she wasn't going to get married anyway.

'Anyone you know?'

'No.'

'How much?'

'Two thousand quid a couple of weeks ago. Two thousand quid last week.'

Christ, thought Duffy. He must really have got something on her.

'Where do you pay?'

'Oh, it's not far. Very considerate, really. End of the drive, turn left, and it's only half a mile or so.'

'Same place each time?'

'Yes.'

Amateurs, thought Duffy, amateurs. Greedy amateurs, mind. 'What's it about?'

'The usual thing.'

'What's the usual thing?'

'Sex,' said Angela. 'That's what everybody means by the usual thing, isn't it?'

'I don't know. I didn't think anyone cared about it so much. I mean, I didn't think anyone paid out for it any more.'

'You don't live in the country,' she said, turning and looking him in the eye. 'You aren't marrying a man who is saving himself for marriage. You aren't having to get through a whole year without sex and finding it difficult. You aren't expected to know how to behave because you're going to give that old baggage up at the House a grandchild. You didn't find it hard to take and you didn't do something bloody silly and stupid just four months before your wedding.'

It was quickly told. Henry had been going through a patch

of keeping away from her. There'd been this nice boy, just down for a week from London, she'd been a bit drunk, well, why not, who's to find out? Yes, at her cottage, and then once again, here at the Hall, it had seemed safer here, and she'd got away with it, she really thought she had. The boy had gone back to London, he'd understood, he hadn't made a fuss, and then three months later, out of the blue, a telephone call from some foreigner. How he was sure she wouldn't want him to spoil the lovely wedding and all that. How he needed some money to go back to his own country.

'Did he have any proof?'

'What, like polaroid photos? He didn't need them, did he?'

'Did you tell anyone?'

'Not about the boy. I sort of told Vic about paying out.'

'Do you think this foreigner sounds like the boy?'

'No. Anyway, he's not that type.'

'Why did you pay?'

'Because I could afford it. Because it was only a few weeks to the wedding. It seemed easier.'

It always did. That was blackmail's false sweetness to the victim. Duffy used to have a dentist who'd say to him, when drilling a cavity, 'Once more and that'll be the end of it.' This was the blackmailer's promise. Once more and that'll be the end of it. But then the drill came back again and again, and there was never an end to it.

'It's getting cold,' she said. They rose and started back towards the house. Halfway across the lawn, she went on casually, 'He asked for another payment tomorrow. But I thought I wouldn't this time. Not if I'm not getting married. Not if I'm coming to a bad end.'

'Have you told him you've changed your mind?'

'Haven't got his telephone number, have I?'

'Pity about that,' said Duffy. Though good in another way, of course.

●

At dinner everyone was a bit subdued. Even Sally wasn't giggling so much; perhaps she hadn't got a good enough offer for the burnt-out bits of her Datsun Cherry. Angela was quiet;

perhaps the fate of Ricky was getting to her at last. Jimmy's absence was also having an effect. It wasn't that Jimmy was good company; he was pretty slow, and all his jokes had mould on them. But he made everyone else feel good company, made them feel bright and witty and sophisticated and successful. They didn't do much, this crowd, thought Duffy, and they really needed the presence of this hopeless estate agent who hadn't knowingly sold a single bungalow.

'Cheer up, you laughing girls and boys.' Damian, of course, was the first to react against the general mood. 'How about getting out the old modelling albums, Belinda?'

But Belinda didn't think this a smart idea. She reacted as if he'd said, 'Belinda, why don't you show us your tits?' – which in a way, of course, he had. Damian tried again.

'My dear Taffy, there must be a really violent gangster film on the box.'

'I don't like that stuff,' said Taffy. 'It's not . . . realistic enough.'

'Not enough blood for you, Taff?'

'No, not that. There's too much for me, usually. It's just, things aren't like that. Not enough goes wrong. Or it may go wrong for one side but not the other. Out in the real world it goes wrong for everyone. It's just a question of making less mistakes than the other side.' Duffy was yawning already. And the other thing the films get wrong is that they don't show villains with phobias. Very delicate, some of our finest criminal minds, they are; got phobias about fire, or dogs, or being locked up, or whatever.

'Was that a yawn I espied?' Uh-uh. Damian didn't miss too much. 'How about a clatter round the green baize, Duffy? Touch of the old in–off and six away?'

'I don't think I'm ready for you yet, to be honest. Give me another couple of days.'

'Well, I can't say I've caught you putting in much practice. Sneaking down in your shortie dressing-gown in the middle of the night, are we?'

'No,' said Duffy. He half-expected Sally to giggle, but she was silent.

'Well, if you don't all perk up a bit,' said Damian, 'I shall sing you "The Dogs".'

'Oh, not "The Dogs".' Even Sally, who clearly went along with everything, registered a protest.

'Yes, "The Dogs", "The Dogs".' In a creamy baritone, with the swanky over-emphasis of an opera singer on television, he began:

'The dogs they had a meeting,
They came from near and far;
And some dogs came by aeroplane,
And some dogs came by car.'

Damian paused. Duffy half-recognized the tune. It was one of those hymns. He didn't have many hymns at his beck and call, to be honest, and he didn't know if he'd ever sung this one. The tune sounded a bit posh for him. Perhaps he'd heard someone else singing it. He was waiting for the second verse, when Lucretia said, 'Damian, you can be a real berk, you know,' and nodded towards Angela.

'God, what long memories people have,' said Damian wearily.

'Actually, I don't mind.' Angela didn't seem to. 'I'm sort of over it now. It doesn't matter.'

Lucretia looked across at Damian as if to tell him Angela didn't mean it. Sally said, 'Go on, Dame, what's next?' even though she had heard the song dozens of times.

'Won't,' he replied. 'You're so *boring* this evening. Damian's going to sulk in the snooker room.' He did a stage pout, and left the room. The evening broke up. Duffy tried to catch Lucretia's eye, but she failed to catch his back. Instead, he found himself in the kitchen with Vic. Perhaps Vic had been a bit quiet at dinner because he was wondering how long he'd have the coppers inviting themselves round for a rummage whenever they felt like it.

'Couple of things, Vic.'

'Sure.'

'The dog business. Anything to do with you?'

'How do you mean?'

'Well, any . . . troubles lately? Could it have been meant for you?'

'Me?'

'A warning or something.'

Vic did his honest-citizen chuckle. 'You don't let go, Duffy, do you? I mean, only another twenty years and I might convince you I'm legit.'

'You and Taffy should stand for Parliament,' said Duffy.

'And the other thing?'

'When Angela told you about being blackmailed, did she say anything else?'

'No, I said.'

'But . . . how did it come up?'

'Well, things don't really come up with Angela, do they? I mean, you may have noticed, she doesn't exactly follow the normal rules of conversation.' Duffy nodded. 'So, we were just talking about something else and out of the blue she said she was being blackmailed. No who, no why, no anything. Shut up at once. Told me not to tell anybody.'

'Guesses?'

Vic shook his head. 'Have you tried asking her?'

'Mmm. She wouldn't tell me a thing.'

In bed that night, Duffy found himself re-reading Basil Berk's restaurant column in the *Tatler*. He'd have to put up his daily rates if he was ever going to afford the Poison d'Or. Half asleep, he found his brain idling over two things: the location of tomorrow's drop, and the location of Lucretia's bedroom.

One of these sites was more easily identified than the other. Duffy was fairly sure they were dealing with amateurs: the time, the place, and the amount of money hadn't changed over three successive weeks. The drop was ordered for three o'clock that afternoon; so he reckoned it was probably safe for Angela and him, quite by coincidence of course, to run into one another at the top of the drive during their morning constitutionals.

Left at the gates, and half a mile took them to a T-junction. Well, maybe not so amateur: that made three directions in which to escape if necessary. On the opposite verge was a large County Council grit-bin, painted green. The sort of object the eye didn't notice for eleven months of the year; only in the twelfth, when snow fell and motorists got panicky, did you suddenly spot it. You might even go across to it out of curiosity, pull up the heavy lid, and wonder why it was empty.

'In there,' said Angela, with a spectacularly stagey nod of the head.

'Keep walking.'

It wasn't a bad place for a pick-up. Nor was it a bad place for hiding in the trees and jumping the postman. On their way back to the Hall they had the argument about whether Angela should be allowed to watch with Duffy. It sounded a terrible idea to Duffy, but Angela, who only yesterday had seemed apathetic about the idea of being blackmailed, now started insisting that as it was her money, she should see where it was going. Duffy gave in.

By one-thirty Duffy was squatting in some bracken about twenty yards from the grit-bin. He had excused himself from lunch, driven off for a pub sandwich, found a hiding-place for the van, and worked his way through some woods to his present uncomfortable niche. With an hour to kill he tried plaiting himself a camouflage hat out of ferns, like the one Jimmy had worn when he'd caught Duffy poking in Mr Hardcastle's shed; but he couldn't get it to stick together, not without cellotape or something. No doubt there was an art to it.

At two-thirty he heard footsteps from the direction of the drive, then saw Angela, unsuitably dressed for a country walk, come into view. She headed straight for the bin, dropped a brown envelope into it, didn't look round (as he had instructed) and started off up the road to the right. Five minutes later, after only a certain amount of crackling undergrowth and shouts of 'Oh, shit,' she was by his side.

'I don't really like the country,' she said, as she patted the ground testingly before sitting down. 'Bloody prickly.'

Duffy grunted, and kept his gaze on the road. Five minutes later, she said, 'It's quite exciting, this, isn't it?' She gave him the eyes, and a half-smile too.

'Shh.' Mum's the word, he'd said to Jimmy, and Jimmy

had replied, 'My mum talked *all the bloody time*.' Angela went quiet.

At six minutes to three, by which time two cars and a motor-caravan had gone past, a bicycle came into view. It was an old-fashioned machine with stand-up handlebars and a basket on the front. The rider looked pretty old-fashioned, too, pedalling along with his knees and elbows out. On his head he wore a deerstalker. If this is anything to do with it, thought Duffy, if this is the postman, or even just a lookout, they're definitely amateur. Probably want the money to pay for new bicycles. The figure got nearer, and was about fifteen yards from the grit-bin when Angela suddenly got to her feet, started waving and shouting, 'Henry, Henry.' She ran down the bank towards the road, crashing through the undergrowth and shouting 'Henry' in an increasingly hysterical voice. The cyclist, now five yards short of the grit-bin, looked up, saw her, cycled straight on and pulled up by the side of the road. Angela started hugging him, which was not easy given the presence of the handlebars.

Duffy swore, got up, kicked away his feeble attempt at a fern hat, and trotted down the slope to the road.

'What are you doing in the woods with my fiancée?' Henry bellowed, and then burst out laughing, as if he was sure there was a reasonable explanation. Duffy laughed back, and tried to think of one. He saw Angela about to open her mouth and quickly got in before she could screw things up further.

'We were looking for Ricky's body, actually. What happened to your car? Broke down or something?' Henry had two cars, and his mother had one, and there was always the Land Rover in emergency.

'Felt like the exercise. Nice day. Thought I'd pop over and see my gel.'

'You are romantic, Henry,' said Angela. She took his arm, and started leading him and the bike up the drive to Braunscombe Hall. Romantic, grumbled Duffy to himself as he followed them at ten paces or so. Romantic! Just because he won't go to bed with you and rides a funny old bike and has a stupid hat on his head. If that was romantic, it wasn't a difficult trick to pull, provided you didn't mind behaving like a prat and a wally all the time.

Of course she'd screwed up the drop deliberately. She'd seen Henry coming and couldn't bear to watch him delving in the grit-bin. She'd rather marry someone she thought was probably blackmailing her than not marry someone because she definitely knew he was blackmailing her. She must be really lost, thought Duffy, nothing but panic and terror gurgling through her all the time. He wondered if Henry knew the ins and outs of this girl who came over all story-book lovey-dovey whenever he hove into sight.

It must *be* Henry, mustn't it? It looked like an amateur, it had to be someone who knew Angela or could find out about her, it must be someone local; and Henry had turned up at the drop at precisely six minutes to three. What did it look like?

Duffy didn't know why he was following them back to the house. He didn't know why he sat with them in the family room, occasionally picking pieces of bracken off his trousers, for half an hour or more. Maybe he was expecting Angela to apologize; maybe he was expecting Henry to confess. The atmosphere during that half-hour was hardly relaxed. Angela was ignoring Duffy, as if to say, you bloody suspect Henry, don't you, you've got the nerve to suspect Henry, haven't you, why don't you piss off? Duffy was ignoring Angela in return, as if to say, you knew, didn't you, you suspected, I bet you recognized his voice, perhaps he didn't even put on a fancy foreign accent, that's why you insisted on coming with me, that's why you screwed up the drop, you bloody guessed, didn't you? Henry sat making polite remarks in both directions, but with a slight frown, as if to say, what were these two doing in the bracken in the middle of the afternoon, and if you really were looking for a dead dog, shouldn't you have had a stick or something so that you could bash down the brambles?

'Got to see to the van,' said Duffy, and left without anyone saying goodbye to him. He stamped across the gravel and up the drive. He marched past the pre-weathered salamander clinging to its pre-weathered globe. For once he was too cross even to notice the smell of the countryside. He got to the grit-bin and wrenched open the lid to retrieve Angela's envelope. There was nothing in the grit-bin apart from grit. 'Bugger,' said Duffy.

It was a half-hour walk to fetch the van, which didn't improve Duffy's temper. He drove carelessly back to Braunscombe Hall and as he turned in at the gates he had to pull sharply over on to the grass to avoid Henry, who was pedalling down the middle of the drive, back erect and knees pointing out sharply like a frog's.

'Sorry,' said Duffy, even though it was a 50–50 case.

'Maybe you *are* after my fiancée,' said Henry cheerfully, then turned round in the saddle, without wobbling, and added, 'Don't forget your lesson.'

'Right.'

When Duffy got back to the family room, Angela didn't wait for him to sit down. 'You bloody think he did it, don't you, you nasty common little person. You bloody think he did it, don't you?'

'If you were so sure it wasn't him, why didn't you wait till he got past the grit-bin? Another ten yards and everything would have been clear.'

'There, you bloody do think he did it, you common little person.' Duffy didn't answer. 'Anyway, I was pleased to see him. Fiancée's prerogative,' she added rather smugly.

Duffy was glad he didn't have to handle these mood-swings in more than a business capacity. One moment she was coming to a bad end and wouldn't get up the bloody aisle, let alone the bloody nave, and the next moment it was all sweet Henry and 'Here Comes the Bride' stuff. Was it pills, or was that just what she was like? Or was she even worse without the pills?

'Henry didn't stay long,' he said as neutrally as he could.

'What the fuck's that got to do with you?' There was a hostile silence. 'If you must know, he didn't have any lights on his bike.'

It was a good two hours before dusk, and Henry's ride couldn't have been longer than forty minutes, but Duffy thought he would let that pass. 'I think you could have let him go the extra ten yards,' he said. 'You see, I went back and checked the grit-bin. The envelope's gone. So it couldn't have been Henry.'

'You incompetent little man,' she shouted. 'Why didn't you stay in the wood? Then you could have seen who took it.' Duffy thought this hadn't seemed a plausible option at the time. 'Anyway,' she went on, suddenly cheerful, 'what's another two thousand?'

'Hang on,' said Duffy. 'You don't mean you put real money in the envelope?'

'Of course I did.'

'Christ. You weren't meant to.'

'What do you mean? You told me we were doing the drop. So we did the drop. And you were meant to hang about in the trees and catch them. Wasn't that the idea?'

'You said you'd decided not to pay. You were meant to put newspaper or something in the envelope. I thought that was obvious. Haven't you ever seen any films or anything?'

'You screwed up properly, didn't you?' But her tone was still cheerful, as if the fact that Henry wasn't the blackmailer had made everything all right again.

'*You* screwed up. Well, we both screwed up. This is hopeless.' Not just hopeless, amateurish. An amateur blackmailer, an amateur blackmailee; and he hadn't exactly been quick off the mark himself, had he?

Before dinner he ran into Sally at the foot of the stairs. As she was brushing past him he said, 'Oh, er, I understand you do the drawing.'

She turned. With her big black eyes and lolloping curls she could be a good-looking girl if she wanted to, Duffy thought; all she needed was to get some focus into her eyes, like now. 'So?'

'Well, just wondered if I could see them.'

'Who's your favourite painter?'

'Have you got any of them around?'

'Who do you prefer? Picasso or Braque?'

'I understand they're very nice.'

'Matisse or Renoir?'

'It must take a lot of skill to make a dog look like a monkey.'

'Jackson Pollock or Pelé?'

'Pelé's a footballer.'

'That's right,' said Sally as she walked off. Half-incredulous, she muttered to herself, '*He*'s asking to see *my* etchings.'

●

Dinner that evening was no more lively an affair than the previous day. Duffy sat well away from Angela, and diagonally across from Lucretia. It looked as if she'd washed her hair. Duffy persuaded himself that she didn't really look posh; no, posh wasn't the word for her, she was more . . . sort of . . . classy. Those clear-cut, slightly carved features, the half-smile, yes, she was doing it again. Once or twice he would catch her eye and she would look back at him. What did that glance mean? Did it mean, frankly you haven't got a prayer, or did it mean, why not give it a go? Mrs Colin had said that Lucretia did less fucky-fuck than Sally; but that could still mean a healthy and democratic amount of fucky-fuck.

When the coffee had been handed round and Mrs Hardcastle had retired, there was the scrape of a chair. Damian was on his feet, a glass of wine held in front of him as if he were preparing to toast someone. 'Gentlemen,' he said, 'I give you "The Dogs".' Sally clapped; Taffy looked perplexed; Duffy glanced across at Lucretia, whose eyes were elsewhere. He looked back and up to Damian, who was addressing him. 'The tune, for strangers to the house and lower-class persons generally, is "The Church's One Foundation".' Damian cleared his throat and began:

'The dogs they had a meeting,
They came from near and far;
And some dogs came by aeroplane,
And some dogs came by car.

'They came into the courtroom
And signed the visitors' book,
And each dog took his arsehole
And hung it on a hook.'

Damian's creamy baritone was briefly lubricated with a sip of wine. Sally was looking up at the singer expectantly; Taffy seemed to be examining his cutlery.

'The dogs they were well-seated,
Each mother's son and sire,
When a naughty little mongrel
Got up and shouted "Fire!"

'The dogs they were in panic,
They had no time to look,
So each one grabbed an arsehole
From off the nearest hook.'

The tune was growing on him, thought Duffy. He wasn't sure about the song.

'The dogs they were so angry,
For it is very sore,
To wear another's arsehole
You've never worn before.

'And that is then the reason,
The dog will leave his bone,
To sniff another's arsehole,
In hope it is his own.'

Damian drew out the last line, with lots of wobble on the final vowel, closed his eyes in a mock excess of emotion, drained his glass and bowed. His face glowed and the end of his nose twitched slightly. Sally clapped again, and Taffy, like an old clubman, tapped the edge of the table with the flat of his fingers and murmured, 'Very amusing.'

'Glad you liked it. My old school song.'

'Where was that, then?'

'The Kennel Club, O Taffy.'

Damian's performance seemed to put everyone into a good mood. If it worked that well, Duffy thought, maybe they should play it instead of 'Here Comes the Bride' when Angela went trotting up the nave. But no one talked about the chances of that event taking place, or about Angela's ordeal in the woods, or Ricky's death, or the spontaneous combustion of Sally's car. For at least an hour, everyone seemed keen to pretend that this was just another jolly evening on the Buckinghamshire/Bedfordshire borders. How did they manage it? All this cheerfulness was starting to make Duffy feel depressed.

The whisky got taken seriously for a while, and then people began to sidle off to bed. Duffy, without knowing how much was his cunning and how much was her complicity, ended up in the family room with Lucretia. They seemed to be alone.

'What did you think of the song?' she asked.

'I thought it could have done with a bit more saffron in it.'

'You're funny, you know.'

'Right.' Had that been a compliment? He could scarcely check with her, could he? Instead, for no reason except that it came into his head, he told her about the football team he played in, the Western Sunday Reliables. He told her about what it was like to be a goalkeeper, the sort of opponents they came up against, the speed of their young striker Karl French, and his hopes for the forthcoming season. He went on about all this with some enthusiasm, then found himself stopping and feeling awkward. 'I suppose I should have asked if you're interested in football.'

'I suppose you should,' she said, with a half-smile. 'I'm afraid I'm not.'

'Why not?'

'Boring, I suppose. All that putting the boot in. I mean, just not interesting enough.'

'Right. Well, tell me about some restaurants then.'

'You don't want to know about restaurants.'

'Why not? Perhaps I could take you to one. In London. You know, up the West End.'

She didn't answer. He got up from his chair and started slowly walking across towards her. Boy, she looked classy, all cool and blonde and wreathed in cigarette smoke. 'Did you wash your hair today?' he asked.

Lucretia burst into laughter. 'I can afford to have it done, you know.' Her response froze Duffy halfway across the carpet, one foot hovering in the air, as if he might put it down on a pressure plate and set off the whole alarm system. She gave him a more or less friendly gaze, compared that is to her fashion-page fuck-off glance.

'Look, I may as well say it, so there aren't any misunderstandings. You're quite funny, but I don't find you at all sexy.'

Duffy's foot did not descend. Instead, he shuffled round through 180 degrees before placing it back on the carpet. Then he walked slowly to the door. As he grasped the handle, he turned and said, 'Is that funny as in funny ha-ha or as in funny peculiar?'

'I'll let you know, Duffy. I'll let you know.'

As he crossed the hall he thought he heard a chuckle, a creamy baritone chuckle. He lay in bed and reflected that in a single day Angela had called him common and incompetent, Damian had called him lower-class, and Lucretia had called him not sexy. He slept badly and six hours later, before anyone else had risen, he was trundling south on the M1 through the morning mist.

When he got back to the flat he felt he needed a bath. No, he needed more than that: he wouldn't mind strapping himself to the top of his Sherpa van and putting himself through a carwash. All those lovely big brushes scratching away at the muck he felt encrusted with, and lots of water squirting, and then big floppy mops polishing him back to normal. He had breakfast and lunch on one plate at Sam Widges, then collected the remains of Ricky from Jim Pringle (who was disappointed that Duffy didn't want him stuffed and mounted). At three o'clock Carol found him bent over the end pages of the *Standard*. He got up, kissed her, patted her bum, smiled and trotted back to his chair.

'Bad as that, was it?' After all these years Carol did not deceive herself that Duffy's behaviour was the result of her new hemline, or that touch of scent behind the ears.

'Romford, Walthamstow or Wimbledon?'

'What?'

'I'm taking you out.'

'Really that bad? You all right?'

'You ever been beaten up with words? It seems to last a lot longer, somehow.'

A few hours later, in the van, Carol finally asked, 'Where are we going?'

'Walthamstow. To the dogs.'

'The *dogs*?'

'We'll have a nice meal. Bottle of wine.'

'Why are we going to the dogs?' Carol was mystified.

'Because *they* wouldn't go there.' Duffy gripped the steering wheel. 'Because *they* wouldn't go there.'

'Sure,' said Carol, not asking, not wanting to know. 'But Duffy, you don't like the dogs, do you?' She looked across at his profile, lower lip jutting and a frown that wasn't caused by the traffic.

'I'm going to learn to like them,' said Duffy. 'I'm sure there's a lot to be said for dogs.'

They parked up the street from the stadium and joined a crowd that was peaceful and anticipatory. A pair of coppers stood on the pavement outside, but they were strictly for decoration: doing the stadium was an easy option. You didn't get football yobbos here; there was even the odd East End family outing complete with permed gran and a couple of kids. Duffy began to relax. No chance of running into Damian or Lucretia here; no chance of catching Henry on his antique bicycle, Jimmy doing his Army crawl around the track, Taffy trying to poach the hare.

Inside, they walked down a dim corridor with heavy glass doors at intervals. They climbed up to a sharply tiered restaurant and looked down through large windows at a track lit half by the evening sun and half by floodlights. Jolly signs dotted here and there said WELCOME TO THE STOW. Beneath them a corpulent man in jodhpurs and a bowler hat led the parade for the first race: he was followed by six men in white coats, like off-duty chemists, proudly showing six dogs of varied colour and elegance. Away to their left the tote board flickered constantly as the odds changed. Duffy caught the arm of a motherly waitress in a tight black skirt and frilly white blouse. As the traps sprang up and the six dogs leapt into the bright lights in vain pursuit of a hare they would never catch and which wasn't a hare in the first place anyway, Duffy popped the cork on the Veuve du Vernay, filled their glasses, put his arm proprietorially round Carol, and murmured, 'Welcome to the Stow.'

'You are a scream, Duffy.' Still, he was taking her out, that was something; and Carol knew not to examine the reasons for it too closely. They ordered the prawn cocktail – Duffy asking for extra sauce as if he were a gastronome who knew that the bottled stuff they served here was especially fine – followed by the rump steak and chips. They looked at their programme, a cyclostyled single sheet of paper with the following Thursday's details on the other side. Nine more races to come, three big ones over 640 metres, the other six over 475. 'Billy's Flyer,' Duffy read out, 'Philomena's Ark, Rockfield Rover, Bernie's Gamble, Ding Along Dell and Desert Dancer. Fancy any of them?'

Carol couldn't decide. Duffy squinted at previous form and announced knowingly, 'It must be between Bernie's Gamble and Ding Along Dell.'

'I'll have Desert Dancer then.'

He grinned and pushed down a switch on the bet-summoner, swiftly bringing a waitress with a large tray to their table.

'A fiver for the lady on number two.'

'Duffy, that's a lot of money. And by the way, you're beginning to sound a bit posh. *A fiver for the lady on number two,*' she mimicked.

He grinned. He still grinned when Desert Dancer was pipped on the line by Ding Along Dell. They ate their prawn cocktails and drank their Veuve du Vernay and backed another loser.

'You know,' said Carol, 'you could have quite a nice time if you let yourself.'

Duffy grunted. He wasn't sure if that was what it was about. Those people up on the Buckinghamshire/Bedfordshire borders – they were all out to have a nice time, weren't they? And look at them. Duffy shook the vision from his head, wolfed a few chips, and tried to concentrate on more important matters. Should he have gone for Rhincrew Doc or Chiming Valley? He hadn't been able to make up his mind, and it was too late now as the stadium lights were dimmed and several thousand faces pointed towards a little row of stalls where six dogs yelped quietly in anticipation. Thirty seconds later the electric hare was being covered up again with a cloth, the six dogs had been recaptured, and Duffy was a bit relieved as neither Rhincrew Doc nor Chiming Valley had got a nose near the hindquarters of Art Grass. At the table behind, a permed gran celebrated noisily.

They walked out through a slurry of discarded tote tickets into the warm night air. The two coppers were rocking on their heels and bidding some of the punters goodnight. There hadn't been a sniff of trouble all evening. The winners were happy; the losers were pretty sure they'd be winners next time round. As they climbed into the van, Duffy said, 'It's really nice there. I could do that again.'

'It's rather a long way.' And she had to get up for the early shift.

'But it's really nice. Nice people, nice dogs, no trouble. Nice food.'

'Duffy,' said Carol, with a teasing sharpness in her voice, 'are you going soggy or something?'

'What?'

'Duffy, what makes you think there weren't as many villains in that crowd as there are in any other crowd?'

'Well, there were whole families and stuff.'

'Yeah, sure, villains taking their families out. Probably a few nice deals going on over the prawn cocktails. I mean, it's a handy sort of place to go, isn't it?'

But Duffy wasn't to be deterred. 'Nah. It's really nice. And you can tell they love those dogs, can't you? Always patting them, stroking them. Probably give them lumps of sugar when they get back to the kennels.'

'I think you ought to see a specialist,' said Carol. 'Do you think it's cleaner than any other sport?'

'Must be,' said Duffy, smiling at the traffic in the Seven Sisters Road.

'I knew a Detective-Constable once, he was on a case with the dogs. Somewhere out Romford way I think it was. Said it was awful the things he found out they did to the dogs to make them run faster. He wouldn't tell me some of them. But it stands to reason. Think what those athletes get up to – and they're doing it to *themselves*. If it was only a dog, you wouldn't think twice, would you?'

'You can tell they love those dogs,' said Duffy warmly.

'But it's about money, isn't it? There was a lot of money

changing hands tonight, I don't know if you noticed. Well, you should have done, quite a lot of it was yours.'

'Do you know what the top prize was tonight? Seventy-five quid plus a trophy, with twenty-five quid to the second. That's peanuts.'

'It's the betting. Same as the horses. It's all about betting. And if there's only six dogs in each race, it's easier to predict than with the horses, isn't it?'

'Nah. If you gave your dog something special to make it go faster, they'd catch you, wouldn't they? They must test the winners.'

'You don't have to do it that way round, Duffy. Say there are two class dogs in a race and one of them's yours. You can't make yours go faster without being caught, so what do you do? You make yours go slower.'

'How do you do that?'

'I don't know. Feed it prawn cocktail and steak and chips the night before. Cut its toenails so that it hurts or something. Then you bet on the other dog.'

'So you bet against yourself?'

'Sure.'

Duffy continued to look a bit disbelieving, as if he declined to let this sour burst of scepticism invade the pleasure of the evening. They drove along in silence for a bit, then Duffy nodded, swerved towards the kerb, braked sharply, causing a protest of horns from behind, pulled on the handbrake and turned to Carol. 'Has anyone ever told you, you might be a genius?' he asked.

She reached across and patted him on the thigh. 'You really are soggy tonight, aren't you?'

7. NEIGHBOURHOOD

Did he have a runner? Had Carol given him a tip and did he have a runner? This was the question Duffy debated as he headed back up the M1 with nothing but a ragout of dog in a plastic bag for company. And if he did have a runner, the next problem was, which race was it in? The trouble with this case was that the runners kept on turning out not to be in the races you thought they'd been entered for. For instance, Angela's dog gets knocked off, but does this have anything to do with Angela? It ought to, and it ought to connect up with the blackmail, but it didn't seem to: the blackmail was a nice regular weekly transaction. What happened to Ricky wasn't being used to raise the stakes.

Then there was the blackmail itself. When Henry had toddled up on his bicycle, it looked as if that put him in the frame, but it didn't. Or take Jimmy and the business up at his camp: that had looked a pretty reliable runner, but it too had gone lame. The coppers had charged him, but even they knew a bit more was needed to make things stick. The only aspect of the case with no obvious runners so far was the car. Well, perhaps it would be the responsibility of a delinquent squirrel after all.

At his meeting with Detective-Sergeant Vine he traded his plastic bag for the information that there was still no information on the Datsun Cherry: they hadn't found any bits of timer, or traces of familiar explosive. It might turn out to be something simple like a bit of rope dipped in tar; one of your good old-fashioned country ways of setting fire to things, none of your city tricks. D/S Vine had interviewed the Datsun's owner, but hadn't got anything out of her, which he suspected was because there wasn't much inside her anyway. Duffy forgot to tell Vine about the encounter by the grit-bin – well, nothing had really happened, had it? – but did venture the opinion that some of the folk at Braunscombe Hall got on his tits. Vine chuckled.

'By the way, anything new out of old Jimmy?'

'Remanded for a week. Sits in his cell and says he didn't do it. He seems a bit potty to me. Might have to get in the headshrinker to take a squint at him.'

'Get him to give the rest of the Hall the once-over while

he's about it,' said Duffy. 'By the way, talking of something completely different, do you get much drugs around here?'

'No, not really. If we do, it comes down from London. We've got a drugs squad, of course, but that's mainly because the local paper thinks we ought to have one. They're on other duties most of the time.'

'So no big local suppliers?'

'Not that we know of. And I think we would know, even if we couldn't make a case. You want me to get the Hall raided by any chance?'

'That's jumping the gun a bit. Just something I'm working on.'

'I'm sure the squad'd like it. They spend most of their time dressing up like hippies and waiting to get approached in pubs. The most that happens is the publican throws them out because he doesn't like smelly hippies in his bar.'

'Well, keep them on hold.'

'Will do.'

When Duffy got back to Braunscombe Hall he didn't give the salamander a glance and he wasn't too careful with Vic's gravel as he pulled up. He was pissed off with being patronized. He'd taken against these people at first, that was only normal, then one after the other – Belinda, Lucretia, Angela, Damian – they'd half-made him quarter-like them. It hadn't been much of a shift, but it had made him uncertain how he saw things. That was bad. It was also unprofessional.

He started by calling Henry and asking if he could come over for a snooker lesson on his 1866 Thurston that afternoon. Good, and sure, he'd be happy to have tea with Henry's mum afterwards. Then he rounded up Damian and Sally, who were loitering over a late breakfast in the kitchen. He took them into the billiard room. The curtains were drawn back, and the morning light made the baize a fainter colour than the spotlights did; the room seemed unfamiliar, colder somehow. Duffy told them to sit on the chintz sofa. Then he stood facing them, his bottom half-perched on the rail.

'I always find,' Damian remarked to Sally, 'that attacks of masterfulness in men are directly related to disappointment in love.'

So he had been listening. Or maybe he'd just been told. Duffy didn't care. That was a day and a half ago. He'd been greyhound racing since then. He wasn't so certain any more that he'd taken to the sport, but he thought he'd keep it in reserve, for those times when he felt tempted to like the wrong sort of people. Come and sit on my lap, Duffy? No, I'm off down the Stow. Listen to my old school song? Sorry, I'm going to the dogs.

'You could get yourselves killed,' he said.

'Oh, God, here we go again.' Sally's tone was sarcastically bored. 'Old spoilsport sticking his nose in. Don't put your heels on the cloth you might rip it. Don't do this, don't do that. Don't have a little fun or you might kill yourself. One drink leads to another, one roll-up and next day you're making with the syringe. Government health warning number twenty-three.'

'I didn't say that,' Duffy replied. He felt Damian's eyes on him, while Sally was looking angrily away. 'I didn't say you'd kill yourselves. As far as I'm concerned you can stick what you like up your nose and you can stick what you like in your arm. I didn't say you could kill yourselves. I said you could get yourselves killed.'

'Speak on, O wise man from the East End,' said Damian.

'I don't think you're making connections. I'm not sure they're all obvious to me, but they ought to be to you.' Damian uttered a stagey sigh – the schoolboy irritated by the pedantic master.

'Did Angela tell you how Ricky died?' They shook their heads. 'Ricky didn't die from being thrown through the french windows.' He paused, and Damian gave him a get-on-with-it twitch of the head. 'Ricky died from being injected with enough heroin to kill a cow.' Actually Duffy didn't know how much more heroin this took than was required to dispose of a dog, but the phrase sounded tasty.

'Poor old Ricky,' Sally wailed, and turned her head into Damian's shoulder on the sofa.

'So you found the body?' Damian, at least, seemed to be taking things a little more usefully than Sally. Duffy nodded. 'But why did they get rid of it in the first place?'

'Someone else did. Someone with a tidy mind that happened along.'

'Someone whose name you're not going to tell us.'

'That's right.'

'So why should anyone do that to Angela's dog?'

'You're not making the connection, are you?'

'What connection?'

'The dog and the car. The dog and the car.'

'What are you talking about?' Sally took her head out of Damian's shoulder. 'Ricky was Angela's dog. And the thing about these foreign motors' – Sally started to grin in a hysterical manner – 'is that they're so frightfully . . .'

'Shut up, Sal. Listen.'

'You walked the dog a lot, didn't you, Sally? You walked the dog as much as Angela did?' She nodded silently. 'They thought the dog was yours. Well, they got that wrong. But they knew the car was yours so they got that right. But you should have made the connection. The third time they won't be after dogs and cars. They'll be after bits of you that break easily. And the time after that you could get yourselves killed. I've seen it all before. Lots of times, and I can assure you it's a lot nastier than when you don't keep up the hire-purchase on the spin-drier.'

Damian looked as if he was going to smirk at Duffy's analogy, but the expression never got going. He turned to Sally and said, 'Maybe we'll have to go to your pater on our bendeds.' When she didn't reply, he turned to Duffy and said, 'Any suggestions?'

'How much do you owe?'

'About eight.'

'Christ. How much did you start off owing?'

'Fifteen.'

'Christ. So,' Duffy went on pedantically, 'you've paid off seven.'

'About that.'

Seven. Six plus one. Three twos are six, went Duffy. Gotcha. 'And who's using?' Damian and Sally looked at one another. 'OK, you're both using. Is it fifty–fifty?'

'No,' said Sally. 'It's nearly all me.'

'I only use it for snooker, more or less,' said Damian ingratiatingly. 'Find it settles the nerves wonderfully. Stops that sort of cue-twitch I see you've still got, my dear Duffy. Makes you see shots you didn't know were on. That plant across the table into the middle pocket – you'd never even spot it without a little help.'

It was Damian's last attempt at a flourish. Duffy went remorselessly on. 'So she uses almost all of it, gives you a little gratuity to help with the snooker. But you're the one who does the shopping?'

'Mmm.'

'Well, if I were them I'd go to work on you first, and probably make quite a mess of you, and if they decided they couldn't get any more out of you, they'd move on to her.'

'I had thought of selling the Datsun,' said Sally. 'Until they blew it up. That's cutting off their nose to spite their face.'

'They're more likely to cut off your nose,' said Duffy brutally.

'Oh God,' said Damian. 'Oh God, oh God, oh God.'

'What are we actually talking about?' said Duffy. 'A variety of substances or just the one?'

'Only coke, for Christ's sake.' Damian sounded angry. 'I wouldn't touch the other stuff. And anyway,' he added with needless disloyalty, '*she*'s the user, not me.'

Sure, thought Duffy. She's the user, you're just the shopper. She's the one who climbs up on the snooker table and takes off her knickers, you're just the innocent fellow with the cue. She's the one who lets down my van tyres, you're the one who suggests it and then bottles out at the last minute in case someone's coming. She's going to be the casualty, you're going to be the survivor; but without people like you she'd never have been a casualty in the first place. Have a taste of this, go on, no, I'm not feeling hungry myself. Bed? You're not on the pill? Come on, let's risk it, be a sport. Have another drink, why not have a double, actually I won't, I'm driving myself. Then the Damians of this world would skedaddle away leaving the Sallies addicted, pregnant, drunk, wrecked. If there was anything to be said for the rough justice administered by the pushers, it was that it treated the Damians and the Sallies with even-handedness.

'So you started off with a bill of fifteen. How did you let it get that big?'

'They have this wonderful system of credit,' said Damian enthusiastically, then stopped. It was obviously a phrase from before the trouble started.

'And you had about a thousand, but that left you owing fourteen, so you had this idea of getting it out of Angela.' He said it as a statement of the obvious. When they didn't reply, he went on. 'I'm not a copper. On the other hand, I'm not stupid. I just don't see why you didn't ask her for a loan.'

'People are funny about money,' said Sally, as if he ought to know. 'Well, she's got it, she doesn't know what to do with it, she's going to get more when she marries Henry. Anyway, it was more fun this way.'

Of course, thought Duffy, I keep forgetting about the fun factor, it's more fun to blackmail one of your friends than just ask her for money which you might later have to repay. That's the big difference between the two ways of doing it: the fun.

'It was a sort of joke, really,' said Damian, almost apologetically. 'To start off with. We tried to think of who wouldn't miss a chunk of cash, and we thought of Angela, and then we wondered what we might have on her. And then we remembered her sneaking off upstairs with some boy here. I mean, we didn't catch them at it or anything, she may have been showing him the view from the roof for all we knew, but we just thought we'd give it a run.'

'So you went to a phone-box and put on your funny foreign accent.'

'Foreign? Oi put on moi Oirish accent, that's all. Tells you how much Angela notices things.'

'And she paid?'

'We couldn't believe it. I kept the folks entertained with some tittle-tattle, Sally pretended to go and lie down with girls' trouble, and sneaked off up the drive. It was all so ridiculously easy. We didn't really believe it, so we just kept going back to the same place.'

'I don't see why you didn't ask her for a loan,' Duffy repeated.

'People are funny about money,' said Sally again, as if pronouncing a rare truth.

'Where do you do your shopping. Up in London?'

'No, no, no. They come to us. It's all very well-organized.'

'What, here?' Duffy imagined a van with a fancy name on the side and a royal 'By Appointment' crest on the front. 'Messrs Smack, Coke & Hash: Purveyors of Narcotics to the Gentry. Deliveries Thursday and Saturday. Credit Allowances.'

'Course not. We do it at the motorway caff.'

Fair enough. One of the usual places. Duffy sometimes wondered what would happen if they cracked down on all the naughtiness – from adulterous hand-holding to criminal meets – that took place in motorway caffs. Would the restaurants survive?

They all looked at one another for a minute or so. 'What's going to happen now?' asked Damian.

'I don't know.' Duffy had no particular reason – or desire – to be soft on them. 'It's up to D/S Vine from here on. Obviously I'll pass on what you've told me. He'll probably want to go over the same ground again. Then it's up to him. He might think it would be a good idea for you to make another payment under laboratory conditions. Or he might just throw you in a cell, of course. It all depends on whether he takes a light-hearted view of blackmail and hard drugs or not.'

'Oh God,' said Damian, 'you're making it sound so *serious*.'

'It was only fun,' Sally repeated. 'Don't you ever have fun?' Duffy didn't answer that. He wasn't altogether sure about fun. Take the dogs at Walthamstow: that had felt like fun, but maybe it was only fun because he'd just been having such a shitty time on the Buckinghamshire/Bedfordshire borders. Sally had another question. 'Are you going to tell Ange?'

'Perhaps it would be better coming from you.' Sally seemed to be one of those girls people always did things for. Well, she could get on with this by herself.

Duffy straightened up. As he turned to go, Damian said,

'Assuming I'm not in the slammer, you won't forget our little grudge match on the green baize?'

'Assuming,' said Duffy. Most people didn't have any sense of priorities, he reflected.

'And I'll do my best to stay off the infamous marching powder beforehand.'

'I can't think why you use it,' said Duffy.

'I can't think why you don't, given the wretched little prod-and-poke game you seem to be managing with at the moment. Gives you flow, that's what it does, gives you flow.'

Duffy agreed that his game required a bit of flow, as well as a few other things – like skill, accuracy, reliability, nerve – but he was committed to getting them in the old-fashioned way. When he turned up for his lesson at Winterton House the gravel made the same posh sound, like some breakfast cereal whispering back to him as he poured on the milk. Henry, in a typical mixture of large-checked jacket, floppy handkerchief, foulard and cavalry twill trousers, greeted him with a punch on the shoulder. 'Who's been going into the woods with me gel, eh?'

'I told you . . .' Duffy hoped that Angela hadn't blabbed to Henry after he'd gone off to look for the drop.

'So you did.' Henry put his large, square, red face closer to Duffy's. 'How much is that doggie in the woodshed, and all that. Eh?'

'Sure.'

'Mother's expecting us for tea at four-thirty, so why don't we get down to it?'

Once again, they went through the house to the gentlemen's quarters, to the darkened billiard room with its smell of old leather and yesterday's cigar smoke. On the sideboard Duffy noticed one of those Victorian decanter units with a lock to stop the servants from sneaking a drink; though, if Braunscombe Hall was anything to go by, the servants wouldn't bother with half-full decanters of whisky. They'd just unload a case of the stuff straight from the wine merchant's van into their own back kitchen. 'An old British custom in the big houses,' as Mrs Colin had put it.

'You rack the balls,' said Henry, who was picking out his

cue. Duffy gathered the reds together and began to corral them into the heavy mahogany triangle. Was it an illusion, or did they sound a bit solider as they clanked gently together? And weren't some of the colours marginally different from those at Braunscombe Hall? The blue ball seemed a little darker, the brown a little redder. Of course: Henry had the authentic ivory balls, Vic the new super-crystallate jobs. Over the last few years they'd fiddled with some of the colours to make them show up better on television. Duffy wasn't sure he approved. He was no traditionalist, but he preferred the feel of the old-fashioned set. He also preferred Henry's immaculate 1866 Thurston to Vic's table, which had more runkles than an unmade bed.

In the cloister calm of the billiard room, with its old smells, its quietly clicking ivory, and its fierce burst of colour in the midst of darkness, Henry became subtly altered. Duffy had seen fat men put on ice skates and acquire a sudden elegance as the blade bit its frozen trail; and something of the sort happened to Henry. A large, rigid fellow who bicycled with knees and elbows out became smoother and neater; even smaller, if that was possible. As Damian would have put it, he had flow. He wasn't flash – he didn't start moving on to the next shot before the pot had gone down – but he had a certainty of purpose about him. He looked at ease.

Duffy was much less relaxed. Henry's confidence made him edgy, and Henry's game made him edgier still. He found himself charging at risky long pots, then ruthlessly pinned back into baulk, then humiliatingly snookered. He had a little run on the colours towards the end, but still had to chew on the wrong end of a 72–28 scoreline.

Then they had the lesson. Henry was very keen on getting Duffy's stance right. He made him take up position and promptly started adjusting him, like a photographer with a model. He fiddled with the splaying fingers of Duffy's bridge hand. He pushed the head down further over the cue. He knelt and shifted Duffy's legs around until his feet were a bit more parallel. He pushed the right hand a few inches down the cue and tried to make the forearm hang vertically from the elbow. Finally, he made Duffy practise locking his hips. This part involved Henry taking him by the waist, slipping his hands down a couple of inches, and tugging gently in a clockwise direction.

Duffy's hips locked, and he found himself in a perfect cueing position; but something seemed to be preventing him from playing the shot. For a start, Henry was half-resting on his back; more noticeably, Henry's large palms, which had been glued to Duffy's hip-bones, had contrived to ease themselves into his trouser pockets. Duffy didn't move. He let Henry rummage around for a while before coughing gently and lining up a brown.

Henry withdrew his hands. 'Just checking the balls were in the right pockets,' he said cheerily.

The lesson continued, with Henry occasionally laying hands on Duffy, who didn't shrug him off but didn't exactly reciprocate. Then they played another frame, which Henry won less easily, though whether this was because Duffy's game had improved or Henry was thinking of other things was impossible to tell. With twenty minutes left before they were expected for tea by Henry's mother, he suggested another lesson. Duffy claimed to have had enough, so they sat down on the creaky leather settle from which men with mutton-chops and big cigars and glasses of port would once have presided over some after-dinner billiards.

'How's Angela?'

'Top-notch. Taken all this stuff like a trooper.'

'I expect you can't wait to get married?' Duffy couldn't resist the question, even if it might be a little cruel, given Henry's recently declared fondness for pocket billiards.

'Rather.'

'Terrible thing to happen to her, though, so soon before the wedding.'

'Fancy old Jimmy turning out to be a psycho.' Henry shook his head sadly.

'You wouldn't have thought him capable, then?'

'Well, that's the point, you can't tell with psychos, can you?'

'Anyway,' said Duffy, 'they'll soon prove whether it was him or not.'

'What do you mean?'

'Well, tests and things.'

'Fingerprints?'

'That sort of thing . . .' Duffy was deliberately drawing it out. 'Not exactly . . .'

'Look, just spit it out. She's my gel, I think I ought to know.'

'Sorry, Henry, it's just a bit . . . embarrassing, really.' Duffy appeared to be broaching a tricky subject with reluctance. 'I was talking to D/S Vine about it. He's very interested in all the latest technology, that sort of stuff. Well, you know what happened to Angela . . . after she was tied up.' Henry looked away and nodded. 'According to Vine, what they can do now is examine it. They've found a way of analysing it. Under a microscope. Sperm,' he said abruptly. 'It's like fingerprints. They can find out where it came from.'

'I've never heard of that,' said Henry.

'Nor had I,' said Duffy. 'Apparently it's pretty new and pretty expensive, so they can only use it in special cases. I mean, someone does a rape in London, they couldn't possibly go round collecting samples from everybody. But in the present case . . . well, Jimmy's denying it, isn't he? It may have happened up at his camp but no one saw him there. Angela didn't recognize him. So obviously they'll make him give a sample and that will clinch it one way or the other.' Duffy paused, waiting for Henry to ask the obvious question. He didn't. 'And of course, if they don't get a match, then that would put Jimmy pretty much in the clear.' Again, no question came. 'And as there can't be that many males who are regular frequenters of Braunscombe Hall, I should think the obvious course would be to come round and collect a few more samples. Eliminate all the obvious candidates, as it were. I'm only guessing. It'd be up to Vine to make the decision.'

Henry nodded and didn't say anything. 'What about tea?' Duffy suggested.

Henry's mother was in the conservatory, surrounded by Kew Gardens. She still had on her pink running-shoes but was now in a cream linen suit with lots of beads round her neck. Except that they wouldn't be just beads, any more than Henry's snooker balls would be made of super-crystallate.

'Still wearing that nasty tie you borrowed from the crook.'

'He doesn't have a criminal record, if you must know.' Suddenly, Duffy felt defensive about old Vic, even if he was a bit of a chancer.

'That's a very narrow definition of a crook. If you had to have a criminal record to be a crook . . . Take Henry, for instance.'

'Mother!'

'Well, you're a crook, aren't you, dear?' Duffy noted that the first time Henry's mother had used a term of endearment to her son was in the same breath as accusing him of being a criminal. Henry opened his mouth, but his mother went on. 'That diseased veal you sold, remember?'

'We didn't know for sure it was diseased.'

'You mean they hadn't actually died?'

'But you can't obey all the Min. of Ag.'s regulations, otherwise you'd go mad. I only did what any other farmer . . .'

'Exactly. All the other farmers are crooks, too. Are you a crook, by the way?'

'Me?' said Duffy.

'You're certainly wearing a crook's tie. You don't mind my asking?'

'No, sure. I'm a crook, too. You can tell by looking.' Duffy was less charmed on this visit by Henry's mum. He took a bite of fruit cake. That tasted posh as well. Where he came from it was cake with bits of fruit in; here it was fruit with bits of cake in. Easy on the flour, you could hear them shouting.

Henry wasn't saying much, and after a single cup of tea Duffy got up to leave. 'So sorry you have to go,' said Henry's mum brightly. 'Do come again. I still want to be told what goes where.'

By the time Duffy got back to Braunscombe Hall, Detective-Sergeant Vine was installed for another session. The analysis on the Datsun had come through but had proved inconclusive: no bomb, no commercial explosives, on the other hand no carbonized squirrel with sharp teeth, and no reports of summer lightning striking at random across the county. A bit of string stuck down the petrol tank, something like that seemed the most likely. An efficient piece of destruction, but less than hi-tech.

D/S Vine had talked to the Datsun's owner again, and Sally had had a small confession to make. Damian had come along, and offered a small confession of his own. But the morning story and the afternoon story – as Duffy discovered when D/S Vine relayed the latter version to him – were about as similar as a video nasty and a kid's pop-up book. There had been some thinking done while Duffy had been away, and it was pretty clear that Damian had been doing it. There had been some thinking, and also some closing of ranks. Angela, for a start, had been squared.

The new account – the one some expensive lawyers might in the future be hired to defend – went like this. Damian and Sally had, they admitted, been a little naughty in the past. They had, because it was part of the life-style of their generation, dabbled in drugs; well, go to London nowadays and you practically get a free sample as you buy your return ticket, you know what it's like, Mr Vine, sir, don't you? They'd done a little coke in their time, and they were prepared to pay for this sin whatever price society demanded. But they hadn't used for a while, in fact they'd given up going to London. They lived quietly in the country with their friends now. The trouble was, London had come to them. They were being blackmailed by someone they had once bought drugs from, someone who had sought them out and demanded money. They'd paid him three times so far, but he was still greedy. The terrible thing was, they didn't have much money between the two of them, and when they'd mentioned their plight to Angela she had insisted on footing the bill. She was incredibly generous, Angela, and said she had lots of money, but it was all getting out of hand. The blackmailers must have seen Sally taking Ricky for a walk and then killed him; they'd set fire to her car; and they probably had worse things up their sleeve. Could Mr Vine help them, please? Perhaps when Damian made their next payment, which Angela was kindly putting up, and which was due to be handed over at the motorway caff the following day?

Duffy whistled when he heard Vine's version. Not bad for

a couple of hours. The best quick-change artists outside the music hall: from blackmailer to blackmailee in the twinkling of an eye. Angela changed from victim to sterling friend as soon as you turned your back. Roll up, roll up, and watch posh people closing ranks! Duffy supplied the earlier account of events and it was Vine's turn to whistle. 'It makes you just want to let them all get on with it, doesn't it?' he said.

'But you won't.'

'Not if they're blowing up cars, et cetera.'

'Sure.'

'After all, we're still after the same person or persons. Then, when we catch them, we'll decide whether to do them for blackmail or pushing.'

'You're going to have to alert London.'

'I know.'

'Pity we couldn't have had that raid on the Hall.' Duffy wished he'd been able to watch Damian being held upside-down by a muscular police sergeant while all sorts of pills and powders and funny tobacco fell out of his trouser pockets. But what hadn't been destroyed before Detective-Sergeant Vine's first visit would certainly have been flushed away by now.

Vine didn't need any help from Duffy in planning things for the next day. He would alert London, get the local drugs squad back off traffic duty, arrange the tail, fix for a takeover vehicle half-way to London, and so on. But perhaps Duffy might like to sit in on the drop; just in case the messenger turned out to be local. Wouldn't do to scare him away with a familiar face. Duffy accepted.

●

He stayed away from the Hall that evening. He didn't want to meet Lucretia in the family room and be told whether he was funny ha-ha or funny peculiar. He didn't want to sit opposite Damian at dinner and find him shiny with self-con-fidence again, all plumped up with how cleverly he'd snook-ered D/S Vine and how he and Sally might be looking at not much more than a suspended sentence, max. He didn't want to run into Angela and start wondering how she woozily sorted out what she thought of her charming friends; nor did he much want to look at her and remember Henry's big red hands sliding into his trousers. 'Just checking if the balls are in the right pockets.' Duffy sat in the motorway caff pushing a lukewarm shepherd's pie round his plate, and sipping at the alcohol-free lager he'd chosen to counteract the effects of the shovelful of chips with which he'd anointed his pie. After a slice of fruit tart and a plain yoghurt he returned to the Hall and went to bed early, taking care not to disturb the others.

'Any advice?' said Damian the next morning when they ran into one another on the terrace. Duffy, keen to get out of the house, had gone for an uncharacteristic walk: an hour or so of plodding head-down through the woods, watching out for nettles and bear-traps, trying not to OD on the country air.

'You mean generally?' Duffy could have got quite enthusiastic when it came to giving general advice to Damian.

'About this evening. My big night. PC Plod has told you, I assume.'

'Right. Don't play to the audience, that's all.'

'What audience?'

'Well, me for a start.'

'You? I am touched. Maybe we should meet for a gourmet Colonel Sanders beforehand or something.'

'You don't amuse me, I'm afraid.'

'Oh.' Damian's face fell theatrically. 'Come on. You used to like me. A bit, anyway. Didn't you? Didn't you think I was brave about the cars?'

'By the way, if there's any trouble . . .'

'Trouble?'

'If there's any trouble, if, say, for instance, they decide to rough you up a little, don't worry. The coppers, who have been thoroughly informed of the esteem in which you hold them, will come running almost as fast as they're able.' That seemed to dispose of the confident expression on Damian's face.

A van prominently marked DUFFY SECURITY probably wouldn't look too clever in the motorway caff car-park, so Duffy drove to the police station and took a lift with one of the tails. He was in position at a table by the door well in advance. At a quarter to seven Damian arrived, to be greeted like an old friend by one of the girls at the self-service counter. After a little ostentatious flirting he took a cup of coffee across to a table overlooking the car-park.

Duffy played with his food and tried to guess from the backs of customers coming past him which was Damian's meet. After about eight wrong guesses he picked right: a short fellow, mid-twenties, in a jeans jacket, who stood rather impatiently in the queue, tapping his foot as he waited to buy a cup of tea and a pork pie. The caff was by no means full, and Duffy noted with amusement how Damian and his meet played an elaborate game of dumb show before they ended up sharing a table. Damian did well: Duffy scarcely noted the envelope change hands. After a while, the runner got up. Duffy rose at the same moment, and spent some time scrabbling in his pockets looking for a tip to leave on the table. His head was down as he did this, but his eyes were not. Five five, he said to himself, dark brown hair over the collar, black eyes, broad face, bump in the nose, thin lips, ring in the left ear, jeans jacket, green T-shirt, black trousers, running-shoes, brand uncertain, but basic colour maroon. Do you see the man you observed on that occasion in court today? Would you point him out, please? Thank you.

Duffy didn't look at Damian, who had been instructed to wait at least ten minutes, and followed the man outside. He didn't need to keep close, because he wasn't tailing him: if Damian's table overlooked the car-park, the car-park equally overlooked Damian's table, and the officers who were to take the first stretch had already examined Damian's meet. Duffy got into D/S Vine's unmarked Cortina and watched the tail begin.

'I hate this bit.'

'Right,' said Vine. 'You set it up and then it just runs away from you. Those buggers in London either screw it all up or they claim all the credit. How did the boy do?'

'All right. I mean he didn't drop the envelope or anything. Looked a bit nervous, but that was what he was meant to be. I don't think the runner had a degree in psychology.'

'Right. Well, it's back to the station, then.'

They left the radio channel open, without expecting to hear much. The runner had climbed into a brown Fiesta and headed off south down the motorway. The coppers, who were under instruction to use as few words as possible, probably wouldn't break radio silence until the first change-over at the Watford Gap, or perhaps even beyond that. Vine and Duffy chatted about the case. Vine confirmed that Jimmy's condition, and Jimmy's story, both remained the same. Duffy asked Vine about the semen test he'd outlined to Henry that afternoon.

'Never heard of it,' said Vine. 'Hasn't reached the sticks yet.' He chuckled. 'Shouldn't think it'll be too popular with the medical fellows. Bad enough taking all that blood and pee. Now they'll be giving out test-tubes with big wide ends or something.'

'What if someone refused to give a sample?' Duffy chuckled. 'Do you think they'd have to . . .'

'Shh.' Vine cocked an ear towards the radio. 'That's funny.'

The brown Fiesta, heading south from intersection 13, had turned off at intersection 11. But it hadn't gone east, and it hadn't gone west. It had rejoined the motorway and was now heading back north again. Vine pulled over and they waited in silence for the next report.

They looked at one another when they heard that the Fiesta had turned off at intersection 13, and was heading straight back into Vine's manor. At first its direction seemed to be Talworth, then Illingham, then, after a bit of circling around, it seemed to settle on Fen Burton as a destination. Vine drove fast enough to get to the Seven Bells free house within five minutes of the brown Fiesta's arrival. He got out and talked to the policeman in the tailing car, then came back to Duffy.

'One of them's gone in after him. Should be another car along in a couple of minutes.'

'I suppose,' said Duffy, 'that as I'm not on duty, there wouldn't be any objection to a citizen having a drink himself.'

'As long as you're not planning to drive afterwards, sir.'

Duffy strolled across the road to the Seven Bells. It was a normal village pub with all the traditional country entertainments like a juke box, a Space Invader machine and a one-armed bandit. To the background of this quiet popping and bleeping and blaring a couple of dozen locals were sinking a choice of eight different beers. Duffy ordered half a pint of something he'd never heard of, found a secluded table, nodded to the nearest drinkers, and looked around. He could almost not quite pick out the plain-clothes copper, who was sitting up at the bar. The driver of the brown Fiesta was in the far corner, pretending to watch a darts game, but scuttling a glance towards the door whenever he heard a noise. After a while he looked up and then didn't look down immediately. Here he comes, thought Duffy, and squinted sideways without raising his head as a man walked past. He wasn't big, but he was strongly built; either that or he had shoulder-pads in his raincoat. He bought a drink and went to sit by his runner. Duffy could see him in profile now and immediately ruled out the possibility of shoulder-pads.

There was always something faintly pleasant about watching a suspect who didn't know he was being watched. And in the present case, the pleasure was more than faint. Duffy watched the figures as they nodded and sipped their drinks; he noticed the envelope being transferred quite openly from one pocket to another; he smiled as the runner got up, hunched his shoulders in his jeans jacket, ducked his head as a farewell, and headed towards the door.

Duffy continued to smile as he got slowly to his feet, a near-empty half-pint mug in his hand. Slowly he walked along the bar, deliberately nudging the copper as he went past. When he reached the corner near the darts players, he said quietly, 'Can I buy you the other half, Taffy?'

At this point things got a bit messy. Taffy half-stood up, a little bit of beer-foam glistening on his jazz-man's beard, and said with an answering smile, 'Why don't I get it?'

Duffy backed off a little but was firm. 'No, it's my turn.'

Taffy, now fully on his feet, politely declined. 'Oh, but I insist.'

Duffy remained untouched by such generosity. 'I really can't let you pay, I'm afraid.'

The conversation stalemated, Taffy resorted to non-verbal communication. Perhaps it was a tactic he'd picked up from *Theories of Social Revolt*. He shoulder-charged Duffy, who might have been knocked flat if he hadn't half-turned and shoved his beer-glass at Taffy's head. The unplanned angle of Duffy's attack meant that the glass skidded off the side of the jazz-man's face but did not break. A long red mark on Taffy's cheek began to pop blood. Both men were half off-balance. In Duffy's philosophy of fighting, if you had a small weapon and your opponent, though unarmed, had a reputation for thumping people with iron bars, then you got your retaliation in first. He pulled back his arm and prepared to mug Taffy more seriously this time, when his fist got stuck up in the air and a rural voice, belonging to someone who thought hooligans should fight in their own pubs, not other people's, said, 'You bloody yob.' The voice's owner bent Duffy's forearm slowly behind his back; Taffy, surprised by such impartial intervention, thumped Duffy once more as he ran past.

The plain-clothes man at the bar obviously thought that showing Taffy his warrant card wouldn't cut much ice, so he tripped him up as he ran and watched unsentimentally as Taffy's fall took him into a glass table full of drinks. Then he sat on his head, shouted 'Police', ordered two of the heftiest locals to hold down Taffy's legs, and waved his warrant card when they hesitated. Everyone panted heavily for a while, then Duffy was frog-marched across the bar by his unseen assailant, who said proudly to the plain-clothes man, 'I got the other one for you.'

'Well, well, well,' said Vine as Duffy, still puffing, settled himself in the front seat of the Cortina a few minutes later. 'Now that is what I call an abuse of hospitality.'

'Poor old Vic.' Not that Duffy really meant it. It was nice to catch someone like Vic being naïve for once.

'Where do you think Taffy got his supplies?' Duffy asked.

'London, probably. We'll have a go, but I shouldn't think we'll get anywhere. He looks a tough nut.'

'It pisses me off that you never find out.'

'Well, if you want someone to blame,' said Vine, 'it goes like this. Taffy bought it in London from someone else, who bought it from an importer, who got it from somewhere tacky in Spain, who had it flown in from the West Indies, who had it flown in from probably Colombia, where it was grown by a peasant who you can't blame because he can't live off any crop apart from that because his land is so poor, and then does that make it the Government's fault, well no because the Government's only a puppet Government, so who's paying the bills and you end up with Washington, and so you blame the American President. Why not?'

'Are you political by any chance?'

'No, I'm just saying you go daft if you start thinking about it. We got two tonight. They may not be big, but we got two, and that's a good night's shopping.'

'Check. You might have a problem with the charges, though.'

'How do you mean?'

'Well, Damian's story, which you're acting on, was that he was being blackmailed. So it depends on how Taffy reacts to that. If he knows he's going down, would he rather go down for blackmail or for drugs? He'd have to weigh up the sentencing, wouldn't he? And if it seemed six of one and half a dozen of the other, he might just want to take Damian down with him.'

'He might.'

'Do you get more for blackmail or for drugs around here?'

'Bit of a toss-up. Depends on the drugs. Depends on which judge you draw. Depends what he had for breakfast.'

'Sounds like a good pay-day for the lawyers.'

Vine nodded. 'I don't think I'd like to be that Damian fellow over the next few months,' he said.

'I'll pass it on.'

Vine dropped him at the station and Duffy picked up the van. It had been a good evening. Something had got solved, and he'd hardly been beaten up. He reckoned the local force should consider recruiting that fellow who had held back his arm. Except he was probably earning more dragging double-decker buses along by his teeth at local fairs.

Duffy returned to Braunscombe Hall with the cheerfulness of someone bearing interesting news. He might just put Damian through it a bit as well. But when he got there, he didn't have the chance. A late-night parliamentary session consisting of Vic, Belinda, Lucretia and a depleted whisky bottle was gathered at the kitchen table. They looked up at Duffy when he came in, but didn't greet him. OK, so he wasn't popular, well, stuff that, thought Duffy. They can bloody well hear the latest about two of their esteemed house-guests.

He had just shuffled his chair into position when Vic said, 'Henry shot himself.'

'Christ. Dead?'

'Oh yes, dead. He wouldn't miss from that range. Gave himself both barrels.'

'I don't want to hear this again,' said Belinda. 'I'll go and see how Ange is sleeping.'

'About six o'clock this evening,' said Vic, answering the unasked question. 'He did it in the snooker room. Didn't leave a note or anything.'

'Billiard room,' said Duffy. 'They called it the billiard room there.'

'His mum found him, apparently. Said there was blood all over the cloth.'

'How's Angela taking it?'

'She just wanted some pills. So we called the doctor and he told us what to let her have, and she's been out ever since.'

'Christ,' said Duffy. 'I didn't think he'd do that.' He coughed, and instead of explaining his heroic role in the capture of a criminal house-guest, found himself explaining his unheroic role in the suicide of a neighbour. He told them about his first snooker lesson, his second snooker lesson, and the conversation that followed it. He told them it all as accurately as he could remember, in preparation for repeating it to D/S Vine. He missed out the bit about Vine never having heard of semen typing.

'You killed him,' said Lucretia at the end.

'No, he killed himself,' said Duffy. 'That's what suicide means. You kill yourself.' It was a point people often preferred to evade.

'You killed him.'

'He did that thing to your friend Angela in the woods,' said Duffy. 'He was quite happy to see your friend Jimmy go down for ten years. And when he thought he might get found out he didn't make it easier for either of them, did he? Or his mum for that matter.'

'His mother's an old cow,' said Lucretia.

'So he did all that other stuff, then?' Vic asked.

'He did all the harassing to start off with. Maybe he thought he'd drive her a bit nutty, then he wouldn't have to marry her. She came to you for protection, and he decided to up the ante. Use more forceful methods.'

'Why didn't he just break off the engagement?' Lucretia was still asking the obvious, and therefore difficult, questions.

'Dunno. Maybe he reckoned people would start looking at him if he did that, start wondering if he was queer or something. Maybe he thought if Angela pulled out or went potty, he wouldn't ever have to marry. Could play the tragic lover with the broken engagement and that would last until his mum died and then the pressure would be off. Look, maybe it's a bit like at the greyhound racing, people betting against their own dogs. It doesn't make sense to you, but it makes sense to them.'

'Oh, spare us your working-class analogies,' said Lucretia.

'Talking of dogs,' said Vic. 'Did he do Ricky?'

'No, someone else did Ricky. That wasn't Henry.'

'Are you queer as well?' The question did not come from Vic.

Duffy looked at Lucretia. 'It depends,' he replied. 'Sometimes I don't think you'd notice the difference.'

'You're queer. You killed Henry and you're queer.' It came with sudden violence, as if she really had fancied Duffy all along and was now relieved to have found a belated excuse for having turned him down. Duffy registered her tone of voice, as you would register a belt round the ear; its possible implications only came to him later.

'Kids,' said Vic wearily, 'that's enough for tonight.'

●

Duffy woke up feeling depressed. It was a beautiful autumn morning, with a crisp sun and the sky a super-crystallate blue; there was a crust of russet on the woods to the south. He had solved a case, and Mrs Colin had brought him breakfast in bed with a smile that seemed to exceed the call of duty. But Duffy felt depressed. He longed to be back in London, where, on the whole, blokes didn't half-rape their fiancées and then top themselves because they felt a stir at tight-trousered bums bent over snooker tables. He remembered Vic's sentimental homage to social mobility and rearranged it while he shaved. England is a place where your Rons can steal from your Vics, where your Damians can blackmail your Angelas, where your Taffies can strongarm your Sallies, and where your Henries will let your Jimmies go to the stake for them.

Most of the morning was spent with D/S Vine. Taffy was still dishing out the expected line about the two thousand quid in the brown envelope being a gambling debt; but the runner wasn't so smart, and Vine thought they'd break through quite soon. Whether they could pin the dog and the car directly on Taffy was the only problem area. He might well have contracted out for these two jobs.

'He claims to have this phobia about fire,' said Duffy, 'so he may have got someone else in. On the other hand, he could just have been lying.'

'Odd how they can't tell the truth, isn't it? It's a sort of habit, I suppose. And the trouble is, it gets infectious. I mean, us coppers sometimes find ourselves telling a few fibs as well, just to see how they react.'

'You might find yourself fibbing about the dog and the car?'

'Always possible. Finding dog-hairs in his trouser pockets, that sort of thing. Course I wouldn't have to do it if he told the truth. By the way, why do you reckon he did the dog? Given that it wasn't Sally's.'

'I thought about that,' said Duffy. 'I guess it was just handy. It didn't have to be Sally's, and it was a bonus that she was fond of Ricky. She was obviously meant to find out what they'd done to it, and then a nasty phone-call. Your turn next, darling, or whatever. Except Vic got tidy-minded and the dog did a runner.'

Two things happened after lunch. As they rose from the table, Damian reminded Duffy about their return snooker match.

'I was thinking of getting back quite soon, actually.'

'You can't let me down. Not now. After all, they might not have a table in the slammer.'

They went along to the billiard room and shut the curtains against the bright autumn sun. Before he broke, Damian melodramatically pulled apart the lids of his right eye with two fingers and put his face up close to Duffy's. 'Look, no marching powder,' he declared. Then, without the help of anything illegal, he beat Duffy by two frames to none. Duffy's heart wasn't in it; besides, Vic's table felt like corrugated iron after Henry's Thurston. He wondered why Henry had topped himself where he had. Was it to do with the lessons, or that argument he'd had with his mum about replacing the cloth? Was it because that part of the house was originally intended only for men? Perhaps it was mere chance – he just happened to be there when the terrible decision made itself for him. Damian set up a third frame and blasted the reds apart. To Duffy they looked like a glistening scatter of blood on an 1866 Thurston. It was time to go. He racked his cue and left Damian to it.

The second thing happened just as Duffy was about to depart. There was a scream from upstairs; a woman's scream, and quite loud. Then there was some banging of doors. Duffy told himself firmly that it was probably nothing more than Sally making up her mind who to do fucky-fuck with. This reminded him to say goodbye to Mrs Colin. He found her in the kitchen. They nodded and smiled at one another for a minute or so, as if neither of them was fluent in English.

He explained to Vic that he'd have to come back to the Buckinghamshire/Bedfordshire borders to give evidence, first at the inquest – though somehow he felt he mightn't be called – and later at the trial. But he thought he wouldn't stay at the Hall if that was all right. On the other hand, Vic might like to take out a regular maintenance contract for the alarm system.

'Oh, I don't think I'll bother,' said Vic. 'It seems to be working pretty well. And I'm sure you'll knock me out a decent price if anything goes wrong. Just for old times' sake.'

Duffy nodded. 'I'll think it over. By the way, what was all that screaming?'

'That was Angela, I'm afraid. They let Jimmy out, he came straight round here. Only natural, I suppose. Wanted to see Angela, well, that was natural, too, wasn't it? She's still in bed, in this little cot in our room, like we told you.' Duffy imagined the scene. 'Soon as old Jimmy sees her, what does he do? Gets down on his knees and asks her to marry him.'

Duffy shook his head sadly and climbed into his white Sherpa van. 'He'll never get anything right, will he?' Then he slid the door shut and did a racing turn in front of the porch which fucked up Vic's gravel properly. He drove fast until he got to the bright brick entrance pillars bearing aloft the family arms of the Blessing-Crowther dynasty: Two Tits Rampant with a weathered ferret crawling all over them. Perhaps they should stick another animal on the unoccupied stone globe, for balance. Like a drowned dog.

●

A few days later, Duffy was carrying his bright yellow laundry-bag up Goldsmith Avenue, Acton W3. It was a dull Sunday morning, and there was a spatter of rain about, but Duffy felt content. He'd had a good breakfast at Sam Widges, and for once it had been his lucky day: the laundromat had disgorged exactly the same number of socks as he'd fed into it. He sucked in the acrid, dusty, fumey air, still loaded with Saturday night's smells, and it tasted good to him. He thought of young Karl French, lean as a whippet, pounding the roads in preparation for the football season. Well, he was a striker, after all. Walking to the launderette with a heavy bag of clothes and walking all the way back again on a full stomach was quite enough exercise to keep a goalie in trim.

Three hours later he and Carol sat over the fish in low-calorie sauce which had survived Duffy's absence uneaten. He was still brooding about his stay at Braunscombe Hall.

'Does it ever strike you that the country's going to the dogs?'

'I think it's always been like this, Duffy.'

'I'm beginning to wonder if it's such a good idea for your

Vics to mingle with your Damians and your Damians to go camping with your Henries.' Carol wisely let this inscrutable utterance pass. 'I mean, down at that place, they were all doing something naughty. They should all have been arrested, all of them.'

'Even that one you fancied?'

'Lucretia? I didn't say I fancied her.'

'You didn't have to.'

Hmm. Carol knew him well and no mistake. Not that it was always too bad, being known well. 'Lucretia,' he said forcefully, 'Lucretia should have been arrested just for being Lucretia.'

'Duffy, you are a scream. But it's all right, you know. Anyway, what do you think of the fish?'

Duffy took a gourmet's tiny forkful and ingested it with a careful frown. 'I think it needs a little more saffron,' he announced.

Carol giggled. 'Do you know what saffron tastes like?'

'Actually,' he replied, with as severe a face as he could manage, 'I haven't the slightest idea.'